When Hearts Collide

Jacinta,
Thank you for your
support! Always
follow your heart :)
Hope you love
the book!

xoxo

Michelle

stay weird
stay crazy ♥

By
Brittney Michelle

2016 © Brittney Michelle

www.itsBrittneyMichelle.com

ISBN (Paperback): 978-0-9863813-3-1
ISBN (eBook): 978-0-9863813-2-4

BM Webster Publishing, LLC.

contactme@itsBrittneyMichelle.com

Dedication

To all of my family and friends who've believed in me when I've said "I'll write novels that'll be turned into movies one day." It's time...

Chapter 1

The world we live in is vast, but the degrees that separate us are often much closer than we realize.

Lightning bolts flashed as thunder boomed across the warm, but gloomy sky on that infamous summer afternoon. It was the early 2000's, on June 26th to be exact, and a day that would change the course of history forever. June 26th began just as any other summer day in Detroit, Michigan. Children ran through the streets chasing after ice cream trucks in their swimming trunks and bathing suits. Adults young and old worked in the blazing heat of the Motor City's various plants, factories, and local businesses. It was a good day, but life, just like the weather, can change in the blink of an eye. By 3pm rain clouds replaced the sun, and a full out thunderstorm darkened the mood of the once sunny day. As rain tap-danced heavily on the rooftop of a small Coney Island restaurant on the city's northwest side, soon started a chain of extremely unfortunate events.

Inside of the Coney Island, the overhead lights flickered once, then twice. Everyone in the restaurant paused in unison, anticipating a complete loss of power. Gratefully, the electricity stayed on, not that it would have mattered much anyway. Business was undoubtedly slower than usual, and the gloomy weather didn't draw many customers inside of the run down establishment. Yet and still, a young black woman worked tirelessly, serving the few customers inside. Her hair was pulled back into a small tight bun, and her frame was petite, yet strong. At the attention of an elderly gentlemen sitting at the bar, she refilled his coffee mug, while he read an article from the city's local newspaper: The Detroit Free Press.

"Gang related violence has lead to a bloody start to the summer in Detroit." the man, Mr. Gaines, read aloud.

The young woman quickly looked up, as the title of the article immediately caught her attention.

"It's a shame if you ask me." Said Mr. Powell, another elderly man sitting to the right of him replied as she refilled his coffee mug as well.

"I know your pretty self ain't involved in all that ruckus?" Mr. Gaines asked with a smile.

The young woman smiled pleasantly and shook her head "no." She looked around for a distraction, and then quickly moved to the end of the long countertop. She wiped her hands on her apron before picking up a few dishes left behind by previous customers.

"Yeah, I didn't think so. You don't look like the type that causes any trouble." Mr. Gaines stated before taking a sip of his piping hot, black coffee.

"Them the ones you gotta worry about. The pretty gals." Mr. Powell joked.

Moments later, an all black SUV with tinted windows, and no visible license plate abruptly pulled into the parking lot of the restaurant. Two large, intimidating men hopped out of the vehicle and proceeded towards the front door. Their builds were that of bodybuilders or club bouncers, but the looks in their beady eyes read nothing but pure trouble. Just as the young waitress cleared the last few dishes from the countertop, she heard a "chime" noise as the door swung open. At the sight of the two men at the door, her blood pressure skyrocketed through the roof. Her soul was completely stricken with fear, and the ceramic dishes in her hands fell to the ground, shattering to pieces. Embarrassed, but more so scared for her life, she ducked down behind the counter before the two men were able to get a good look at her. The two strange men took one step inside of the restaurant and paused while scanning the perimeter of the room.

"Is CJ here?" one of the men asked, while trying to look past the swinging doors that lead to the kitchen.

"Oh CJ... yeah she's..." Tina, a fellow waitress began to say until the young lady, known as CJ, pinched her leg from her crouched down position on the floor.

After feeling the pinch, Tina glanced down towards CJ, and immediately discerned the look of helplessness in her big brown eyes.

"Oh yeah, CJ... She's, she's off today," Tina stuttered. "Yeah, she didn't come in. Maybe y'all should try again tomorrow? Maybe..."

The two men looked at one another and shook their heads in unison, as if they knew Tina was lying.

"Yeah alright, we'll let you slide only because we have other business to handle this afternoon."

"Yeah, but when you see CJ, tell her Big D's partners came through looking to collect on his investment." the other man said without a smile or ounce of pleasure in his voice as he cracked his knuckles.

"Um, okay... yeah... I'll let her know, when I see her, tomorrow." Tina replied confidently as the two men pivoted and headed out the building.

As the door slammed shut, Tina stared out the window in complete utter confusion. The moment the SUV left the parking lot, she yanked CJ up by her collar.

"You have some explaining to do!"

"It's really not that serious Tina." CJ replied with an attitude as she swept the pieces of the broken dishes on the floor.

"Not that serious?" Tina replied, raising her voice a tad.

She didn't realize that Mr. Gaines and Mr. Powell were both tuned in.

"Told you them the ones you gotta watch out for." Mr. Powell chuckled.

"Have you never heard of discretion?" CJ mumbled, as she turned and walked through the double doors that lead to the kitchen.

"My bad, Miss Attitude." Tina replied as she followed a few steps behind CJ. "Excuse me for not knowing that you had an appointment with the Black Mafia today. Got you hiding behind counters. Who are those guys? What do they want?"

CJ leaned against the wall, which was covered in peeling paint, and grabbed her cell phone from her back pocket.

"Nobody." she replied as she looked down at her phone.

The phone was cracked after having been thrown against a wall a time or two before. On the screen were seven missed call notifications from an unsaved number.

"Joe I'm going on break!" she yelled to her manager who was on the other side of the kitchen frying chicken wings, and filling up to-go boxes.

Tina shook her head as she watched CJ frantically grab an umbrella that hung around a door handle. She quickly slipped out the back door to the deserted alley behind the restaurant. Although it was hot and muggy outside, CJ didn't care. Quite frankly, she was just too afraid to care. With a puzzled and confused look on her face, she dialed the unsaved phone number and slowly raised the phone to her ear. After about two rings, a raspy male voice echoed on the other end.

"So you really think you can run away from me, huh?" said the familiar angry male voice.

"How did you get this number?" she asked, her voice cracking with fear.

"Ha. Now you should know by now that you will never, ever escape Big D. You can change your number and your address as much as you want, but I'll still find you. You think I'm playing games? Well, let me make one thing perfectly clear for you CJ. You don't pay me my money, before 6:30 tonight like we arranged, then you might as well kiss your kids goodbye. You'll be swimming with the fishes before you can even find out what I've done to them."

Click.

Before she could respond, Big D hung up the phone, just like that, leaving her to listen to nothing but silence and her thoughts. CJ wiped tears from her eyes as she paced back and forth in the rain. Suddenly, the thoughts and emotion became too much to bear, and she fell to her knees into a muddy puddle.

"How did I let this happen?" she thought.

"You alright young lady?" a voice asked from nearby.

Startled, she jumped up from her knees at the sight of a homeless man sitting next to a garbage can. She didn't answer his question, just simply nodded her head and walked back inside of the restaurant. Before she could gain her composure, she noticed that Joe and Tina were already waiting for her. Tina stood proudly with her arms folded across her chest like Joe's sidekick.

"What in the world happened to you?" Joe asked, as he looked up and down at her dripping wet clothes and pants covered in mud.

"I tripped outside Joe. I'm alright, nothing serious. The ground was, it was slippery. I'm just going to finish up my tables since my shift is just about over."

"You know what..." he began, while shaking his head and setting his towel down on the counter, "I think you could use some time away from this place. Something's just not right with you lately and I ... it's just... it's bad for business."

CJ's eyes began to water again, and her defensive reflexes immediately kicked in.

"What are you saying Joe? Are you trying to fire

me? I'm the best waitress you have in this place." she said as she stared at him in disbelief.

"Wait a minute now." Tina said with an attitude.

"Don't you start Tina," Joe began, "now, CJ, business is slow. I don't need all these waitresses in here, and I can't afford to keep paying y'all. Trust me, it's not personal. I think you're a nice girl, and I appreciate your work ethic, but I really think you need some time off. You know, to focus on you. And not only that, I'm really worried about your wellbeing. You haven't started doing that...."

"No, I am not doing drugs Joe. And I ain't been drinking either. You know I'm just trying to do the right thing. I'm clean Joe. I swear! I'm just trying to raise my kids man and survive in this city," she pleaded as her voice shook violently. "but you can't fire me Joe. I know I've been moody lately, and late and stuff, but I promise it's just been so much on my mind. I really need this job, man. I need this money."

"I'm sorry, but my decision has already been made. I know the cycle. You were probably out there using those drugs on your break. You have all kinds of dangerous people riding by here all times of the day and night. It's just too much of a liability keeping you here. You need to get some help CJ. Now I know a doctor who can help you get the..."

Before he could even finish his sentence, CJ ran through the double doors of the kitchen in tears. She grabbed her purse from a hook on the wall and purposely knocked over a glass on the counter, shattering yet another dish into a million tiny pieces.

"CJ!" Joe yelled one last time, an effort that went unnoticed.

CJ was too upset to listen to anything else that he had to say. By the time she marched out the front door, her tears had transformed into rage.

"I can't believe this man just fired me, what am I gon' do? How am I gon' feed my kids? Talking 'bout I'm on drugs, ain't nobody on drugs no more. Everybody knows I'm clean! People always wanna bring up the past." she yelled loudly as she rushed angrily to her rundown, black 1991 coupe.

She yanked open the door, and viciously pounded her hands on the seat cushion as she sat down. She yelled and yelled until her screams reverted back to tears. The waitressing job was her only source of income, and for a woman in her predicament, being broke was not an option.

After a few minutes she glanced at the clock on the dashboard that read 4:55pm. She sighed and shook her head as she stuck the key in the ignition.

"It's going to be a wet, and stormy one for Detroit today. With high winds and slippery road conditions, we encourage you to stay off the roads this evening." said the radio newscaster.

CJ quickly pressed the knob on the dashboard,

shutting off the radio altogether. As she reversed out of the parking spot, she pulled an envelope stuffed with cash from her purse. She removed a handwritten note from the envelope and glanced at it as she drove down the street. Rent $700, Electricity $200, Groceries $250, Kids $350. A million thoughts raced through her mind as she sped off down the road, and in that moment she decided that paying her countless bills was indeed out of the question this month. She quickly crumpled the note and threw it out of the opened window onto the street.

"Everything else will have to wait. I gotta get Big D his money." she thought.

After driving a few more blocks, she stopped at a red light at the intersection of two busy streets. As she sat with her hands firmly gripping the wheel, she glanced to her right and noticed a group of men standing outside of one of the many neighborhood corner liquor stores. She refocused her eyes on the stoplight for a moment, but her curiosity pulled her attention right back to the men. She shivered and rolled her neck and shoulders as she tapped her fingers against the wheel. Seconds later, when the light turned green, she was still stuck staring at the men.

"Beeeeeeeep." honked the driver behind her.

CJ quickly turned her steering wheel to the right, and pulled into the corner store's parking lot. The group of men locked their eyes on her vehicle as she slowly crept over to a parking spot. Her heart began to beat faster and faster as she placed the car in park.

"It's not too late to just go home..." she thought briefly before making eye contact with one of the young men in the group.

She took a deep breath as the young man, dressed in sagging blue jeans and a white undershirt jogged over to her vehicle. She grabbed a one hundred dollar bill from the envelope on her lap, and quickly stuffed the rest in the pocket on the back of the driver's seat. The young man, who was no older than 18, walked up to the driver's side window and leaned down so he could see her face.

"You lost or something?" he asked, with his hand gripping a gun on his left hip.

"You know why I'm here." she replied with a stone cold expression across her face.

"What you need? How much you working with?" he asked.

With the $100 bill between her pointer and middle finger, she held her left arm out the window at a 90-degree angle. With her right hand, she flicked her inner elbow using her index and middle fingers. The young man grabbed the cash, then signaled one of his partners. His partner, who was about twice his age, looked around as he walked slowly to the vehicle.

"CJ... long time no see, my baby..." he said once he realized who was in the car. "I thought you forgot about us over here on the Ave." the man chuckled deviously as he leaned through her window.

"I've been around." CJ replied in an unbothered tone.

"Mmm hmmm..." the dealer began. "China White." he whispered to his younger partner.

His younger partner nodded his head before hustling off to an alley behind the corner store. A minute or two later, he returned to the car with a small package tucked in his fist.

"Be easy." he stated as he reached his arm through her window, and dropped the small package in her hand.

CJ had a lot of issues, but the epitome of which was her longtime addiction to heroin. She stared at the illegal substance, brownish in color and extremely potent, and shook her head in shame. Just as she was about to drive off, she looked up at the liquor sign and paused. She stuffed the tiny package into the glove compartment, and reached behind her, pulling a few extra bills from her backseat pocket hiding spot. She stuffed the money into her bra as she opened the car door.

"Good Afternoon." the store clerk, a middle aged Middle Eastern man stated after she walked into the store.

She nodded her head, but didn't say a word. Instead, she headed straight to the vodka bottles. She scanned the section, and quickly grabbed the first cheap bottle she laid eyes on. As she grabbed it from the shelf, she felt chills race up her spine. She quickly approached the register, and tossed a $10 bill on counter.

"Keep the change." she replied as she walked out the door.

5:20pm.

As CJ made her way through the neighborhood, raindrops lightly dropped against her window shield. She rolled up her manual window as she headed towards Joy Road, the street that lead to her older sister's neighborhood. She stood the liquor bottle upright between her legs, and twisted off the cap with one hand. The burning sensation of the liquor trickling down her throat provided a sense of comfort, as her mind slowly went numb. She needed to escape the noise. Although the radio was silenced, even the natural sound waves vibrating through the air were too much for her to handle. Her thoughts were screaming at her louder than the radio ever could.

"Screeeech!" was the sound her tires made as she burned rubber against the pavement.

"Almost missed my turn." she mumbled under her breath as she turned onto Wyoming Street.

She breathed heavily, as she slowly brought her car to a halt a few blocks from her sister's house. She covered her face, and then gently hit her forehead with the palm of one hand repeatedly. Raindrops continued to dance against her window, but the serene water provided no peace. She twiddled her fingers together as she contemplated her next move. After less than 10 seconds of internal reevaluation, she opened the glove compartment and felt around for a plastic bag that contained a plastic spoon, a needle, a lighter, and a few cotton balls. With the plastic bag in hand, she reached back in the glove compartment and pulled out the small package of heroin. She dropped both on her lap, and sighed a sigh of frustration mixed with disappointment. She'd come a long way, but unfortunately, the drugs always seemed to find their way back to her. In the heat of the moment, she ignored her innermost thoughts, and emptied the contents of the plastic bag onto her lap. She pulled a shoelace out of one of her gym shoes and tied it around her left bicep. She looked out both windows to see if anyone was looking, and then proceeded to cook the heroin, right there in her car. She placed it on the spoon, and poured a few drops of water on it from a half filled water bottle she'd found on the floor beneath her feet. Then, she carefully lit the bottom of the spoon with a lighter. After waiting a few moments, she dropped a cotton ball in the spoon like a pro. She proceeded to extract the heroin out of the cotton ball with her needle, until she had sucked up enough for her liking. She nervously looked out her window again, before pressing the needle through her skin.

"Oh, how I've missed you." she mumbled as she

injected the heroin into her arm.

She sat smiling in the same spot for about 10 minutes, with her head back against the headrest. Once she was good and high, she put the car back in gear and drove a few blocks down Wyoming before turning onto Belton, and then Normile Street. She parked in the driveway of a nice looking house with tan shutters. As she untied the shoelace from her arm, she stared at her reflection in the rearview mirror and rolled her eyes. Severely inebriated at this point, she stumbled her way down the driveway, and up the front stairs to the porch. She struggled to keep her balance as she banged her fist on the wooden door. Within seconds, a woman, about 35 years of age with natural sandy brown dreadlocks opened the door.

"Sis, I told you I'd watch your kids until 5:30. It's 6:00! Come on now, I'm late for bible study class. CJ, you know I hate being late." she fussed without ever looking up from the book she held.

"I'm sorry. They got me working... overtime... at work." CJ replied as she peeped around the kitchen corner. "Where my babies at?" she asked.

"They're back there in the den." her sister said, as looked around for her keys.

She looked up for the first time, and noticed the redness in her younger sister's eyes.

"CJ, are you high?" she yelled. "I know you are not out here usi..." she paused and then lowered her voice, "I know you are not out here using drugs again are you?" she whispered with authority.

"Re-lax sister. Ain't nobody using no drugs." CJ slurred.

"...and is that alcohol I smell on your breath too? Oh my God, My good Lord, I cannot believe this CJ." her sister gasped as she grabbed CJ by the arm.

"Look. Girl. Stop judging me. Just give me, my kids so I can go... so you can go." CJ snapped as she yanked her arm from her sister's grasp.

"I cannot believe you could be so selfish? You're out here shooting heroin and getting drunk when you have a 6 and 7 year old to take care of?"

"I didn't come here to hear you lecture me. Sis. I'm grown, okay. I'm pretty, sure, I can handle my own. Life." she replied as she stumbled over her own two feet and laughed.

"Evidently you can't. You are 25 years old, still doing the same stuff you were doing at 16. Let me go find my keys, so I drop you right back off at the rehab center. Don't you dare walk out that door, you hear me?" she yelled as she ran up the wooden stairs.

"Think she gon' put my niece and nephew in danger, she is out of her mind..." her sister huffed as she stomped up the stairs.

CJ rolled her eyes and quickly ran into the den. She smiled when she saw her kids, the only peace she had in her crazy world. She carefully picked up her son from his spot where he was sleeping on the couch, and motioned for her daughter to get up.

"Come on Babygirl, time to go with mommy," she said to the little girl, who's curly poof ball on top of her head matched the baby doll's she was playing with.

The little girl quickly got up and followed CJ towards the door.

"Mommy, you ain't gon' tell TT goodbye?" she asked, referring to her aunt, CJ's sister.

"Didn't I tell you to come on NOW?" she snapped back.

She grabbed her daughter's hand and yanked her body towards hers, as they quickly ran out of the house towards the car.

"It's raining, Mommy. I'm all wet now!" the little girl cried as rain poured over her head.

"Just get in the car." CJ yelled.

She placed her son in the backseat and buckled him in, before getting into the driver's seat.

"CJ get back here!!!" her sister yelled with all of her might from the opened upstairs window. "Come back inside NOW!!!"

"Buckle your seatbelt." she instructed her daughter as she backed out of the driveway, liquor bottle in hand.

Her tires burned rubber against the pavement

again, as she sped off down the block.

"CJJJJJJJJJJJJJJJJJ." her sister hollered.

"Just let me be..." she whispered.

She ignored both her sister's cries and the shouts of her own conscience as she drove away.

"People think they can control my life, they got another thing coming." she whispered.

A few seconds later, her phone rang again. She looked at the clock, which read 6:05pm, meaning she had less than 30 minutes to deliver the money to Big D before she'd have a whole lot of trouble on her hands. She quickly pressed ignore, and turned the phone face down on her lap. She threw the almost empty liquor bottle on the floor as she merged onto the I-94 freeway.

"Babygirl. Grab me all of the money out of the seat pocket in front of you." she ordered her daughter.

"If I hurry up, I can still make it to Big D..." she thought.

"It ain't no money back here, Mommy." the little girl said as she felt around the seat pocket.

"What you mean it ain't no money back there? Look again. This ain't the time to play games little girl."

"I'm not playing games. It's not back here, look." she repeated with an attitude.

CJ abruptly pulled over to right and exited via the nearest ramp. She stopped at the first stop sign, quickly turned the corner, and parked. She leaned over the backseat and felt inside the back pocket, only to find that the money was indeed missing. In a pure state of shock, she turned around very slowly, and stared out the window in a cold, hard, emotionless daze. It was then that she realized that the drug dealers had robbed her when she went inside the liquor store.

"Sneaky, greedy mother fu..." she began to whisper until her phone made another noise, this time with a text message alert.

She opened the message, and to no surprise, all it read was, "15 minutes." CJ stared lifelessly out the front window. She was scared, upset, and confused on what to do next. Now that the money was long gone, she was sure that she'd be murdered by Big D, and that her kids would soon be in harm's way. In a fit of rage and panic, she attempted to do the only thing her intoxicated brain could think of at the moment...escape. She yanked the gear into drive, and pressed her foot as hard as she could against the gas. Her heart pounded inside her chest as she floated down the street at reckless speeds.

"Slow down Mommy!!!"

Her daughter's screams woke her son, who too began crying hysterically. Once again, CJ did not respond. At this point, her mind was completely elsewhere. Although she could hear her children's screams of terror, her own anxiety of what was to come blurred their hopeless cries. She flew down the slippery street, approaching 80 mph. No longer present in the moment, but completely lost in her fears. The rain poured harder, obstructing her view. Out of nowhere, her hand slipped, causing her to lose control of the vehicle.

"Ahhhhhhhhhhhh!" she and her children screamed as the car swerved sharply onto a heavily populated main road... CRASH!

Chapter 2

"I'm just saying. Men and women are just different. We see the world inversely and we process what's going on in life from two totally different vantage points. A man sees a beautiful sunset as that, a beautiful sunset. A woman sees that very same sunset and turns it into how many hours she has left in the day to finish cooking, cleaning, and catching up on her shows." said the beautiful young lady with a gorgeous smile, and curly poof ball on top of her head.

She clinched a heart shaped locket with the initials "C.J.C." engraved on the front, as she leaned in towards the microphone.

"You lost me there, Londyn." the handsome young man next to her replied.

"Okay, basically. We think things through. So let's look at relationships for example. A girl meets a great guy, someone she sees as a possible suitor. So, she wants to date him. If she likes him, she's willing to put all others aside for the very purpose of trying to make it work, because that's the logical thing to do. You men on the other hand, will meet the girl of your dreams, and mess it up just because you're too dumb to realize she's your beautiful sunset... Y'all will miss out on her, and say it's cool."

"...No, actually logic will tell you that if you miss the sunset on the east coast, there's another one coming up on the west." he replied.

"Why pass up on something good?" she asked.

"Eh... it happens... There will always be another girl. I'll settle down when I'm like 34,35...."

"See Ricky, that mentality is exactly what's wrong with the male population today. Our parents and grandparents weren't thinking in that mindset. Shoot, at 22 or 23 they were married and on baby number 3..."

"That's true Londyn, but its 2015 my baby. Our parents' and grandparents' generations were both totally different than ours. Times have changed. At 22, my grandfather had already been working in the plant for 6 years, been promoted, and was more than able to support his family. So yeah, why not settle down at that point? At 22, I can barely afford to feed my own self 3 times a day, let alone do all for my girl that I as a man feel like I should be able to do. College and settling down just doesn't sound all that appealing to most guys."

"I just disagree... So you're telling me, that if you were to meet the woman of your dreams tomorrow, in class... you wouldn't settle down just based on the simple fact that you're still in college? Even if she was perfect?"

"Exactly..."

"Unbelievable..."

"Nah, I'm playing Londyn... In all honesty if I were to meet that perfect girl, and deep in my heart I felt she was loyal enough for the ride, I'd definitely have to step up to the plate. All jokes aside. That's just if she's really a rider though. No time to be out here getting played and what not."

"Understandable. Relationships are definitely built on trust and support. If you don't have that, you don't have anything."

"Exactly, so if I find a woman who's really down for me... one who I know without a doubt is there for me and only me, then she'll get the title and the ring. Once I'm in it, I'm in it for the long run, so that's why I'm not in a rush. "

"Okay ladies, y'all hear that? Even the worst of them have a soft spot." Londyn giggled into the microphone.

"The worst of them?"

"Just kidding Ricky."

"Yeah sure you are." he replied sarcastically. "I have a question for you though man..."

"Shoot..."

"Why is it that girls claim to want a good guy... will put up with all types of bull crap from the type of guy they claim to hate, and then turn around and punish the good guy for all the stuff the old guy did... when they never even made the old guy pay for what he did to begin with?"

"That is a question for the ages, but most definitely for my next show. Well, that's all for today folks, I hope you enjoyed today's topic on love and relationships. My time is up now. Thanks for listening to Real Talk, with yours truly Londyn J, and my special guest of the day, my boy Ricky Daniels AKA Slick Rick AKA aaaaall the ladies love him! Ha ! DJ Rokk is up next. Keep it locked right here on the one and only FM 97.5 WZYB. Warrior Pride Baby! I'm out."

"Great Show Londyn!" The manager of East Lincoln University's WZYB radio station, Paul Roberts said as he walked past the studio.

"Thanks Paul!" 21-year-old Londyn James replied as she removed her headphones and sat them down on the booth.

She let out a huge sigh of relief as she had just finished another week as a radio personality on her school's campus radio station, a job she'd held for the past two years. She smiled and stared in a daze at the wall of a picture of a beautiful woman sitting in same very booth she was sitting in... earphones on, and microphone positioned right in front. The stunning brown skinned beauty's skin glowed and her personality shined through her huge smile in the photograph. Londyn couldn't help but wonder what the topic of discussion was on the day that photograph was taken. However, before she could finish her thoughts, she was interrupted by the sarcastic antics of her best friend, Reagan Graham.

"Clap - Clap - Clap." was the sound of Reagan entering the studio with a dramatic slow clap. "Oh my goodness, congrats to myyyyy best friend, Miss Londyn James. Go best friend, that's my best friend. The only *single* woman in the world who can hold a three-hour conversation on love & relationships, but can't keep a man for five whole minutes. If only these folks knew what I knew." she said with a sarcastic and playful grin.

"Shut up Reagan..." Londyn said with a sly smirk, "and for the record I'm single by choice, thank you!" she finished as she folded her arms under her chest.

"HA! No ma'am, you're single because you won't give a guy a fair fighting chance unless his name starts with Per and ends with Fect."

"Oh lord, please spare me Reagan." Londyn replied as she picked up her black Michael Kors bag and headed towards the studio doors.

She purposely walked at a fast pace in hopes of leaving her annoying B.F.F. behind as quickly as possible.

"You can run from the truth but the truth is still true, Joan Clayton!" Reagan giggled as she put on her studio headphones and huge Rayban sunglasses. "Showtime!" she smiled as she flipped her long box braids and blew a kissy face at the air.

Reagan was most definitely a character. A wild personality that most either completely loved, or completely hated. Londyn shook her head in embarrassment as she pushed past the studio's double doors and walked outside. It was a gorgeous summer night at East Lincoln University, commonly referred to as ELU, in the heart of midtown Detroit, Michigan. Although it was about 8pm, students still filled every area of the beautiful, modern campus. Some rode their bikes along the bicycle path, while others made their way to the student union for dinner or student organization meetings. Although they were only about two weeks into the new summer semester, professors were already piling on the workload, so Londyn needed to get home and study as soon as possible. She walked down the crowded sidewalk towards the student parking lot, still thinking about what her best friend had just said to her.

"I'm not that picky," she mumbled under her breath. "Geez, can a woman just have standards?"

"Talking to yourself?" said a deep voice

creeping closely behind her.

Startled, Londyn turned around quickly and almost dropped her purse.

"Don't do that Antonio!" she squealed as she pushed her younger brother's shoulder away from her. "You almost gave me a heart attack. Don't run up on people, fool. You almost got popped." she giggled.

"Londyn, now you know you can barely swat a fly." he laughed, while snatching her car keys from her hand.

"Yeah, okay loser. Just give me back my keys!" she yelled as her big, little brother held them up high, far above her reach. "Ugh what did I ever do to deserve this?" she sighed as she gave up and walked towards her car. "Of all the colleges and universities in America, you just had to apply to my school."

"Here, take your funky little keys then, punk! I got a date to get to anyway." he replied.

"Oh yeah? Which one of these little fast girls are you going out with tonight?" Londyn asked as she snatched back her keys.

"Miranda Reynolds!" he said while licking his lips and rubbing his hands together slowly.

Londyn rolled her eyes as she unlocked the driver's side door and hopped into her 2007 White Ford Focus. She rolled down the windows and chucked the deuces to her younger brother as she pulled off quickly.

"Don't catch nothing." she yelled out the window.

Londyn and her brother were close, as in they could tell each other everything, but they didn't necessarily get along all the time. Antonio was only about one year her junior, but he took the term "annoying little brother" literal, for almost all of the 20 years he'd been on this planet. Nonetheless, they still belonged to a very tight-knit family. Their father, Gerald James was a military veteran and mechanic who loved Muhammad Ali, and all things Prince. Their grandmother founded Hattie May's Sugar & Spice Bakery in the heart of the city, and at 89 years old, still baked fresh pies and cakes a few days each week. As of last Christmas, The James' household gained two new additions: Tammy, Gerald's new wife, and Sabrina, her five-year-old daughter. As to be expected in any newly blended family, Londyn and Tony were still adjusting to their newfound stepmother and stepsister.

Londyn drove out of the parking lot and down the street towards her on-campus apartment. She turned on the radio to her campus' station to catch a bit of her best friend's show.

"I mean honestly, if you ask me, LeBron is not better than Kobe. I mean, and I'm not even saying that because Kobe has 5 rings. It's just a proven fact, Kobe is the best since Jordan. FLAT OUT." Reagan stated.

"Man, What? There have been plenty of guys with skills as great as and better than Kobe Bryant.

Look at the stats, man." chimed in David, star quarterback at ELU.

"Like who? And Do-Not-Say-LeBron!" Reagan argued.

"KG!" he stated quickly and confidently with a shoulder shrug.

"Whaaaatt. D, dawg. Good Day. You don't know anything about basketball, you freaking football jock. Folks, this is the last time y'all will hear my boyfriend on MY show!" Reagan said as she yanked the microphone from David's face. "I mean you could've at least said Steph Curry. As a power forward, I think I know a little more than he does, when it comes to basketball, especially stats." she said into the microphone.

"No you really don't." he laughed from his seat. "You average like 3 points a game, and your defense is weak, babe." he snickered.

Reagan immediately looked at her boyfriend with disgust. She quickly moved the microphone away from her face and whispered, "So you trying to embarrass me now? For real David? You just gon' talk down on me like that?" she began to say before remembering she was still live on air. "Umm, sorry y'all... we have to go to a quick music break, so listen to this new joint from the homie Big Sean. DJ Rokk, back after this........ Boy are you out your mind?" she asked while throwing the microphone away from her face.

Londyn laughed and shook her head as she pulled into a parking spot in front of her apartment.

"And she wonders why I choose to be single." she said aloud as she got out of her car and walked up the short sidewalk to her front door.

Once inside, she kicked off her gym shoes, dropped her keys on the countertop, and removed her ponytail holder all practically at the same time. As she tussled her natural curls, she walked over to the fridge, only to be disappointed by the lack of food inside. She closed it, sighed, and then opened it again, as if something could have magically changed in the last 5 seconds. After closing the door for the second and final time, she opened the freezer and grabbed a pint of Cookie Dough ice cream. The breeze from the freezer felt soothing as it blew against her warm face. She closed her eyes for two seconds, realizing that this was the first moment she'd actually relaxed all day long. The sound of a dog barking in the hallway snapped her from her daze, so she shut the freezer door and walked down the hallway to her bedroom. She pressed past the door, and plopped down on her queen-sized bed, which was covered in pink and white pillows. Stretching all four limbs across the bed, she rested her head against the wooden headboard. She glanced over at her Economics book on the nightstand, and rolled her eyes before grabbing it and placing it on the bed next to her lap. As much as she hated to study, it had to be done. She opened the top drawer on her nightstand and grabbed a red notebook with the East Lincoln University logo engraved on the front. While pulling the notebook out of the drawer, she stumbled across a photo booth picture. She picked it up and stared long and hard at the romantic collage of pictures of her and a tall, curly haired man.

"Ugh..." she chuckled sarcastically as she tossed the picture onto her nightstand, just missing the drawer.

She shook her head and opened her Economics book to page 47. Tapping her pencil on the edge of her notebook, she began to read and take notes, while eating a spoonful of ice cream in between each page.

After about 30 minutes she became restless, and turned on her flat screen television, which sat directly across from her bed on a brown wooden dresser. She flipped through the channels for about 25 seconds before stopping on the Lifetime channel. On the screen was "Waiting To Exhale," the classic romantic drama she'd seen a dozen times before.

Within 15 minutes she was knocked out cold, ice cream in one hand, Economics book in the other.

Chapter 3

At about 3:00 in the morning, Londyn awoke to a loud banging noise coming from the front door of her apartment. Frightened, she reached down beneath her bed and felt around for the baseball bat she kept for protection. Tightly gripping the bat, she walked slowly into the hallway, careful to avoid making any noises with her feet. She slowly crept up to the door and gazed through the peephole, while her heart beat a millions times over.

"Ugh." she mumbled in an irritated voice, before quickly opening the door.

"It's 3:00 in the morning Tony, do you really have to bang on the door like the police?" she asked as she stood face to face with her brother.

"Sorry sis, I just wa..."

"Hold up." she interrupted as she looked

behind her brother and noticed that he did not come alone. "I know you did not bring this fool to my house."

"Pause, are you still in the same clothes from yesterday? That's nasty Lo." Tony replied, ignoring her question.

"Why would you bring him here?" she asked with an attitude and look of confusion on her face.

"Umm, are y'all just gon' keep talking about me like I ain't standing right here though?" the uninvited guest butted in.

"Yeah, you, you just stay quiet right now." Londyn snapped as she waved her hands in the air in total frustration.

"Wow. I guess ex-boyfriend's don't get no love around here." he replied.

"Emphasis on ex." Londyn replied.

"Look man I'm just trying to do what I gotta do." Tony replied as he nodded his head in an attempt to get his sister to catch his drift. "You feel me?"

Tony stepped closer to her and whispered, "Look sis, I'm just trying to do what I gotta do to stay in the Mu's good graces so I can make sure I make this next line... and look at him, he's wasted. I don't want to take him back to the dorms because the RA is a snitch, and I know he'll tell Coach Fred."

"I just don't see how any of this involves me, Tony." Londyn replied.

"C'mon Lo, we have football practice in the morning. If I take him to the Dog House, those guys are not gonna let me leave. You already know how that goes. I'm not trying to deal with all that tonight. Just let us lay low here, alright. Please?"

"So you're selling your own sister out for the sake of getting into a fraternity. Unbelievable." Londyn said as she walked away from the opened front door.

"Lo, you're just about the only person that can keep him under control," he said as he pulled Londyn closer so that he could whisper into her ear. "THIS MAN was about to be in the party with nothing but a crown royal bag on! I'm talking came out the bathroom with no clothes on."

"You owe me Tony..."

"I know, I know." Antonio replied as he walked past Londyn, plopped down on the comfy suede couch, and pulled a blanket over his shoulders.

"What happened to Miranda Reynolds?" Londyn asked.

"Man. We just couldn't see eye-to-eye. She thought I was gonna be all up on her at the party. She was all in my personal bubble and whatnot, trying to make it seem like I was her man or something."

"Tuh." Londyn replied as she turned to walk down the hallway to her bedroom. "I hate men." she whispered.

"So I'm sleeping with you LoLo?" her ex-boyfriend asked while walking towards her.

"Those days are long gone, Justin." she replied as she gave him the "talk to the hand" motion, and walked into her room, slamming the door behind her.

She quickly jumped back in the bed and buried her face in a pillow in frustration.

"I'm gonna kill Tony." she mumbled.

A few seconds later she heard a light knock on the door.

"WHAT?" she groaned from underneath the covers.

The door crept open and Justin stood pitifully in the doorway.

"Umm... You think I could get a pillow... ma'am?" he asked while chuckling under his breath.

Without even lifting her head she reached for the pillow next to her and threw it towards the door at her drunken ex- lover.

"Can I sleep with you baby?" he whined.

"Get ouuuuutttt!" she yelled.

"Man this some bull." he complained as he slammed the door shut.

She looked over to her dresser and saw the photo booth picture of the two of them on the nightstand, and flicked it to the ground in disgust.

★

"Beeeep beeeeep beep." the alarm clock sounded at exactly 8:30am.

Londyn hit the off button and dragged herself out of bed. She made her way down the hallway towards the bathroom, then paused and walked towards the living room. Not to her surprise, it was empty, as Tony and Justin were running laps across the football field by now. She shook her head and walked into the bathroom to get ready for a long day of studying.

★

By 1pm, Londyn was still sitting in the campus library, focused on notes covered with statistics and complicated calculations. After studying consistently all morning, she was in dire need of a break. So, she picked up her cell phone and called her best friend.

"Hey Reagan. What are you up to?"

"Nothing much girlie, sitting here with David watching him play 2K. I'm bored, let's do something." Reagan responded.

"I'm in the library studying for these Calc and Econ exams. I swear if I wanted these types of classes, I would have majored in business... graduation requirements are so petty."

"Ugh. Boooooo, no fun. Look, I'm trying to go out tonight! There's a kickback at K16 later, you trying to go?" she asked, in reference to the townhouse where a few of the members of Beta Kappa Epsilon lived.

The townhouse was known across campus as "K16" because of its address.

"I really need to study." Londyn groaned.

"Girl, bye. Study all day and then take a break for once in your life. I'll scoop you at 10."

"Alright fine, I'll go." she replied before hanging up.

While Londyn was not really the bookworm type, she was determined to pass all of her classes so that she could graduate on time. She was attending ELU on full ride scholarships and grants that would only cover 4 full years of school. Anything after that would have to be paid out of pocket, so finishing on time was a must. However, one summer night off was just what she needed to ease the stress.

At 9:28pm Londyn stood barefoot in front of her opened closet. Like a normal girl, her closet was filled with tons of clothes, but even still she always

seemed to struggle finding an outfit to wear. She didn't want to be too dressed up, but on the flipside, she didn't want to look too casual or underdressed either. After flipping back and forth through the same rack of clothes over and over, she pulled out a pair of dark jeans and a black and white striped loose flowing crop top shirt. She got dressed, swooped her hair into her signature curly poof ball, and applied a little mascara and lip-gloss. Less than two minutes after she stepped into her black sandals, Reagan was outside honking her horn.

"Let's gooooo!" Reagan yelled out the window of her black Chevy Impala, while still honking continuously.

Londyn came outside and locked her apartment door while shaking her head at her obnoxiously loud best friend. She rushed over to the car, in hopes that her sense of urgency would make Reagan stop honking her horn. As she opened the passenger door and sat down Reagan squealed.

"Ahhhh well don't you look cute, you fine!"

Londyn smiled as she pulled the sun visor down so that she could look in the mirror.

"Aw thanks Reagan. I guess it's been a minute since I've gotten out the house for real. I figured I might as well at least try to look somewhat decent."

"Well you did that honey!" Reagan replied as she swiftly pulled out of the parking lot onto the street.

"So, what did you get into last night? Were you at the library again?"

"No... but, girl let me tell you what happened."

"Oh, yes, story time!"

"Right, so tell me why, at like 3 am last night, my brother came pounding on my door and had Justin with him?" Londyn replied with an anxious look on her face.

"Shut up! You lying!" Reagan screamed, taking her eyes off the road to catch a glance of Londyn's facial expression.

"No. I'm dead serious, Reagan. Justin was completely wasted after going to some party off campus. My brother didn't want to go back to the football dorm because you know they're not supposed to be partying during camp... and he didn't want to take Justin back to the frat house because he didn't want to have to deal with all that pre-pledging stuff."

"Wowwwwwww. I can't believe that fool Justin really had the nerve to come to your house though. So what did he say when you kicked him out?" Reagan asked.

Londyn quickly turned her head and looked out the window, to avoid answering the question.

"Well? Tell me?" Reagan continued.

"Umm.. see, I kind of, sort of, didn't kick him out, per say..." Londyn replied as she shifted her weight towards the door.

"Londyn Marie James. Are you freaking kidding me right now? You let that scrub stay at your house? After the way he treated you?"

"What was I supposed to do, he was drunk?"

"Girl, kick that bum to the curb the same way he did you."

The car fell silent as Londyn's face dropped in shame.

"Do you still want to be with Justin?" Reagan asked with a stern tone in her voice.

"Absolutely not."

"Then why are you still letting him use you? I mean this man played you like a dog. I wouldn't even be acknowledging his presence if I were you."

"Like I said, I only let him stay as a favor to Tony." Londyn replied as Reagan put the car in park on the curb in front of K16.

"Well... I sure hope you ain't let him smash?" Reagan asked.

"Nothing happened Reagan. He slept on the couch, or in the loveseat. Shoot, I don't really know. But it wasn't in my room." Londyn responded offensively before abruptly getting out of the car.

Reagan could sense the tension as she grabbed the keys from the ignition. She shuffled around the front of the car quickly enough to lightly grab Londyn's shoulder.

"Listen Lo, I know I can come off a little harsh sometimes."

"You think?" Londyn asked sarcastically as she rolled her eyes and looked off to the side.

"I'm just trying to look out for you. You deserve a man who will appreciate you. I just don't want to see you heartbroken again."

"Well you have nothing to worry about because like I said, he's old news." Londyn stated as she turned and walked towards the house.

Reagan decided to let it go, and followed her best friend up the sidewalk towards the front door. They had different opinions on how to handle certain situations, but this one wasn't worth the argument.

Londyn and Reagan walked into the crowded townhouse, where the kickback was already in full swing. K16 was filled with ELU students socializing, laughing, and drinking. Infamous red plastic cups sat on every table and empty surface, and the smell of burning hookah coals filled the air. You'd think they were in a club due to the high tech surround sound speaker system that blasted the hottest Hip-Hop and R&B music through the air. Everyone who was anyone was there, including Greeks in their fraternity and sorority letters, student athletes, marching band members, and those without any association at all. The Beta's were pretty cool with everyone on campus, so they always did a great job of bringing the whole minority community together under one peaceful roof.   Like always, Reagan grabbed a drink and disappeared into the crowd, swaying with the music. Reagan was a "life of the party" type of girl, whereas Londyn was more reserved and selective with whom she let see her party side. Within seconds, she noticed Reagan was already in a basketball player's face, laughing, flirting, and dancing. Her boyfriend David was at work for the night, meaning Reagan had a free night to roam and play the field, in her mind at least.

Londyn caught up with a few classmates and friends as she made her way through the party. She stopped abruptly when she mistakenly bumped into the back of a guy's left arm who was sitting down on a loveseat.

"Oh my bad, I..." she began to say, until she realized the guy she had bumped into was none other than her ex, Justin.

In his lap, was a girl laying against his chest, as his right arm was wrapped tightly around her waist.

"Oh. Justin. Sorry. Um, hey, I didn't realize that was you there..." she flustered.

"What up doe?" he replied with a quick head nod, and then immediately redirected his full attention to the girl sitting in his lap.

Slightly embarrassed, and unsure of exactly what to do in such a moment, Londyn did what anyone would do in such an awkward situation. She faked a phone call.   Pretending to feel her phone vibrating, she grabbed it from her purse, and abruptly walked away as she engaged in a fake conversation with herself. She said excuse me to various people as she made her way through the crowd towards the back patio. Her only mission at that moment was to get to a place that was far out of Justin's sight. Once outside, she ended her fake phone call and leaned against the balcony railing that overlooked the pond in the backyard. With her back to the party she took a moment to breathe and think. As much as she hated to admit it, she thought about the fact that Reagan was absolutely right.

"I shouldn't have let him stay in my house. Less than 24 hours ago, he was trying to sleep in my bed, and now he's acting brand new." she thought.

She couldn't blame anyone but herself for ending up in this predicament. She couldn't even fault her brother, as he was just trying to be a good friend. As close as she and Tony were, she never explained to him the extent of what Justin had done to hurt her. Had he known what really happened, she knew he would have acted out on her behalf, thus completely blowing his chances of joining the fraternity he'd longed to be apart of for years. Tony dreamt of pledging ever since he watched their father and his frat brothers march around their apartment in their shiny gold boots so many years ago. She didn't want to be the reason her little brother missed out on partaking in that family legacy, so she downplayed the demise of their relationship for his sake. Besides that, this wasn't the first time she'd allowed herself to be used by her ex. About 4 months prior he called her asking for a ride to the airport, 10 minutes before he needed to leave. She dropped everything and picked him up after he whined about how his car had broken down, and claimed that if he didn't catch this flight he wouldn't have been able to see his mother again for the next 2 months. So she took him to the airport, only to find out via Snapchat the next day that he was actually meeting up for a quick vacation in Cali with his cousins and ex-girlfriend from high school. Meanwhile, his mother was home in New Orleans. He was pretty much a pathological liar who used and abused Londyn before, during, and after their breakup. He absolutely took her kindness for weakness. He knew it, and worst of all, she knew it. As she stood there on the balcony she reflected on why she always came to his every beckoning call.

"I've gotta start standing my ground. I can't let another dude run over me..." she mumbled.

"Is this spot taken?" a deep voice asked out of nowhere, snapping Londyn from her daze.

She glanced to her right only to find herself completely taken aback by the tall, handsome, dark chocolate stranger standing beside her. She turned around so that her back could lean on the railing, and he did the same.

"This party is lit huh?" he asked.

"Um, yeah it's pretty cool." she replied, still smitten by how handsome he was.

He pulled out his cell phone and started typing a text message. As his head was facing downward, she began to look him up and down. She'd never seen him before. In fact, she'd never seen anyone quite like him. His confidence was appealing, and his charisma was captivating. He stood tall next to her petite frame, at about 6'3", 200 pounds, all muscle. He wore long khaki shorts, a red and white Detroit Vs. Everybody tee shirt, white and red retro Jordan 4's, and a fitted cap with the Detroit Red Wings logo on it.

"So...?" he asked after clearing his throat.

"Huh?" Londyn replied in a soft voice, as he snapped her out of her daze once again.

"I said do you go to this school, or are you just visiting?" he asked politely.

"Oh, I'm sorry. Yeah I go here. Do you go here?" Londyn replied in a soft angelic voice, knowing good and well that he definitely did not attend ELU.

"Nah, I'm actually starting my senior year next semester, at The University of Boazer. I'm just home for the weekend. I grew up in the city and my family still stays in this area."

"Oh wow that's really cool," Londyn responded with a flirtatious grin. "Boazer huh? That's impressive."

"Yeah, well I started off at Mizzou my freshman

year, then transferred back home to save a few dollars. I always wanted to go to U.B. though, but you know how it is at 17 or 18... you just want to get as far away from home as possible. So I took the first opportunity I could find and ran with it."

"Yeah, I can definitely understand that. I always dreamt of going to Spelman, but money and scholarships said otherwise." Londyn giggled. "So, after high school I just decided to stay right here at home."

"So when was that, like last month for you?" he asked with a slick grin on his face.

"Funny." she said sarcastically with a giggle. "Nah, I'm actually a senior now too, thank you very much."

"Oh okay." he replied as he looked off into the party with a smile.

"So are you graduating this year?" she asked.

"Nope, I still have one more year. I'm in a 5-year program... Engineering."

"Wow. U.B. *and* an engineering major? Check you out." she said as she flirtatiously brushed his shoulder.

"Just trying to be more than a statistic." he chuckled. "So what about you. What are you majoring in?"

"Broadcasting. I'll be done in May. Thank God!"

"That's what's up!" he replied before turning to look around at the party again. "So what are you, like 21?"

"Yep, I just turned 21 a few weeks ago."

"Happy Belated!"

"Thank You." she replied with a cheesy grin, still very nervous to be standing there talking to him.

After a few seconds he turned his body towards Londyn and extended his arm for a handshake, "I'm Shane by the way."

"It's nice to meet you, Shane." she replied as she shook his hand. "My name is Londyn ... Londyn with a Y."

"The pleasure is all mine Miss Londyn with a Y."

Chapter 4

The next morning Londyn sat alone in the corner of the campus cafeteria eating a late breakfast. In front of her sat a plate of blueberry pancakes, bacon, eggs scrambled with cheese, and hash browns. A few moments later, Reagan arrived at the table with nothing but a class of grape juice and a granola bar.

"That's all you're eating?" Londyn asked with a confused look on her face.

"Yeah... I need to lose 5 pounds..." Reagan replied sadly.

"What, why? You're already tiny." she asked, while her mouth was stuffed with food.

"Girl. David's evil stepsister Tia is getting married next month, and that girl has literally like zero friends. So David's stepmom is begging me to be in the wedding, and now I have a month to fit into the bridesmaid's dress that was originally supposed to be for David's stepsister's, half brother's cousin's baby mama Candice, but she's pregnant again and showing soooo now she's kicked out the wedding and I have to replace her. Can you believe that?" she said all in one breath.

Londyn laughed and almost choked on her food as Reagan sipped her juice.

"I just can't believe how equally ratchet you and David's families are."

"Okay, first of all Londyn, I'm not ratchet okay. Now I know I might be a little hood, but ratchet I am not. David and them, yeah they ratchet! Thoroughbred ratchets. My baby had no chance. Even his grandmama is out of control."

The two of them laughed and giggled at the thought of it all.

"Ha! Remember in 9th grade when the big TV in the den at your house would get all staticy, and your mom took off the antenna and replaced it with wire hangers?" Londyn asked.

"Hahahaha yes, I swear I will never forget that type of stuff!"

"Ratchet." Londyn giggled

"Don't call my mama ratchet! She is resourceful! Now David's mama is ratchet. They drink out of reused glass jelly jars for cups at his mama's house girl! With the label still half on!"

"Ahhhhhh!" Londyn exclaimed, laughing loud enough for everyone in the cafe to hear, "Y'all are both crazy! But you know what, it works for y'all. Y'all were like made for each other. As much as y'all argue and bicker, at the end of the day, I know he really does care about you."

"That's real Lo... Yeah I guess we are kind of a match made in heaven! I prayed my whole life to meet someone like him. It's crazy that I actually found him."

Londyn's face dropped into a confused frown. "Reagan... You've known him since we were 14. What do you mean you prayed for him your whole life, you've known him your whole life."

Reagan and David met during their freshman year in high school. They flirted for a year or so, before becoming a couple towards the end of their sophomore year. They were the true definition of high school sweethearts.

"Nah, it's different now Lo. I mean, yeah I knew him growing up, and even though we've technically been together for 5 years, back then it was just puppy love. We were just going through the motions. It wasn't until college that I felt like I actually got to know the real him. Well, I guess that's when we actually started to get to know our own selves you know?"

"I'm just happy y'all made it this far. Soon enough y'all are going to be getting married and having little babies and stuff! Aww I can't wait! I guess

I'll just be the single bridesmaid at the wedding. Make sure you pass me the bouquet." Londyn said sarcastically as she twirled the remaining food around on her plate with a fork.

"Londyn... girl, ain't nobody trying to jump the broom nooooo time soon. Plus I'm not having kids until I'm 30. So stop all that foolish talk. You are beautiful and smart... a little crazy, but in a good way! There's no doubt in my mind that you're going to find an outstanding guy one day. I just can't wait to meet him! He's gonna be the bomb girl..." Reagan replied as she bit the last chunk of her granola bar.

"I guess..."

"No, seriously! Just be patient Lo... I might play around about how I think you need to loosen up and date more but really, when the right one comes along, you'll know. You shouldn't have to date around and talk to 50 guys just to find the right one. He should be the one looking for you."

"Yeah, you're right Reagan. Sometimes I just wonder you know, like, is it me? Am I the reason why I can't seem to find a decent guy?"

"Girl bye. You can't find a decent guy because there's only like 2, maybe 3 single ones left on the planet. Why do you think I keep David on such a short leash? I'm not letting him go so he can run into the arms of some lonely heifer looking for a good man..." Reagan exclaimed as she rolled her eyes.

Londyn gave her the evil side eye look and laughed.

"Oh, no offense." Reagan replied with a giggle.

"None taken."

"I just wish that dumb, ignorant son of a... ugh... Justin hadn't done you so dirty." Reagan exclaimed with balled fists. "Maybe then you wouldn't feel so insecure and be so hard on yourself when it comes to these dudes."

"Maybe so... I just think," Londyn started before taking a deep breath and a long pause, "I just think it would've been easier you know... if... if I had my mom growing up. It was just so hard." she said as tears began to fill her eyes. "Don't get me wrong, I always had my Granny, but there's nothing like having your mom around. Sometimes I just wonder what it would've been like to be able to go to her and ask her questions about guys, and about life... I miss her so much."

"Don't cry Lo... You're going to make me cry too..." Reagan replied while passing her best friend a napkin to wipe away her damp eyes.

"I'm sorry... It just hurts." she replied as she wiped away the tears. "I guess since the anniversary of her death was just a few days ago, she's really been on my mind. Even though I was too young to really know what was going on... it's like I can still see it all in my head," she began to say with a blank stare, "the accident scene, and how mangled the car was... the funeral... everything."

"Well they say kids have crystal clear memories... and that even as a little kid, you're able to repress memories from your childhood, especially traumatic ones. I learned that in my psych class. Maybe they're just leaking through your subconscious." Reagan replied.

"Yeah I've heard that too."

"Well, even though your mom isn't here to help you make all of those tough decisions about life and guys, I'm sure Tammy would be more than happy to help you wi..." she began to say before Londyn's unpleasant facial expression made her stop mid sentence. "Or.... not," she continued.

"It's not the same." Londyn began. "My dad brings this random lady and her daughter into our family and I'm just supposed to welcome them with open arms? You know he only knew her for like all of 6 months before he proposed. Tony and I barely even knew her name before they walked down the aisle!"

"Right...right..." Reagan said, suddenly at a loss for words. "Well, for the record Lo, just know you always have me, and my mom too. You know I'll share. I know it's not the same, but just know we're always here for you Babygirl."

"I know." Londyn replied with a half-smile.

"Now wipe those tears away! It's Saturday. It's

the weekend. It's time to turn up!" Reagan said as she did a little dance in her chair.

Londyn giggled and continued to wipe the tears away.

"Speaking of turn up... Did you have fun at the party last night? That boy was cracckkinnn, wasn't it?" Reagan asked, trying to lighten the mood.

"Yeah it was cool... I had a really good time."

"So did I, since I didn't have David breathing down my neck the whole time. I swear I love my man. I really do, but sometimes, I just be wanting to tell him to just back off for two seconds! We can't even be at a party at the same time without him trying to see who I'm talking to, and what I'm doing... or who I'm..."

"....I met someone...." Londyn interrupted.

"Wait... what?" Reagan asked and then paused.

"...a guy, I met a guy...at the party." Londyn replied nonchalantly.

"You mean to tell me, we just had this long convo about you not finding any guys when you actually met one last night? You are so irritating Londyn!" Reagan giggled.

"Well, I mean I don't know if he's a good guy. He doesn't even go here."

"So what do you know about him? What's his name? What school does he go to? What does he look like? Is he fine? I need answers girl! Details!" Reagan asked attentively, eyes opened wide.

Londyn moved her breakfast tray to the side and twiddled her thumbs.

"Well, his name is Shane and he goes to school at U.B."

"Ohhh, University of Boazer! Classy."

"Right? Same thing I said! He's a senior, engineering major... tall, like about 6'3"... chocolate..."

"But is he fine?"

"Yeah girl... he's really fine." Londyn said with a smile.

"Okay... like... Reggie Bush fine... or like Usher fine?"

"hmm... Michael B. Jordan meets Idris Elba fine." Londyn replied.

"Lawwwwdd!" Reagan exclaimed, fanning herself and pretending to pass out in her chair.

"I know right! I swear I legit couldn't stop staring at him. He was super cool though."

"So did you get his number?"

"No."

"LONDYN!!!"

"Whaaat? He didn't ask! I didn't wanna look like a thirst bucket... Queen Bey says never chase a man."

"Yeah well Queen Bey is fabulous, she can

afford to say that... you on the other hand should've slid him that number! Give me your phone!"

"Wait?"

"Oh, not that you're not fabulous..." Reagan replied as she playfully snatched Londyn's phone from her hand.

"What are you doing?" Londyn asked as she leaned across the table.

"Was he a Beta?"

"No... Wait, I don't know... He did have on red though, now that I think about it."

Reagan looked up and rolled her eyes as she mumbled under her breath, "I swear you never pay attention to any important details."

"Reagan. What the heck are you doing?"

"I'm on Instagram, chill homegirl." she replied.

About thirty seconds went by as Reagan made small talk and flipped through Londyn's phone. She quickly stopped on a picture of a group of Beta's at the party the night before.

"Are any of these guys him?" she asked as she slid the phone across the table towards Londyn.

Londyn picked up the phone and stared for a few seconds at the photo.

"Yeah that's him right there on the far right. You're a stalker, how did you find him so quickly?"

"I mean, first of all if he had on red at a Beta

party then chances are he was one of them. I figured that Instagram would be the most obvious place to start and so I just went on Chris Taylor's page. You really have to get your CSI skills up Londyn. Every girl needs them."

"You're a creep!"

"Whatever, that's what social media is for! To creep! Use your resources!" she exclaimed as she picked up the phone, pressed a button on the screen, then slid it back to Londyn.

"Oh my God, you followed him? Reagan are you crazy, why would you do that?"

"What?" Reagan asked with an attitude.

"He's going to think I'm some kind of stalker following him out of the blue... or a creep for finding his page the very next day! Ughhhh. My life is over." Londyn sighed, burying her face in her hands.

"You are SO melodramatic. Sitting here talking about him isn't going to get you anywhere. I just gave you a little push. You'll thank me later." she laughed as she picked the phone back up off the table. "Now let's finish this investigation."

With a sly smirk on her face, she scrolled through his posts for a few minutes, making comments and slick remarks every so often.

"Okay, so he's a Beta... obviously. He's single, no kids, a few groupies here and there, but that's to be expected. I mean, the man is sexy... goals in life, a good head on his shoulders, and he loves the Lord. Looks like we've got a keeper. Won't he do it! Praise Him! Hallelujah!" Reagan stated as she raised one hand and quickly patted her feet on the ground as if she was in church.

Londyn gave Reagan a look that indicated she thought her best friend was beyond psycho.

"You got all that... from Instagram? Give me a break!"

"Seriously Lo. You can find anything you need to know about a person on these sites. Don't believe me? Ask the girls who were killed by that social media killer!"

"But, they're..."

"Exactly... They didn't do a thorough background check."

"You're nuts Reagan. Absolutely nuts. How'd you figure all that stuff out about him from pictures anyway?"

"Easy... I scrolled up a few months to around Valentine's Day time, no romantic pictures of him wining and dining a girl. Checked his tagged photos, no pics of a girlfriend shouting him out as her Man Crush Monday... SINGLE. No pics with cute little babies, reposts about baby mama drama, or anything like that, therefore no children. Groupies, yeahhh they're commenting on every thirst trap he throws at him, heart eyes, kissy faces, all that... and as far as him having goals in life, a good head on his shoulder, and being a good Christian man, well you can see all that from the bible verses and quotes he posts. See!" she said as she flashed an example to Londyn.

Londyn rolled her eyes and buried her face back into her hands.

"My best friend is absolutely insane..." she mumbled.

"Yeah, well this insane best friend of yours just got you a follow back from your new boo." she said proudly.

"What?" Londyn gasped nervously as her headed quickly popped up.

"Yeah, he just followed you back... andddd it looks like he wants to see you again too."

"Give me that!" Londyn squealed as she grabbed her phone from Reagan.

Reagan was right. Not only had Shane followed her back on Instagram, he'd also tagged her in a picture. She clicked on the notification and saw that the picture he tagged her in was a flyer for The University of Boazer Summer Greek Fest yard show.

"Hey beautiful, @LondynNoBridge, you and your girls should come through tonight. Our yard show starts at 8pm on the outdoor Webster Hall basketball courts." Londyn read out loud with a huge Kool-Aid Smile.

"Wellllllllllllll?" Reagan asked.

"Reagan... I have a test to study for remember!!! Econ! Monday!"

Reagan snatched Londyn's phone and began to type a response to Shane's comment. She read out loud as she typed: "... Hey @BigShane93! Sounds like fun... see you there, smiley face." she said with a slick grin. "Don't play Londyn... this man is fine!"

Chapter 5

"How much longer?" Reagan asked while fidgeting in the passenger seat.

"GPS says 20 more minutes. We've only been in this car for like 15 minutes girl. Relax!! Why are you so anxious?" Londyn asked from the driver's seat of her car.

"I'm not anxious, I just hate car rides. I never go anywhere that isn't less than 10 minutes away. You know that!"

"Well, if I'm not mistaken. This little trip was your idea in the first place, Reagan!"

"Yeah well that's when I thought U.B. was closer... Did they move?"

"The Campus???"

"Yeah?"

"No... you're crazy..."

"Oh, well, it didn't seem this far away the last time I went. Maybe you just drive slow." she giggled.

"Everybody can't be a speed demon like you, Reagan! My dad isn't the Police Chief of Detroit. If I get a ticket, there's no getting out of that one... and besides, A 35 minute drive is not far at all..."

"I guess. Ugh... Bree is knocked out and I have to use the bathroom." Reagan complained in reference to their mutual friend Breanna Martin who had fallen asleep in the backseat.

"Don't talk to me!" Londyn laughed as she turned the up the volume on the radio.

About 15 minutes later they arrived at their destination. Londyn parked her car in a parking lot filled with students, faculty, parents, and U.B. fans. The three of them got out of the car and began to walk towards the big crowd of people surrounding the Webster Hall basketball courts. The yard was filled with Greeks everywhere-- much more than what they were used to seeing at ELU. While ELU was a relatively large campus, U.B. was a division 1 member of the "Big 10," and was known for being one of the best public academic universities in the country. The Annual Summer Greek Fest was a large popular event that the entire U.B. Greek Council sponsored every summer. There were usually lots of high school college tours, alumni, and current students there to check out the campus and have a good time. It was something like homecoming, minus football.

Heads turned as Londyn, Reagan, and Bree made their way through the crowd. Londyn wore a cute loose fitting full romper, wedge heels, with her signature curly poof. Reagan wore a fitted maxi sundress, wedges, and a blue jean jacket. Her long black box braids draped well past her shoulders. Bree wore her sorority line jacket over a midriff shirt, super tight jeans, and heels. Her long straight extensions laid flat against her back.

"Hey, I see some of my Sorors up there on the hill so I'll catch up with y'all later on." Bree said as she walked towards her sorority sisters who were excitingly screaming her name from a short ways away.

Londyn and Reagan said goodbye, and then walked over to a set of bleachers where they'd be able to get a good view of the yard show. The show was about to start so the bleachers were almost full, but they managed to find two open seats just before the show began. As the music blasted from the speakers, the various Greek organizations began to stroll onto the courts.

"You see Shane?" Reagan asked Londyn.

"Nah..." Londyn replied as she looked into the crowd. "There's too many people down there."

"Oh wait, look, there goes Chris and them!" Reagan said, pointing towards the group of ELU Beta's standing on the court.

"Oh yeah, and I think I see Shane, right there!" Londyn smiled.

She couldn't help but stare like a giggly teenager at the man she knew little to nothing about, yet still felt so drawn to. He stood with such self-assurance, while still maintaining a sense of humility. All she could think about was how she wanted to know more. How she wished she could just have another conversation to figure him out. The voice of the host on the microphone abruptly interrupted that thought, as the show officially kicked off into full swing.

The show was far more entertaining and exciting than anything Londyn and Reagan experienced at ELU on a normal basis. Representatives from all of the major black Greek organizations stepped and danced, and the minority band even came and showed out. A local Detroit comedian by the name of Comedian Elroy did a great job hosting the event and interacting with the crowd. Soon enough, the show was over and the crowd that once filled the bleachers emptied onto the basketball courts. As Londyn and Reagan made their way through the crowd, Reagan couldn't help but to notice Londyn's wandering eyes.

"Girl... if you don't stop being scary and go over and talk to that man!" Reagan laughed as she pointed in Shane's direction. "I'm gonna go find Bree."

Londyn smiled as she began to walk over to

where he was standing.

"Kids these days..." Reagan giggled as she turned and walked the opposite way.

Londyn slowly approached the crowd of people Shane stood conversing with, when he looked up and noticed her from the distance. She could read his lips as he said "I'll check y'all a little later," shook hands, and quickly walked towards her with a huge smile on his face. They both paused a little as they locked eyes and walked towards one another. For some odd reason, Londyn's heart was beating faster than normal, and she really had no idea why.

"Londyn with a Y... Nice to see you." Shane said as he reached in for a big bear hug.

"Nice to see you too Shane... thanks for letting me know about the show... y'all did y'all thing out there! I enjoyed it."

"Haha, straight up? I'm glad to hear that! Just a little something we threw together, you know, had to let the shoulders loose on em..." he smiled while biting his lip and gripping his chin.

"Oh lord!" Londyn giggled, "You didn't even tell me you were Greek!"

"Yeah I know... I tend to keep a low profile."

"Yeah I feel it, well I'm really glad I came out. Definitely a different scene than ELU."

"You're in Boazer territory now, my baby. It's a whole different jungle." he laughed.

"I see, I see..."

"So you staying for the after party, or you gotta head back?" he asked.

"Umm... I don't know.. I..."

"ahem..." said a voice from behind.

Londyn turned around to see Reagan standing there with a smirk.

"Oh, Shane, this is my best friend, Reagan. Reagan, this is Shane."

"Nice to meet you Shane, I've heard a lot about you." Reagan replied with a huge smile.

"Really?" he replied with a confused grin.

"Yeah!"

Londyn quickly elbowed Reagan without Shane noticing.

"Oh, I mean... not from Londyn," Reagan began. "because that would be weird, seeing that you two just met yesterday... Umm yeah I just heard about you from, other ... people. Yeah... Umm yeah, I gotta go find Bree. I think she's looking for me."   Reagan replied nervously before awkwardly walking away.

"Your friend is funny." Shane laughed.

"Yeah she's something else, that's for sure." Londyn replied while slightly rolling her eyes.

"So, the party...?" he asked again.

"Oh yeah, I don't know... We should probably

be getting back to campus. Will it be worth my time?"

"Oh of course. It's Greek Fest, this party is about to be crazy... and I was hoping I'd get to hang around my new crush a little longer." he replied as he flirtatiously brushed her hand.

"Crush huh?" she blushed.

"So, are you staying?"

"Yeah, I guess I'll stay... this party better be worth it too!"

"Oh it will be, no doubt about that. I wouldn't steer you wrong pretty lady." he said with a wink and a smile.

"I can't believe Londyn Marie James is actually letting us stay for an after party. I mean what is this, the end of the world or something? I just knew you were going to tell us it was time to hit the road." Reagan said from the passenger seat of Londyn's car as they drove through U.B.'s campus."

"Shut Up" Londyn responded.

"Ahh leave her alone, Reagan." Bree squealed from the back seat. "Let her get her cake bake session on..."

"Whaaaat? What are you talking about?" Londyn asked as she looked in the rearview mirror at

Bree.

"Girl, you don't have to play dumb with me. I saw you over there laughing and smiling and chatting it up with Solo... mmmm hmmm, you ain't slick!" Bree laughed.

"Ahhhhh, my girl." Reagan screamed as she high fived Bree.

"Okay first of all, who the heck is Solo?" Londyn asked as she breezed through a green light.

"Umm... Shane Solomon... Solo... Sexiest Beta in Delta Phi Chapter... Engineer... Model..."

"You didn't tell me he was a model!!!" Reagan squealed.

"Well for one I didn't know! And y'all are doing the absolute most right now..." Londyn replied.

"Okay, not like a real model. He just has pictures on the school's website, like for the bookstore, or housing or something." Bree laughed.

"Oh, well we've barely held a full conversation. I don't even know him like that!" Londyn replied as she glanced at her GPS and made a quick right turn.

"But, you'd like to get to know him though...wouldn't you." Bree asked as she scooted her shoulders forward in between the driver and passenger's seats.

"Pause... How do you even know all of this about him Bree?" Londyn replied nonchalantly.

"Girl... everybody knows Solo...and because... that's my sands, and if you want I can hook it up for you..."

"Thanks, but no thanks Bree...I can handle it on my own." Londyn replied with a smile.

"Well alright then." Bree replied as she scooted back against the seat.

"She told you huh?" Reagan replied with an instigating laugh.

"Well I just have to warn you. Solo is a ladies man. He's a player for real. Broke my homegirl's heart." Bree stated as she looked at Londyn in the rearview mirror.

"Yeah well what does that have to do with Londyn?" Reagan asked with an attitude as she looked over her shoulder.

"Nothing... I'm just trying to forewarn the girl! Dang, Reagan. I mean, he's all good if you're just looking for a little summer fling... but if you're on the relationship hunt, you can forget about it, homegirl... Believe that." Bree said as she rolled her eyes.

"Yeah whatever, it's not like she's trying to marry the guy. She's just trying to have a little fun. Shoot, anything is better than that other nig..." Reagan began.

"Stop it," Londyn said, cutting her off mid-sentence before she could continue bashing Justin. "I told you, I'm over him."

"Right..." Reagan replied sarcastically, "Anywho, my man is coming up here for the party so y'all better be on S.A.T. patrol..."

"S.A.T. patrol?" Bree asked.

"...You know, spot a trick..."

"Reagan!!! What is up with you today? You have got to find some chill, bro." Londyn replied.

"Sorry." she laughed.

A few minutes later they pulled up to the party venue and circled the lot several times before finding an open parking spot.

"Mannnnn this line is wrapped around the building! I'm looking way too cute to be standing in anybody's line for an hour." Reagan complained as she looked out her window.

"Chill girl, I'll text my Sorors and they'll let us in, no worries." Bree replied as she pulled out her cell phone.

The three of them quickly exited Londyn's car after a few last minute mirror checks. They began to approach the venue door and surely enough, within minutes a tall skinny girl in a white and purple line jacket signaled Bree's attention.

"They're good, they're with me." the girl said to the huge bouncer at the door who then stepped aside and let them past the roped off entrance.

Parties at U.B. were always epic. Strobe lights

were shining, black ice was blowing, and the dance floor was filled with thousands of college kids having a grand ol' time. The DJ had already gotten the party started as the crowd jumped up and down to the sounds of the Detroit classic "Come Roll" by Blade Icewood blasting through the speakers. Londyn and Reagan stood on the side of the dance floor as the Greeks strolled past. Londyn looked around and saw handsome guys all over the place, but no signs of Shane anywhere. Nonetheless, the exhilarating scene excited her. She and Reagan danced playfully on the imaginary guys behind them until the DJ stopped the music abruptly.

"Everybody say ayyyeeee!" he yelled.

"Ayyyyeeee!" the crowd repeated.

"Everybody say U.B. Greek Fest"

"U.B. Greek Fest" the crowd yelled.

"Aight, aight, y'all turnt up in here. But I think it's time to slow it down a little...How many of y'all remember this one?" he asked as the beginning of Jodeci "Freak N U" faded in, then quickly stopped.

"Aahhhhh!" the crowd screamed in disappointment.

"Haha, yea its that time of the night where y'all need to find your girl before she get snatched up by these smooth frat boys! Fellas, if she doesn't know this song, she's too young for you bro!" the DJ joked before starting the song back up again.

Just as Reagan was about to dance on her next victim, her boyfriend David popped up out of nowhere and pulled her hips toward him. She looked back and gave him a smooch before they started to dance on one another. Bree jumped into the stroll line with her sorority sisters, leaving Londyn to stand alone. Everyone around her quickly partnered up to dance, causing her to feel extremely awkward. She searched for an empty chair or wall corner that she could shuffle over to, but was caught off guard when the Beta's began to stroll past. They were so smooth, so coordinated, and so fine. Each one sensually stroked the hand or waist of a random girl as they shimmied past in tune with the beat. As she stared, she spotted Shane near the back of the line. He too looked extra suave as he shimmied his shoulders and winked his big, brown eyes at the women who stood on the sideline, gasping for attention. That is, until he locked eyes with Londyn. As the stroll line continued to move forward, Shane stopped when he got to Londyn. He looked her up and down and began to shimmy right in front of her. Londyn blushed as he stepped out of line, grabbed her hand, and pulled her body closer to his. His frat brother tried to pull his shoulder to get him to come back to the stroll line, but at this point, his attention was completely on Londyn. As they slowly began to rock side to side with the beat, their eyes locked and they were instantly caught up in each other's gaze. Londyn grabbed his hands, turned her body so that her back was against his chest, and began to put her best dance moves to work. Their bodies slowly grinded in unison through that song, and the one after that. They were lost in each other's presence, as if nobody else was in the room, but them.

Chapter 6

The sun beamed down Londyn's face as she made her way across campus. Dressed in a forest green and gold ELU tee, jeans, backpack, and big purse in hand, she looked up at the beautiful sun and smiled. It was Wednesday, meaning only one more day left of the school week, and two days left of her workweek. She successfully knocked out her Econ and Calculus exams, so the rest of the week would be smooth sailing. She pulled her iPhone out of her purse and checked her unread messages. There was one from her brother that read, "come over to my place after work please. I need help w/ a paper," and another from one of her classmates asking about a homework assignment for her Broadcast Journalism class. Four days had passed since she and Shane had their "love in the club" connection, and it was beginning to feel as if it never even happened at all. Once again, Shane didn't ask for her phone number. He didn't send her a DM on Twitter, or comment on any of her Instagram pictures. It was like he forgot she even existed after the party that night. Sunday afternoon after church, she and Reagan had a long talk about all of the possible explanations as to why he hadn't tried to contact her. The discussion ended with Londyn deciding that he probably had a girlfriend anyway. Reagan agreed with Londyn's speculations, and backed up her statement with accusations of seeing an upset girl at the party eyeing them during their epic dance.

"That girl was probably his girlfriend, and he probably just wanted to get as many girls to come to the party as possible. Don't trip over him Londyn. If he wanted to contact you, he would. You don't have to wonder and contemplate on what could've happened. Like you said, you don't even know him. So no need to waste your time trying to play detective."

Londyn thought about it, and decided that Reagan was right. After all, she didn't even know much about this "Solo" character. So, no need to sweat it. Although, like any girl would, deep down inside she couldn't help but wonder if she'd somehow turned him off. When she left the party Saturday night, he gave her, Reagan, and Bree a hug and told them to drive safe. Londyn just knew he was going to give the classic line "here take my number down so you can let me know that you made it home safely," but he didn't.

"Oh well!" she said to herself as she opened the

heavy studio door of WZYB.

It was time to put in another 5 hours of work. As she walked down the long hallway that lead to the main recording booth, her co-worker, Brittany Jankowski, yanked her arm and pulled her in the opposite direction.

"Britt, where are we going?" Londyn giggled as she shuffled her feet to keep up.

"Look at this!" Brittany exclaimed as she pointed towards a bouquet of pink roses in the break room.

"Awwww those are so cute! Did your boyfriend send you those?" Londyn asked as she walked into the room to take a closer look.

"My boyfriend? Yeah right, I'm lucky if that dude even sends me a good morning text, let alone flowers." she said as she rolled her blue eyes and tucked her blonde hair behind her ears. "Those are for you!"

"WHAT?" Londyn exclaimed with a confused look of excitement on her face as she walked into the break room.

She quickly picked up the envelope that lay next to the vase. Surely enough, there was her name written in cursive. She leaned over, smelled the roses, and smiled. By this time, a small nosey crowd had formed in the doorway. Before Londyn could even open the envelope, Reagan came bursting through the crowded door.

"O-M-G. I heard you had a secret admirer. Did you read the card, who is it from? Open it!" she exclaimed as Londyn looked at her with the "calm down" face.

Londyn pulled the card out of the envelope and began to read the front.

"Thinking of You, Someone Special. Someone who..." she began.

"Forget that, who is it from?" Reagan asked as she snatched the card from Londyn's hands and opened it. "Awwwwwwww, it's from Shane!" she shouted.

"Give it here!" Londyn exclaimed as she took the card back. "How'd you even know someone sent me flowers so quickly?" she asked.

"You know Brittany Spears' big mouth can't keep a secret." she said, flashing her cell phone call log.

Brittany laughed as she leaned in to get a closer look at the flowers and cards.

"What does it say?" Brittany asked.

Londyn smiled again and began to read the handwritten message on the inside of the card aloud.

"Miss Londyn with a Y,

You are without doubt the most beautiful woman I've ever laid eyes on. If you'd give

*me the time, I'd just like to get to know you,
and hopefully you'd like to do the same.. ;-) ..
Give me a call pretty lady. 313-456-8887.*

Sincerely,

Shane D. Solomon Jr."

"Oh My God Lo!!!! O-M-G!" Reagan screeched.

"You guys don't think it's creepy?" Londyn asked as she reread the note silently.

"No! It's very thoughtful!" Reagan replied.

"I mean, it's not like he sent it to your home address!" Brittany exclaimed.

"Right. I mean, you told him where you work right?" Reagan asked.

"No..." Londyn replied.

"Okay, maybe it is a little creepy then." Brittany giggled.

"Ugh. It's not!" Reagan began, "Y'all are so unappreciative. That's why chivalry is dying because of ungrateful tricks like y'all."

"Shut Up!" Londyn and Brittany replied in unison.

"Just saying..." Reagan said as she rolled her eyes. "You have pictures of you at work at the studio all over Facebook and Instagram. Anyone with decent sense and Google Maps could find out the address to send some flowers!"

"It is definitely a nice gesture, that's for sure." Londyn said as she leaned down and smelled the flowers again, "I guess I'm just shocked, in a good way though."

"See, I knew I liked that guy..." Reagan smiled.

"Wait a second, who is this guy anyway?" Brittany asked with her eyes opened wide.

Both Londyn and Reagan looked at each other, giggled, and walked away.

"What?" Brittany yelled.

"Britt... you know you couldn't hold water if you were a fish tank, boo!" Reagan giggled as she walked out the break room.

Later on that night, as Londyn wrapped up her radio show, she couldn't help but smile at the thought of Shane. She didn't know what to expect, especially after Bree claimed he was such a player, but she couldn't help but feel quite special anyway. No one had ever sent her flowers before. Once she finished her show for the night, she locked the door to the studio booth and made her way towards the exit sign. She gave the sound engineer a quick salute, and pushed open the double doors leading to the outside. The warm summer breeze gently hit her face as she gazed at the sunset. With her cell phone in one hand, and Shane's card and flowers in the other, she quickly dialed his number. She sat down in her car, and closed the door, but was immediately startled by a strange hand knocking on the passenger door window. She let out a quick squeal, before realizing the person outside was none other than Reagan. As she rolled her eyes, she quickly unlocked the door for her best friend.

"Don't you ever do that ever again in your life Reagan, I almost peed on myself. Why does everyone always try to scare me when I leave that freaking studio?"

"You're just paranoid!" Reagan said with a giggle as she slammed the door behind her.

"Who are you calling?" she asked as she pointed at Londyn's phone, which was now sitting in her lap.

"Awww shoot!" Londyn exclaimed as she quickly pressed the red "end" button to hang up the phone. "I definitely didn't know I was calling him!" she said nervously.

"Who?" Reagan asked.

"Shane!" Londyn replied.

"Well why'd you hang up?" Reagan yelled.

"I don't know! You scared me! It through me off!" Londyn replied in panic. "Oh lord, he's calling back! What do I do?"

"Answer it, duh!!!" Reagan exclaimed as she reached over and pushed the green "answer" button.

Londyn looked at her with frustration, and brought the phone to her ear.

"Hello?" she said in a soft angelic voice, while frowning her face at Reagan.

Reagan shrugged her shoulders and flashed a devious smile.

"Hey, did someone just call this number?" asked Shane's deep voice from the other end of the phone.

"Hey Shane, it's Londyn. Sorry about that, I think my signal just faded or something weird." she lied as she continued to look at Reagan.

"Oh hey Miss Londyn. How are you?" he replied with a huge smile.

"I'm great, thanks to you. Thanks so much for the flowers, and the card! That was so sweet of you!"

"Oh no problem pretty lady. I was hoping you wouldn't think I was a stalker or a creep or anything like that."

"A creep? Nah, not at all. It was really sweet." Londyn said with a giggle.

"HAAAA!" Reagan laughed loudly and ignorantly.

Londyn slapped her best friend's thigh and brought her pointer finger in front of her lips to silently signal her to be quiet. Reagan continued to be loud and childish so Londyn asked Shane if she could place him on hold for a second.

"Sure thing." he replied.

She clicked mute and then laughed.

"Get out! Now!" she said while laughing uncontrollably.

"Daaaaang! You get a new boo and start acting brand new already, huh?" Reagan said with a giggle as she opened the door and got out of the car. "I'll call you later girl."

Londyn laughed and took the phone off of mute as Reagan closed the door.

"I'm sorry, are you still there?" she asked as reversed her car and drove away.

"Of course..." Shane replied.

"Good... but yeah, thanks so much for the flowers. That was really special."

"No problem, Beautiful. Make sure you water them and all that good stuff. Don't be killing my flower babies now. We have to be like co-parents for them."

"Oh wow, you are so silly. I'll take care of them as if they were my own kids."

"You got kids?" he asked.

"Wait, no... it's just an expression." she said quickly.

"I know I'm just messing with you..." he replied.

"You got kids?" she asked.

"Yeah 3."

"Really?"

"Yup. All by the same mother though." he replied.

"Oh...wow...oh okay." she nervously responded.

"Nah, I'm playing... but what if I did though?" he chuckled.

"Then I'd say you'd definitely have your hands full, sir." she giggled with a sigh of relief.

"Nah, no kids for me... not yet at least, one day."

"Yeah same here... one day, not too soon though..."

"Oh yeah most definitely... Once I find a wife."

"Agreed...." she replied. "So... I have a question for you."

"What's up?" he asked.

"How in the world did you know to send these flowers to my job?"

"See I knew that was gonna come off as creepy. Dang."

"Nooooo! I was just wondering..."

"Haha. Well honestly, when I saw you at that kickback I was just star struck. It was just something about the way you carried yourself. You just have this confidence about you. Actually, it's a bit intimidating, but then I saw you smile or something at somebody and I was like okay yeah, she's cool."

Londyn giggled at his response.

"For real, you'd be surprised at how many women just don't smile, but anyhow, my boy Chris saw me staring at you I guess, and he told me your name..."

"Ohhh, so you already knew my name before you even came up to me huh..."

"Gotta do the research in order to fully assess the situation at hand, you feel me?"

"I feel you... creep."

"Ahhhhh nah here you go!"

"I'm just kidding."

"Well, Chris told me you were Londyn from the radio, the good girl... Then he told me I didn't stand a chance."

"Whatttt, seriously?"

"Yeah, that's a good thing though. People think very highly of you Miss Londyn."

"Thanks. So why'd he say you didn't stand a chance, you must be one of those player types. You seem like such a nice guy."

"Player types? Nahh... and I am a nice guy! I mean to be honest, I've made my share of not so good choices in the past. Hurt some feelings along the way, but who hasn't? I've grown up a lot... taken a lot of time to myself to mature and focus on being a better man."

"That's real... I can definitely respect your honesty."

"So what about you? You look like a

heartbreaker!" he chuckled.

"That's funny! I'm so not though!"

"I find that hard to believe..."

"Why so?"

"Because, all pretty girls are heartbreakers..."

"Well that's definitely not a good mindset to have!"

"Ha! You right, you right... thou shalt not pre-judge the pretty girl."

"Too funny." she laughed.

"So are you off work now, you in for the night?"

"I'm actually sitting in my car right now... outside of my brother's dorm. I promised him I'd help him with a paper he has to write." she replied.

"Oh word, well don't let me hold you up! I actually have some studying to get to tonight myself."

"Oh okay... well it was nice talking to you. Thanks again for the flowers and the card. It really made my day."

"Not a problem at all. But umm, one quick question though, before you go."

"Sure what's that?" she asked.

"....Well, I'll be on your side of town again this weekend. My boy is playing at this jazz bar on Friday and I was wondering if you'd like to join me?"

"Like a date?" she asked.

"Yeah... exactly, like a date."

"Aww, Shane... that's so nice of you... but I can't go... I'm married."

"Huh?"

"Totally kidding... payback for the 3 kids stunt you pulled earlier."

"Wow you had me fooled for like .5 seconds... a sense of humor... I like it..."

"Good...." she giggled.

"So...." he asked after a short pause.

"Sooo, yes. I'll come with you."

"Alright, it's a date." he agreed with a smile.

"Definitely a date."

"Okay, cool... well, I'll catch up with you later this week with the details and everything... Lock my number in, and you have a good night pretty lady."

"You too sir!"

Londyn quickly hung up the phone and smiled. Although it was a tad bit early to call it, she was feeling rather smitten by Shane's charming personality. He was very thoughtful, a characteristic that was unfamiliar in Londyn's prior dating life. Nonetheless, he was still "a new guy" and according to her beloved grandmother, new people must be kept at arm's length distance until they've proven themselves trustworthy.

"Even a snake's skin looks pretty 'til it bites!" was one of the many countless lessons wise Grandma

Hattie had instilled in Londyn and her brother at a very young age.

Nonetheless, Londyn was completely intrigued. She forgot to wipe the huge Kool-Aid smile off of her face, and when her younger brother opened the front door to his dorm he noticed right away.

"You must have gotten some action because I know you're not smiling this hard to see me." Tony said sarcastically.

"Eww. Shut up!" she laughed as she pushed her way through the doorway into his dorm room.

"Can a girl just be happy to see her little brother?"

"No... actually, no you can't be this happy because I literally just saw you 12 hours ago. Why are you still smiling so hard?"

"I'm not!" Londyn exclaimed.

"Then why are you walking around looking like you just left candy land?"

"Chill out bro. I just had a good day. I'm in a good mood I guess."

"Well I'm glad to hear that, because you've been a real debbie downer lately, you know that right?"

"What! No I haven't!" she replied as she plopped down on his bed, and kicked off her Jordan gym shoes.

"Uh yeah, yeah you really have. But for real, what happened today sis? Why are you so geeked?"

"Welllllll, if you must know. It started with me killing my exam this morning. I definitely scored at least a 90% or higher."

"Good stuff sis! That's what's up." he exclaimed as he reached over for a fist-to-fist pound with his sister.

"... and then my crush sent me flowers to my job..."

"Whoa, whoa, whoa. Time out. Flag on the play, flowers to the job? Your crush? Who is this buster?"

"This guy I met last week at the Beta kickback."

"Dang sis, one of those pretty boys though?" he asked as he shook his head. "So you just gonna leave the Bruh's and head over to candyland, literallyyyy, huh?" Tony joked, making a reference to the red and white canes that Beta men often carry.

"HA! Tony. You're not even Greek yet, you have no "Bruh's" first of all. Second of all, nobody is in candyland. We're just cool. I mean, it's only been a few days. I don't even know why I'm even bringing it up."

"Because my mans pulled the ultimate slick boy move by sending flowers to the job of a girl he just met. That's what's up, Lo. Don't run him away, we all know how you are."

"Wowww, really Antonio?"

"Look, if I don't keep it real with you then who will? It's all love knucklehead."

"Yeah whatever!"

"So does this mystery dude have a name? Address? Zip code? Social Security number? You know I'ma have to run a background check on this pretty boy. He light skin ain't he?"

"You are crazy!" Londyn giggled. "His name is Shane. He's from Detroit, and he goes to U.B."

"Word... That's what's up. So when are you seeing him again?"

"Well, we're going to a jazz bar this weekend."

"Typical pretty boy ish."

"Stop hating." she interrupted. "You could probably take a few notes from the kid!"

"Aye don't be saying all that now. You just met dude, let's not get too deep, thinking he got it going on already. Play it cool. You know how little bro taught you." he said with a stern head nod and raised eyebrow.

"Of course. I learned from the best." she replied as she smiled and nodded her head in response.

Chapter 7

Over the next few days, Londyn and Shane talked on the phone, FaceTime, and texted rather frequently. Although they'd only known each other less than a week, their personalities clicked right away. When Saturday morning came along, Londyn was more excited than she cared to admit for her date that evening.

"Sooooo, did you figure out what you're going to wear tonight?" Reagan asked Londyn as she and a few of their friends sat on Londyn's bed.

"Kind of... I have it narrowed down to five outfits." Londyn replied with her eyes opened wide.

"Five???" Reagan exclaimed as she hopped up off the bed. "Looks like we have some decisions to make!"

"Shoot... she's better than me, I never decide on

an outfit until about 5 minutes after I was supposed to be somewhere." their good friend Chanel giggled.

"Where are you going?" Bree asked.

"To a jazz bar... On a date." Londyn replied slowly.

"With Solo?" Bree asked with an attitude.

"Yes... Is that a problem?" Reagan asked.

"Tuh... just playing with fire that's all. I mean, we all know you're a lover Lo... I just don't think you're cut out for a guy like Solo." Bree added while painting her nails.

"Such a hater, " Reagan responded. "anyway, are you going to at least do something with your hair?" Reagan asked.

"What's wrong with her hair?" Chanel asked.

"Yeah, what's wrong with my hair?" Londyn asked in an offensive tone.

"Oh... I just assumed you'd use at least one of the many inventions Madame CJ Walker created. Can we see it straightened for once?" Reagan laughed.

"I think her hair is cute like that!" Chanel said in her cute baby voice.

"It's cute. I mean don't get me wrong, I'm team natural all day." Reagan said as she flipped her box braids over her shoulder and raised her fist in the air, "...but it's okay to switch it up every now and then."

"It's unhealthy to straighten your hair all the

time." Bree chimed in.

"Londyn, don't listen to them. They're not your real friends!" Reagan giggled as Bree reached over and hit her in the face with a pillow. "It's cute, but that's how we always see you. It's a date for crying out loud. Spice it up boo!"

"Okay what about this one?" Londyn asked as she changed the subject, pulling out a pair of jeans and summery top.

"Nah... too casual for a jazz bar." Bree replied.

"Alright, how about this." Londyn asked as she pulled out a fitted black dress and blazer.

"Wayyyyy too fancy. Y'all ain't going to the opera." Reagan laughed.

"Ugh." Londyn replied as she dug through her closet. "Clearly, I haven't been on a date in a while."

"How long has it been?" Chanel asked.

"Like 6 months at least. I went out on this awkward double date to the movies with my cousin and these two guys from her school, but that's about it."

"Oh wow!" Chanel giggled as she quickly popped up from her position on the bed and looked through Londyn's closet. After a few seconds, she pulled out a long flowing maxi skirt and a tribal corset top.

"Try these on." she said while tossing the

clothes to Londyn.

Londyn disappeared into the bathroom and returned a few minutes later wearing the long flowy skirt that still had a price tag sticker attached. The skirt was a coral pink color made of sheer, dainty material. The multi-colored tribal print corset top beautifully complimented her petite frame.

"Yaaassssssss. You better werkkk!" Reagan squealed.

"Super cute!" Chanel replied as she passed Londyn a handful of jewelry and the perfect wedge sandals to match.

"I absolutely LOVE it! I never would have even thought to put all of that together!" Bree exclaimed.

"Welllll, I'm not a fashion design major for no reason." Chanel giggled. "So what do you think Lo, can you rock it?"

"Most definitely!" Londyn replied with a smirk as she posed in front of her floor length mirror.

"Yeah well just be careful Lo." Bree stated.

"Is he really that bad Bree?" Londyn asked as she continued to frolic in the mirror. "He seems like such a nice guy."

"They all seem nice at first." Bree stated plainly.

"Okay. I mean what's really the deal Breanna? You were all gung ho for hooking Londyn up with

Shane until she told you she didn't need your help. Now all of a sudden he's the devil in a Beta jacket?" Reagan snickered.

"Chill on me Reagan. Can I not look out for my girl? Solo is a cool dude, don't get me wrong. I love him dearly. And yeah I know I said I'd put her on, but then I really thought about it... and I think he just might be too much for her, that's all."

"Yeah, whatever. Listen, Londyn is a smart girl. So I don't think she has anything to worry about. If this guy really is some type of heartbreaker then he's got a whole lot of people to answer to. In the meantime, Londyn. Just have fun child. You deserve it." Reagan stated as she placed her hand on her best friend's shoulder.

"Suit yourself." Bree mumbled under her breath.

At about 7:45pm, Londyn stood in front of her bathroom mirror, as she applied her last few touches of mascara and lip-gloss. She'd taken Reagan's advice and spiral curled her hair into loose flowing curls. It'd been months since she straightened her hair, so she was definitely feeling herself, and her hang-time. Just as she turned off the bathroom light, she heard a knock at the front door. She paused nervously, and took a deep breath before walking towards it. She looked through the peephole, and then opened the door slowly, and carefully not to appear too anxious.

"He is so fine....." she thought as she looked Shane up and down.

He wore khaki slacks, a red and white patterned collar shirt, and a Hermes belt. His white teeth glistened as he looked at her and smiled.

"Hey, you're right on time." Londyn said with a smile as she tried to contain her excitement.

"Wow. You look beautiful Londyn!" he replied as he pulled her hand towards him and blessed it with a quick peck.

"Why thank you, Mr. GQ." she replied flirtatiously.

"So are you all ready to go?"

"Yep, just let me grab my purse!" she replied as she shuffled back into her bedroom.

As she began to walk towards him from her room, he looked at her and smiled.

"Keys?"

"Keys! Right." she giggled before going back into her bedroom to grab her house keys from her nightstand.

He was intrigued as he glanced around the quaint, clean apartment.

"Alright. I think I'm ready for real now!" she

giggled as she walked towards him.

"Cool."

He stepped aside to let her walk through the apartment door first. As she turned the key to lock the door she caught him staring at her from the corner of her eye. She smiled a bit and then turned to look at him.

"You... are absolutely beautiful." he said with a huge smile.

"Thank you Shane. But stop it, you're making me blush."

"I can't... stop being so beautiful then."

"Ha... I can't..." she replied with a smirk as she turned and walked ahead of him towards the car.

He smiled and shook his head as he followed her towards his sparkling white Dodge Charger. She stopped on the sidewalk in front of it and smiled.

"Is this you?" she asked as she pointed towards the car with the fraternity license plate frame holder on the back.

"Nah... actually this is me over here." he said pointing to the rusty broken down gold hooptie parked right next to the Charger. "Can't really afford something that fancy."

"Oh... I'm sorry! I didn't mean to assume." Londyn said with an embarrassed expression on her face.

"Nah, I'm playing girl. That's all me." he said as he beeped the horn on the Charger with his keypad.

"You play too much!" she giggled as she playfully hit him on the arm.

"My bad pretty lady.   You'll learn I'm a bit of a jokester." he replied as he opened the passenger seat door for her.

"It's okay... I kind of like it."

He chuckled and closed her door before walking around to get in on the driver's side. She leaned in and opened his door from her seat, which caused him to smile a bit. As he pulled out of the parking lot, he finagled around with the radio system, skipping through numerous XM radio stations in search of the perfect sound for the mood.

"What you know about this here?" he asked as a classic Tupac song began to play.

Londyn giggled and started rapping the lyrics to "That's Just The Way It Is" without missing a single word.

"Ahhhh, she up on Pac!" Shane cheered with excitement.

"Man, whatttt? Tupac is the G.O.A.T!" she replied before continuing to sing along with the chorus.

Shane joined in, and the two laughed and bobbed their heads to the beat as Shane floated down the highway.

"This girl is different..." Shane thought.

★

From outside of the jazz club, Londyn could hear the smooth sounds of instruments coming from the second floor windows of the venue. Shane gently grabbed her hand as they walked to the front of the line outside the door. The doorman immediately shook Shane's hand and moved to the side so that the two of them could walk right in.

"Oh you got some clout in here I see?" Londyn asked with a smile.

"I come here often." he replied with a nonchalant smirk. "They know me a little bit."

The pair walked through the restaurant and up a flight of winding wooden stairs. Once they reached the top floor, they walked past the band and sat in a little corner booth for two. Black tablecloths covered each tabletop, and dim lighting gave the place a chic feel. Each table centerpiece was made with a serene waterfall base lamp.

"This place is dope! My mouth is watering, it smells so good in here." Londyn stated as she looked around in amazement.

"It is isn't it. It's real low key, that's why I love it... not too many people are up on it yet."

"I see. I can't believe I've never heard of it before." she began to say as their petite, pretty, young waitress approached the table.

"Hello! Welcome to Mojo's Lounge... How are you all doing tonight?"

"We're doing great. Thanks for asking." Shane replied.

"My name is Lauren, and I'll be taking care of you two tonight. Can I start you off with some drinks or appetizers?"

"Umm, I'll just take a water for now." Londyn replied as she looked up from the menu.

"Make that two waters." Shane said with a slight smile.

"Two waters for the lovely couple, coming right up." the young waitress replied before walking away.

"Oh... we're not a..." Londyn began, as Shane let out a small burst of laughter.

"We must look good together if you've got people thinking you're my girlfriend already."

"Ha Ha," Londyn laughed sarcastically, "You'd like that wouldn't you."

"I might." he replied as he sensually bit his bottom lip.

Feeling slightly embarrassed, Londyn smiled and quickly changed the subject. "So... what's good here? What do you recommend?" she asked as she stared attentively at the menu.

"It depends... are you more of a wings and fries type of person, or steak and potatoes?"

"Definitely wings."

"Well, in that case, you have to try the Mojo's Classic. It's pretty decent! I get it every time."

"He's right! That's our house favorite! You get 5 whole wings fried with our classic seasoning, a basket of our signature butter garlic fries, along with a caesar salad." Lauren butted in as she sat their ice-cold waters down on coasters.

"Hmmmm, can I trust you? I hope you have good taste." Londyn asked with a smile as she glanced at Shane.

"I picked you out of the bunch didn't I?"

"Awwwwwww." Lauren cooed as she covered her mouth and squinted her eyes as if she was about to cry.

Londyn and Shane both turned towards her at the exact same time, and stared at her with the *"Really? Could you chill out?"* face. She immediately took the hint and proceeded to take their orders.

"Oh, sorry... ha... Yeah so, do you both want to go with the Mojo's Classic?"

Shane looked up and glanced at Londyn to allow her to go first.

"Yeah I'll go with that... and a strawberry margarita please." she stated as she flashed her ID.

"I'll have the same, but with a Coke please." Shane added.

"Alright, so I have two Classics, 1 strawberry margarita, and 1 Coke. I'll go put that in for you all right now. Enjoy the performances tonight!"

"Thank You!" they both replied in unison.

"So I'm the only one drinking tonight? Now I feel like a lush. I want to change my order!" Londyn giggled.

"Oh, it's cool, don't feel that way. But nah, I don't drink. Alcoholism has been a pretty consistent issue in my family so I never really dabbled in it too much. Just a personal decision though, no judgment."

"Well, that definitely sets you apart from most. I never thought I'd meet a college man who doesn't drink. I respect it."

"Well, I'm not your average guy." he said with a smirk and a wink.

"Oh really... do tell!" she replied as she stirred her straw around her water glass.

"For starters, I'm probably one of the most focused guys you'll ever meet. I was blessed to discover my passion in life at somewhat of an early age so that really keeps me focused and on track as far as my goals, and where I'm headed in life."

"That's awesome! So what is it that you want to do?"

"Well, you know, I'm majoring in engineering. Environmental engineering actually. I want to develop solutions for different environmental and public health issues like pollution and unsafe drinking conditions. Plus work with companies to ensure they're complying with federal regulations. All that. Probably sounds boring I know…"

"Noooo. That's pretty cool!"

"Ha, you think so? Most people give me the side eye when I say that. I know it doesn't sound like the most interesting career off rip."

"But I'm sure it's very rewarding! You'd be potentially improving the quality of life. That's a commendable way to use your degree for sure."

"Thanks. That's the way I look at it. I'm all for making the world a better place."

"That's awesome. We need more people with that mindset. Everyone these days is so focused on themselves. I mean, what ever happened to unity and coming together for a common good? Now it's just about who can make the quickest dollar."

"I definitely agree. So what about you? What's your post-grad plans?" he asked.

"Well…I have this crazy idea to become the host of some big-time talk show, like 20/20…"

"That's what's up!"

"Yeah. I want a platform where I can talk about real world issues and give thought provoking interviews... and get the answers from people that the world wants to know, but nobody knows how to get. I probably should've minored in Psychology or something because I'm always trying to pick someone's brain..."

"That's dope Londyn... so you like to get in folks' heads?"

"I do! It's a blessing and a curse sometimes... it's like I can never really take people for who they are on the surface. I always have to try and figure out their motives. You can't really judge a person's actions when you don't understand their thought process behind it."

"So does that mean you're trying to figure out my motives and all that right now? Is your brain sending all those busy signals trying to connect the dots and all that?"

"Oh most definitely, you better believe it." Londyn said with a giggle and a smile. "I've got my eye on you sir..."

"I like that... keep it on me." he replied just as their waitress came and sat their warm plates down in front of them.

"This smells deeeelicious." Londyn exclaimed as she extended her hands across the table towards Shane's.

He wasn't sure if she was trying to hold his

hand, or if she was doing some sort of weird stretch. Part of him wanted to interlock his hands with hers, but another part of him didn't want to embarrass himself if those were not her intentions.

"Let's say grace." she said, answering his inner thoughts of confusion.

"Oh! Right." Shane replied as he gently grabbed her hands, and bowed his head.

"Dear Heavenly Father, we come to you in thanks for allowing us to cross paths and enjoy each other's company tonight," she began.

Shane slowly glanced up and peeked at Londyn whose head hung low, and beautiful eyes were closed shut. He smiled and closed his eyes again, bowing his head.

"Thank you for the food we are about to receive. Let it be nourishment to our bodies and bless the hands that have prepared it in Jesus' name. Amen."

"Amen." he stated proudly.

At that very moment Shane could tell that there was something very different about Londyn Marie James. He pondered in amazement as he stared deeply into her brown eyes. Although she hadn't said much, she'd said enough for him to see that she was special, and unlike any other woman he'd ever come across.

"*Is it her calm, sweet demeanor?*" he wondered. "*Or maybe her ability to so eloquently articulate her words?*

Is it the fact that she's so confident, graceful, and sure of herself? Or maybe it was how she took the initiative to pray over their food?" he thought.

"What?" Londyn asked as as Shane awkwardly stared at her.

"Huh?" he replied.

"You're staring at me..." she laughed.

"Oh sorry, it's just that you got hot sauce on your face." he quickly replied while pointing at her left cheek.

"Oh!" she screeched as she quickly dabbed her right cheek with a napkin, "did I get it?"

"Nah!" he chuckled while she wiped a little higher on her cheek.

"Okay, what about now?" she asked.

"Here, let me help you with that." he replied as he reached across the table and gently brushed the hot sauce off of her left cheek with her napkin.

She smiled, slightly embarrassed, while staring into his eyes. He realized how sappy his actions must have seemed, so immediately sat back in his seat. He turned his attention toward the live band, and Londyn followed suit.

As the date went on, the two new friends enjoyed both the nights' entertainment and each other's company.

"What happened to your friend? I thought he

was performing tonight?" she asked.

"Oh yeah he is, he'll probably be one of the next acts." he replied with a gentle smile.

Just as he finished his sentence, one of the performers on stage hit her last note, and the crowd began to clap. The host for the night, a local young hip-hop artist by the name of Mia Moore came back to the middle of the stage.

"Give it up for Lady Bell everybody! Wow, wasn't she amazing!" Mia Moore asked as the performer took a quick bow and exited stage left.

"Next up we have a crowd favorite... singing one of my favorite songs by the legendary James Brown. Please give it up for Miss Melody Rain, singing "It's A Man's Man's Man's World.""

"I'll be right back." Shane stated as he quickly removed his napkin from his lap and stood up.

"O....kay." Londyn could barely utter before he raced away from the table.

She assumed he was taking a trip to the restroom, however to her surprise he marched right up to the stage and took a seat at the piano. Her eyes opened wide as she stared at him with her full-undivided attention. Then, a tall, skinny chocolate girl walked up to the microphone in the middle of the stage. She was stunning. Her red lipstick brought out the red flower that stuck in between her large soft curly fro. Londyn wondered not only who she was, but who she was to Shane. However, that thought was cut short when the pretty lady opened her mouth and sang with power and grace.

"Whoooooooo!" the crowd erupted as she took a short breath before repeating herself, this time accompanied by Shane on the keys.

Londyn was pleasantly surprised as she listened to him create such a beautiful melody with his fingers. He managed to play the song in a way that was unlike any other way she'd previously heard. It was as if his passion and soulful vibes were passing through his fingertips onto the white keys, then reflecting off of the black keys to her ears. Just another hidden layer to the mystery man she was so eagerly interested in getting to know. Although she was naturally talented in figuring people out within the first few moments of meeting them, she may have finally met her match.

As the song ended, Miss Melody Rain received a standing ovation from the audience. She thanked her fans with a head nod as she returned the microphone to its stand and walked off stage. Shane followed quickly behind her and headed back to he and Londyn's table.

"Soooooooo you weren't going to tell me that you were the friend that was playing tonight?" Londyn squealed as she reached in for a hug.

"Haha. I just wanted it to be a surprise...." he replied bashfully.

"Well you definitely surprised me alright! You're just full of all types of surprises Mr. Solomon."

"Well I tried to tell you I wasn't the average guy..."

"I'm starting to see that!" she smiled. "So do you do shows often?"

"Every now and then... Melody Rain is my cousin. Her real name is Tanisha. We just do it for fun here and there. Don't want it to feel like work... you know? Takes the enjoyment out of it."

"Right, right. I can definitely understand that."

As the night went on, the two engaged in great conversation. They talked about everything under the sun from current events, to their spirituality, to classes, and the frustrations of college. Their conversations flowed effortlessly, and their chemistry was so strong that you'd think they'd known each other their entire lives. As intrigued as Londyn was by Shane's charming character, he was equally, if not more captivated by her beautiful personality.

"Favorite artist?" Londyn asked.

"Easy. Tupac," Shane replied. "You?"

"Hmmm. It's a tie between India.Arie and Juvenile." Londyn giggled.

"Wow, what a contrast." Shane chuckled.

"Yeah... I have two sides to me I guess." she laughed.

"I feel it... hmmm, okay favorite TV show?" he asked.

"The Bachelor."

"Really?"

"Really!" she exclaimed.

"Interesting." he chuckled.

"You?" she asked.

"Besides anything on ESPN?" he laughed.

"Yes, besides ESPN."

"The Wire... or Martin, if I'm in the mood to laugh!"

"I love both of those," she giggled. "Favorite movie?"

"Paid in Full. I can relate to Ace Boogie."

"How so?"

"He was a man with a brain who knew how to make a way out of no way. Reminds me of myself."

"I dig it." she replied.

"Yeah. So are you an only child?" Shane asked.

"Nope I told you I have a younger brother, remember? He goes to my school. Unfortunately." she giggled.

"Ohhh right, I forgot you did tell me that the other day. Why do you say unfortunately? You two don't get along?"

"We do, I was just joking. It's weird being at the

same school with your sibling though. I always feel like he's somewhere near by watching my every move." she laughed.

"Haha, that's too funny. So it's just the two of you?"

"Well... yes and no..."

"What?"

"Well," she began before pausing, "my dad recently got married, and his wife has a 5-year-old daughter, so I guess that means I have a step-sister?" she said while rolling her eyes.

"You don't sound too happy about that."

"Eh.... Long story I guess..."

"I see...." he said, hoping she'd elaborate further.

"Yeah... but, like I was saying... it's super weird having my brother on campus. Especially at parties. He's always somewhere creeping on me." she giggled as she quickly changed the subject.

"Aw, little big bro huh? Yeaaah, that's how I'd be if I had a sister. Well if I knew my sister I guess I should say." Shane replied, appealing her request to redirect the conversation.

"What do you mean?" she asked.

"My sister on my mom's side and I grew up in different households. She grew up with her pops, and I haven't seen or talked to her since I was a kid. Then

I'm sure I have at least a few siblings by my dad, but I've never met them." he replied.

"Oh wow."

"I know right...nothing but drama." he replied.

"So what's the story? Why don't you talk to them?" Londyn asked.

"Well... I don't talk to my dad at all. I'm a product of a sticky situation. I don't know if you want to hear all that?" he replied.

"I'm listening. Judgment free zone here."

"My parents met in the streets. They were from two different neighborhoods and weren't supposed to associate with one another, but they fell in love. They risked their lives to be with one another, and it caused all kinds of chaos between their respective cliques. It got messy, people died. My mom thought my dad died at one point, and she took some pills to try and die with him. Yeah, it got crazy."

"Wait...?" Londyn asked with a puzzled look in her eyes.

Shane blurted out in laughter, and Londyn threw a french fry at him as soon as she caught on to his joke.

"I knew that story sounded familiar. You're irritating. Romeo and Juliet, really?" Londyn chuckled.

"Mannnn.. You should've seen the look on your face though. Too funny."

"It's not that funny." Londyn replied with a giggle.

"Nah, but in all seriousness, I've never had a close relationship with my pops, and I really don't know why. He just never really took the father thing seriously. He's a street cat, and was always in and out of prison. His father wasn't there for him, and I guess history just repeated itself. It sucks, but it is what it is, right? I turned out fine without him."

"Wow! Really... that's terrible. When is the last time you heard from him?"

"Um.... Wow, it's been a minute... I'd say maybe about 12 years ago. I randomly ran into him at this concert with my aunt. He was with some chick. It was awkward... really awkward..."

"Dang man... I'm sorry to hear that... So what about your sister? You said she lived with her dad?" she asked.

"Yeah, we lived together on and off, until I was 10, when my mom passed."

"I'm sorry..."

"It was a long time ago... I've been able to deal with it. My Aunt Kathryn, well I call her Aunt Ryn, did a great job stepping up to the plate and raising a little bad knucklehead boy from the city. She gave me a life my parents probably couldn't have ever given me, that's for sure. She's really all I got... well she and one uncle, that's my dude."

"Wow... how did your mom pass? If you don't mind me asking?"

"She had a brain disease..."

"Oh no...."

"Yeah... I don't really know all of the logistics of what happened, but she pretty much just left us one day." he said as he fidgeted around with his fingers and cracked his knuckles.

"Oh wow..." Londyn replied at a loss for words as she realized that they actually had something major in common.

"Yeah... but enough about me... what about you? What was life like growing up for little Miss Londyn? You seem like you were your parents' little princess!" Shane joked, with a cheesy smile.

"Not exactly..." Londyn replied.

"Oh really? Well, do tell...No judgment zone, remember." he responded as he removed his napkin from his lap and placed it on his empty plate.

His eyes were attentively focused, and his face showed an expression of genuine concern.

"Okay, well... my mother passed away a few weeks after my 7th birthday."

"Wow that's rough."

"Tell me about it... She died in a car accident. She was driving and... well... it's a long story... I don't really even like talking about it actually. I always get real emotional about it this time of year... anniversary, you know how that goes..."

"Understandable... You don't have to talk about it..."

"Okay... well yeah, my parents were actually separated while my mom was pregnant with my little brother Tony. They were really young... probably too young to be married with kids anyway. Not to mention my dad was a total jerk back then..." she stated as Shane listened carefully, hanging on to her every word. "He was just really immature. Growing up the youngest of 9 kids, he got away with a whole lot of nonsense as a child. He was the baby and I guess they never really forced him to grow up. So, once he and my mother's relationship started to fall apart, she packed up and left. She didn't have a whole lot of money, so once she gave birth to Tony, the 3 of us stayed with different aunts, or with my grandmother... that is, until my mom passed away..."

"Where was your dad that whole time?"

"He was out and about, in and out of college... in and out of work... living life..."

"Oh gotcha.." he replied.

"Yeah... so after the car accident, my dad was forced to take us in. My Granny was like 75, I think... way too old to be taking care of 6 and 7 year old little kids. So he dropped out of college, got a little raggedy apartment in the city, and tried to play daddy. That didn't work for long though, because the environment was too crazy, and he was still way too immature. So my Granny rescued us within like two months, and took us back in with her. We ended up living with her fulltime for 7 years until I was 14 and Tony was 13."

"Wow... I would've never guessed you went through all that, just by looking at you!"

"I could say the same thing about you." she replied with a half smile. "You can't judge a book by its cover."

"Sure can't. So you said you stayed there until you were 14? What happened after that?" he asked.

"Well... I guess it took my dad looking at his then 80+ year old mother taking care of his two kids as he ran around like a fool, to realize that he needed to pull his life off of the ground. So he got it together. Long story short, he went back and finished college, joined the military, and came back to help my grandmother raise us."

"Wow, that's amazing!" he replied. "So, everything worked out with y'all after that?"

"Yeah, for the most part. I mean, we still have our issues, but overall we're good... we've come a long way."

"And what about your G-Ma?"

"My Granny is good... out here living life like she's 60 instead of 89."

"89!"

"Yes 89, and still lives in her own house, and cooks Sunday dinner for us every other Sunday. You'll have to meet her one day... she's quite a character."

"I get to meet grams huh? You must like me..." he smiled as he sipped his Coke and winked.

Londyn smiled bashfully and playfully rolled her eyes as she took a long sip of her margarita. The two of them took turns staring without the other noticing. Their connection was ever so strong, and neither of them could hide it.

"That's crazy though... I never would've imagined that you grew up that way. You wear it well...gracefully I mean." he stated.

"You too." she replied with a slight smirk.

"We're soldiers..." Shane stated as he reached out with with a balled fist.

"Soldiers!" Londyn replied as she returned the pound.

Another hour passed as the two engaged in more intriguing conversation. So intriguing that before they knew it, they were the last couple in the whole room. It wasn't until the bus boy began sweeping past their feet, that they realized just how late it was. By that point, the band had already started to pack up, along with a majority of the building staff.

"Oh wow, what time is it?" Shane asked as he patted down his pockets in search of his cell phone.

"2:09," Londyn answered, "definitely time to

get going." she giggled.

"Yeah, I think so too... Our waitress is probably mad that we're still here." he chuckled as he pulled some cash out of his wallet to cover both the bill and the tip.

"You ready?" he asked.

"Yessir..." Londyn replied as she arose from her seat.

Shane quickly extended his hand towards hers. She smiled and placed her hand in his as they walked towards the exit sign, down the stairs, and out the door. The two walked hand in hand towards Shane's car when he suddenly stopped in his tracks.

"Did you forget something?" Londyn asked with a concerned wrinkled expression.

"No, but I want to show you something... Can I?"

"Uhh, sure." Londyn replied with a wide stare. "What is it?"

"Just trust me..." he replied as they pivoted, and began to walk in the opposite direction of the car.

"Are you cold?" he asked.

"Nah... I'm fine." she replied.

"You sure, because I have a jacket in the car!" he replied while pointing over his shoulder towards the car with his thumb.

"No its cool! I'm okay..." she replied as she

lightly grabbed his arm and draped it around her shoulder, causing him to flash a cheesy grin.

They walked a few hundred feet until they reached the long fenced in walkway that stretched the length of the Detroit riverfront. The river looked so still and calm. Tranquilizing, in the most peaceful of ways. The two of them leaned up against the railing and stared outward across the dark sky that hovered over the massive body of water. They didn't say too many words, just basked in the marvelous scenery of downtown Detroit. The GM Renaissance Center stood tall like a flashlight in the midst of the other tall buildings. The enchanting lights of Canada, a country foreign, yet so close shined brightly in the near distance. Shane looked over at Londyn again, and couldn't believe how captivated he was by her beauty. Her skin glistened under the bright moon, and her curls swayed softly with the light breeze.

"My Aunt Ryn used to bring me out here all the time when I was younger." he began as he gazed off into the night sky. "We'd come out here and look at all the boats and the people across the water in Canada. I always thought they were having the time of their lives. She brought me down here to calm down. I was just a troubled little kid. I'm talking getting kicked out of school, fighting, gang banging, stealing. I had no motivation to live a positive life without my mom around."

Londyn gently brushed her hand against his

arm, before sliding her arm around his so that their inner elbows were intertwined. She didn't know what words to say at the moment, so instead she just continued to listen attentively.

"No matter what craziness was going on at home, at school, or in the hood, when she brought me out here, it's like everything in the world seemed okay. I really don't know why either. I don't know if it was because at the time, I was getting the one-on-one attention I needed, or if it was just being near the water. Either way, this scenery, this park, this serenity, it let me escape."

"And that's why you want to save it huh? The environment. That's why you want to be an environmental engineer." Londyn replied, as it all began to make sense.

"That's part of the reason I guess. That, and I've always been a nature geek. Not too many forests or rivers in the hood," he chuckled, "so when I'm out in nature I feel like I'm in a whole new world. I think I'm a country boy deep down."

Londyn giggled and looked off into the dark sky.

"Let's make a wish!" she suddenly exclaimed as she reached in her purse.

"A wish?" he questioned.

"Yeah a wish, like they do in the movies!" she replied as she handed him a shiny silver nickel from her purse.

She closed her eyes for a few seconds, and tossed her coin over the railing into the river. Shane looked at her like she was a tad bit ludicrous, but nonetheless he decided to follow suit. He was about to toss the coin over the fence when Londyn quickly grabbed his hand, stopping him.

"No!" she exclaimed. "You have to close your eyes first, and make a wish!"

He shook his head in disbelief, but followed her request nonetheless. After closing his eyes for a few seconds, he tossed the coin in the water. Ripples formed quickly and then disappeared.

"What did you wish for?" he asked as he turned to look at Londyn's pretty face.

"I can't tell youuuu! Everyone knows that if you say your wish aloud, it won't come true." she giggled.

"That's ridiculous!" he chuckled, "We're not 10 years old."

"Well, better safe than sorry." she replied.

"You have to speak things into existence."

"Oh really... well what did you wish for Mr. Solomon?" she asked with a sweet smile.

He stared deeply into the dark scenery ahead and smiled.

"You..."

Chapter 8

"Then you really told her you wished for her? Bruuuuuh? Like real life? Mannnn you such a sucka, dawg." Shane's good friend, and fraternity brother Xavier Ellis laughed as he stole the basketball from Shane, mid-dribble.

"It just slipped out man... I shocked my own self." he replied with arms opened wide in a defensive position, as the two battled in an intense game of one-on-one at the Webster Hall Basketball courts.

"Well did you smash?" Xavier asked.

"Nah X, it wasn't even like that. She's a good girl. I can tell. I'm not even on that tip."

"Yeah right. I know you, Sands. You're always on that tip." Xavier replied jokingly as he dribbled in between his legs.

"Whatever yo." Shane stated as he knocked the

Brittney Michelle

ball out of Xavier's hands, and shot it from near the free throw line, "Kobe!" he yelled as the ball sunk through the net.

Xavier stood with his hands on his knees, breathing deeply. "Foul man, you tried to knock me down."

"Don't be a sissy, man. Flopping is illegal." Shane replied as he cockily dribbled the ball.

"Yeah whatever, I know you ain't calling me a sissy. You the one out here having long walks on the beach, singing love songs and what not." he replied as he opened his hands wide, ready to catch the ball.

"And? What's wrong with that?" Shane asked as he bounced the ball to Xavier, and quickly jumped into a defensive stance with his legs firmly planted and arms raised high.

"Nothing. It's just that there are so many beautiful women out here, why be stuck with only one? It's unnatural." Xavier yelled as he quickly maneuvered around Shane towards the hoop, and shamelessly dunked the ball.

He held on to the rim, swinging his legs, before jumping down.

"Ahhhhhhhhhhh! You see that Solo? You see that." he boasted while firmly clapping his hands together.

"You fooling yourself today, yo." Shane replied with his hands in the air, ready for Xavier to pass him the basketball, "Check!"

"I'm just trying to keep it one hunnit with you man." Xavier replied as he attempted to steal the ball from Shane. "I ain't mad at you though, boy. Smooth talking these ladies. That's how the Beta's do. We're professional ladies' men."

"You're really making a big deal out of nothing."

"Well you're the one telling me you sent the girl flowers to her job, took her on a nice little date, wishing on shooting stars, and still ain't hit? I'm just trying to see if I need to check you into the hospital, or buy you a wedding gift. You tell me which one is it homie?"

Shane quickly pump faked around Xavier and shot a long 3-pointer. *Swish!*

"Nothing but net baby. Your ankles okay? I ain't break 'em did I?" Shane boasted as he walked off the court and sat down on the bench.

"Oh you gon' ignore the question. That's cool! Where y'all registered at? Target?" Xavier laughed from the middle of the court, hands up in the air.

"Jokes..." Shane mumbled as he shook his head and laced up his shoes tighter.

"What? I can't hear you?" Xavier yelled.

"I said you got jokes!" Shane yelled back as he grabbed his book bag from the sidewalk and wiped the sweat from his forehead with a small white towel.

"Oh you said you gotta go wish on some more shooting stars. Ah ha... aight sands! I'll catch you later!" Xavier chuckled.

Shane wasn't really offended by Xavier's comments. Xavier was definitely a jokester, and was always the first to clown anyone, especially when it came to their women. Of the three people on their line, X was the only one who could never get a decent girl to take him seriously.

As he walked down the sidewalk away from the court towards the Brusley Center, the most populated "central" area of campus, Shane pulled his "Beats by Dre" headphones out of his book bag and placed them over his ears. If there was anything he loved as much as being out near the water, it was being lost in the world of music. Brusley was a tad bit crowded, per usual for the middle of the day, with a few too many people for his liking. Although his peers affectionately knew Shane as Solo due to his last name, to him it took on a more significant meaning: Solitude. No matter how popular or well liked he may have appeared to be, inside he was an introvert who more often than not preferred to be alone with his thoughts, away from the chaos of campus life. As he stood at the campus bus stop, he reached his left hand in his pocket and pulled out his iPhone. He scrolled down through his text messages until he reached Londyn's name. Placing his thumb on the "compose message" button, he began to type a message and then stopped. The bus was quickly approaching, so he stood up and stepped closer to the curb. It wasn't uncommon for U.B. students to utilize the bus as their primary mode of transportation throughout and around the large campus. Shane quickly found an open seat near the middle of the bus next to a window and plopped down. He looked outside for a few seconds, before suddenly remembering that he was about to text Londyn. He reached for his phone and scrolled back to the unfinished message. As he stared at his phone, he contemplated whether or not to send her a text.

"Maybe Xavier is right." he thought. *"Am I moving too fast with Londyn? Will she even take me seriously?*

After all, he was known for being the big man on campus. The guy with all the ladies. His reputation wasn't one he was proud of, but nonetheless it seemed to follow him wherever he went. One thing was for certain, he was not too fond of rejection, and was worried that that was exactly how this situation would play out.

"Man, forget it." he mumbled as he quickly clicked Londyn's name and brought the phone to his ear. It rang a few times before he heard her soft voice on the other end.

"Hello?" she asked.

"What's up Londyn with a Y?"

"Hey Shane, how are you?"

"I'm good, I'm good. Just wanted to check on

you and see how your day was going and everything." he asked as he nervously shifted his body weight in the hard bus seat.

"Aww thanks for checking on me. I'm fine, about to walk into class."

"Class on a Saturday?" he asked, sounding rather puzzled.

"Yeah, well it's an aerobics class. I needed an extra credit, and Saturday was all that worked for my schedule."

"Ohhh okay, I got you... makes sense. Well, just hit me up later, or whenever you're free... if you can of course."

"Oh yeah, I definitely will for sure.   What are you doing today?" she asked.

"Just a little studying... probably kick it with my frat brothers later, nothing too major. I'll be free."

"Alright. Cool. Well I'll talk to ya later suga." she joked.

"Haha, yeah aight. Bye pretty lady." he stated as he hung up the phone and smiled.

He was so caught up in his own world, that he didn't even notice the girl sitting right next to him. He jumped slightly when he looked over and saw her sitting there, deviously smiling. Her long hair stretched past her chest on her tiny, petite frame, and she had big brown eyes that captivated people at first glance.

"Kyla... how long have you been sitting there?" he asked.

"Oh, long enough to hear you flirting with your new little girlfriend. Who is that? The girl I saw you caked up with all night at the party last weekend? Mmmph." she replied as she rolled her eyes and folded her arms with an attitude.

"So you watching me now?" he asked.

"Oh, I'm always watching you Solo. You can play games with all these little groupie girls if you want to. But just remember that can't none of them, do you like I can." she replied as she pursed her glossy lips and grazed his chin with her pointer finger.

"...Don't act like you forgot." she whispered in his ear before getting up and walking toward the bus exit.

Shane didn't say a word, and instead just turned his head in the opposite direction. The bus slowly rolled to a stop, and Kyla flipped her hair over her shoulder.

"Oh so you can't even say bye?" Kyla asked.

Shane chucked the deuces without even looking up at her face. Kyla immediately rolled her eyes and continued towards the door. Once the coast was clear, Shane looked up and sighed of relief as he watched her small, yet curvaceous figure step off the bus. He reached up and pulled the hanging cord to alert the bus driver that the next stop was his.

A few minutes later, the bus came to a screeching halt, and Shane gathered up his belongings and hopped off. He hiked up the parking lot of his apartment complex towards his old brick building. Lightly tapping the hood of his car as he walked past, he stepped onto the sidewalk that led to his front door. As he opened the heavy metal door, he wrinkled his nose at the smell of cigarette smoke and dogs. He nodded his head at a neighbor coming down the short flight of stairs that lead to his apartment. Once up the stairs, he unlocked the door and stepped into his domain. His apartment was squeaky clean, down to the glistening dishes in the dish rack near the sink. His shoes were neatly aligned in a row near the front door, and his DVD collection was stacked neatly parallel to his flat screen TV. Not your average messy bachelor's pad, but after all, Shane wasn't the average bachelor. He stretched out on the comfortable leather sofa in his living room, and laid his head back on a pillow to take a nap. However, as soon as his eyelids closed, his phone began to vibrate in his pocket. He pulled it out, only to see the name "Kyla" flashing across the screen.

"Ughhhh." he groaned with irritation as he threw the phone down on the couch near him and closed his eyes once again.

After a few seconds it stopped vibrating, but then started again quickly. A voicemail. He shook his head and ignored the message without even listening to it. He didn't want anything to do with Kyla Evans;

the sneaky, conniving, Delilah that had caused nothing but trouble in his life over the years that they'd known one another. She was the closest thing he'd had to a girlfriend in college, but their awkward love affair eventually went sour. They were bad news for each other, and everybody knew so. Seconds later his phone vibrated again, so he angrily sat up and grabbed the phone.

"Yo, what do you want?" he sternly asked.

"Well that's no way to talk to the woman who raised you, now is it Shane?"

Shane's eyes opened wide as he pulled the phone from his ear to actually look at the caller ID.

"I'm sorry Aunt Ryn. I thought you were someone else."

"Well who's got my baby so upset that you have to answer the phone like that? You alright, nephew?"

"Yes ma'am. I'm fine. I promise. It's just that crazy girl who won't leave me alone, that's all."

"Crazy huh... and does crazy have a name?"

"Kyla..."

"Ohh Kyla... you know, that Kyla, she used to be such a sweet, sweet girl."

"Not really."

"Oh yes, hunny. I remember when you first met her back when you got to Boazer. You thought she was the best thing since sliced bread." she giggled.

"Ha ha, funny Auntie. Well things change and people change. She isn't all that sweet and innocent as you think. She just won't let me live. It's like whenever she even thinks I might have someone new in my life she just pops up and tries to raise all types of hell."

"Watch it..."

"I'm sorry. She wreaks all kinds of havoc auntie." he said in a playful proper tone. "But, when I'm alone though, she's nowhere to be found. You can't tell me that's not crazy."

"People do a lot of things that may come off as crazy when they're jealous Shane. The girl is just hurting and doesn't know how to deal with it. Young love will have a girl acting out of character, and playing with fire. You just need to make sure you're not out here fanning the flames, you hear me."

"...ain't nobody thinking about that girl."

"Yeah, well you just make sure you're not out here throwing mixed signals to the child. And same for all them other little fast girls running around out there. Don't blame it on them when you're the one sending those late night text messages talking about some, 'Hey Baby... you up?'" she laughed as she mimicked her nephew in a dramatic tone.

"Aunt Ryn, for real?" he chuckled.

"Yes for real, I know how you young boys do. Don't call them crazy in public when you're throwing bait in private."

"Okay, check this though. She was never even my girlfriend. You & I both know that. I don't even know how she got all attached like this, when we were never even together. She was messing around with other guys the whole time anyway. I don't know why she wants to act like I'm her property now."

"...and that's exactly why you young, unmarried kids don't need to be out here bumping and grinding, is that what y'all call it? ... knocking the boots."

"Aunt Ryn this is not the 90's."

"Well whatever, I'm old school. You know what I mean. I know exactly what your little fast tails be up there doing in those dorms. I was young once! You need to be careful."

"I am... I promise..."

"Mmmm hmmm... and you need to take yourself back to the city and go to church. Everybody has been asking about you. Mother Rosa and Deacon Brown especially. They both called me and said they haven't seen you in months, Shane. Then they started asking questions about Carmen, Brian, Evelyn, and the rest of the family. Quite frankly, I wish they would stop being all up in my business, but you know that's really beside the point." she began to ramble.

"I'll be there soon."

"Mmm hmm... you better. You've been reading that bible right? Studying the word..."

"Every night."

"That's my boy!"

"I wish you would just move back home though, mannnn. Nobody told you to move down to Houston and forget all about me."

"Boy, now you know ain't nobody forgotten about you. You're my baby boy. I got you always and forever. You can call me whenever you need me, no matter the time of day or night. You know that right?"

"Yes ma'am." he replied with a smile.

"And you handle things with Miss Kyla too. You just have to be straight up with her, and tell her it's not going to work out with the two of you, if that's how you really feel."

"She's crazy... she ain't gon' listen." he replied again.

"Yeah, well why don't you just try it."

"Aight. I'll try." he replied as he shook his head.

"I love you."

"I love you too, Aunt Ryn."

"Bye nephew."

"Bye."

He laid his head back on the couch and stared at the ceiling for a few moments. He was in deep thought reflecting on what his wise aunt had just advised him to do. So, he picked up his phone again and played the voicemail that Kyla left.

"Look Solo. I don't know what you think you doing out here trying to embarrass me on the bus. You ain't right, man. How you gon' play me like that? Embarrassing me in front of my girls at Greek Fest. Dancing all up on that little thot the whole night. For real? That's the best you can do? I mean, I know she ain't doing you like I do. But at the rate you're going, you'll never get the chance to see what that's like ever again. But I know you want to though. You know you can't leave all this alone. How you gon' be in my bed one night, and all up on her the next? Man. I hate you... but, call me back though."

Shane shook his head as the message played and buried his head in his hands. As if he wasn't irritated enough, his phone rang again. This time it was one of his childhood friends, Emmanuel Jefferson, also known as, Man-Man.

"Hello?" Shane asked as he answered the phone.

"Whattttttt Upppppppp Solo."

"What's good, Man-Man."

"Aye, I'm just trying to see what you on bro. You ain't been in the hood in a minute, what's good?"

"Oh, I'm cool bro... just been focused on school. You know how it is."

"Nah, I don't know nothin' bout that life bro... but I do know that it's getting real, real hot on the block."

"Word... What's going on?" Shane asked as he

sat upright.

"You remember Dayon and Juno, right? The twin brothers that used to stay over there on the Ave, next door to Tiara."

"Yeah I remember, what about them?"

"Well, Dayon just got out. Word on the streets is he coming after my whole Brighmo' squad... but we got something for em." Man-Man replied as he pointed his fingers in the shape of a gun.

"Why?"

"Well, it started 'cause they robbed Juno when Dayon was in lockup. Ha! They so savage man, they sold everything they copped from Juno on they own block. The twins bout broke as hell now cause the crackheads just come straight to Lyndon instead of..."

"No, fool," Shane interrupted, "I meant why are you even involved? This don't even concern you. You ain't from Brightmoor."

"Right. I know that, but you know my people stay over there. Look if anything goes down in they hood, then that's automatically my business. You gotta come home and have my back bro. Dayon and Juno gon' have they whole lil set with 'em. I ain't letting my boys go down like that, not on my watch. It's gon' get real."

"You trippin', Man-Man. Don't get caught up in some mess that don't even concern you bro. It's not worth it."

"Look I ain't trying to hear all that! You coming, or nah?"

"Nah, didn't I tell you I'm trying to focus on graduating?"

"Oh so now you just Mr. Integrity, huh? You used to be the main one out here on the block defending what's yours, but now ever since you been up at that school, and joined that fraternity you act like you too good for the hood. What cause you got some new frat brothers now, you don't need your real brothers?"

"Dawg, you tripping. For real. Chill out."

"Yeah aight. I get it."

"Dawg, you don't even have to be in that mess bro! If it ain't about West Warren then it's really not your concern bro. Just stay out the way."

"Man whatever, they had my back, and so I'm gon' have theirs. I'm loyal unlike some people. Hit me up when you come to your senses." Man-Man said as he hung up the phone.

Thanks to the voicemail from Kyla, and the conversation with Man-Man, Shane was now overly frustrated, and falling asleep was no longer an option. All he wanted to do was live life stress free, go to school, and graduate.

"People always trying to drag me down..." he mumbled to himself.

He picked up the remote and turned on the

television to BET, where the Martin episode when Tommy got into a major accident after he and Martin hadn't been speaking, was playing. After the episode ended, Shane started to reconsider whether or not he should help Man-Man after all.

A few minutes later, his phone began to ring again. To his pleasant surprise, he realized that it was a FaceTime call from Londyn. He quickly answered it, and Londyn's pretty face appeared on his screen. Her hair was up in a high bun, and she was dressed in her cute Nike workout gear.

"Hey Pretty Lady." he said with a huge smile.

"Hey Handsome." she flirtatiously replied.

"How was class? I see you with your workout gear on okay, okay."

"Haha, it was greaaat. I think I'm about to go run a few laps around the track while I'm on campus since I got my blood flowing and everything. Might as well, right?"

"I need to hit the gym myself! Let some of this stress out."

"Stress? What's wrong, school?"

"Nah, school is decent. It's just some other stuff back home. No big deal though."

"Oh okay, I see..."

"Yeah... Seeing your pretty face just made my day all the way better though."

"Stop ittt."

"What, I'm serious."

"Thanks..." she giggled.

"Yeah... but what you got up for the night? It looks like I might have to run back to the city tonight to take care of some things... I might need a roll dawg."

"I'm not doing anything. Just another boring Saturday night. What do you have in mind?" she giggled.

"Oh just a little something..." he replied with a grin.

"Uh oh. I don't like the sound of that? Don't be out here getting me in trouble Shane!"

"Oh nah, of course not. I don't get in trouble!" he laughed.

"I'm just kidding! But yeah, I'm not doing anything. I'm down, we can hangout."

"Cool. I'll let you know when I'm headed out that way."

At about 6:30pm, Shane arrived at Londyn's apartment. Just as he pulled into a parking spot, he noticed a text message from Man-Man.

"Aye if you coming bro just meet us at Dorian

grandma crib bro."

Just as he was about to respond, Reagan came bursting through Londyn's front door.

"Bye girl!" Reagan yelled as she headed towards her car.

She stopped when she saw Shane, who was quickly getting out of his car to greet her.

"Heyyy Solo. Good to see you again. How's life?" she asked with a smile.

"Life is good. How you doing girl?"

"I'm great, bout to go home and attempt to write this theology paper, ugh." she grumbled. "You better take care of my girl tonight. Bout time somebody got her out the house."

"Haha... I got you." he chuckled as he walked up to Londyn's doorstep where she stood in the doorway waiting.

"Wassup pretty lady?" he asked as he greeted her with a warm hug.

"Hey handsome..." she smiled with a smirk.

"You ready for a little adventure tonight?"

"Ummmm... I'm not sure... I'm scared..." she giggled.

"No need to be scared when you're with me." he replied, still face-to-face and arm-to-arm with her in a hug.

Londyn blushed and looked off to the side

before gently pulling away from his embrace.
"Can you come inside for a second? I just need
to put my clothes in the dryer before we go so they
won't get all sour..." she said, quickly changing the
subject as she turned and walked into her apartment.

"Sure no rush at all..." he replied as he followed
behind her.

As Shane entered her apartment he glanced
around at the décor. Once again, he noticed how neat
and tidy her apartment was. A definite turn on for a
super organized guy like Solo. Everything in her
apartment was modern and color coordinated, giving
a very mature adult feel to the place.

"Your apartment is dope." he stated as he sat
down on the couch in the living room.

"Thanks," Londyn replied as she opened a
closet door in the hallway, which housed her stacked
washer and dryer unit, "Reagan's mom helped me
decorate. She loves that kind of stuff."

"You need any help with that?" Shane asked as
he quickly jumped up from his seat on the couch.

"No... no. I got it... stay right there." she replied
with her palm facing him. "I can't have you out here
seeing my unmentionables." she giggled.

"Yeah, true. If I'm washing your dirty drawers
then we go together!" he chuckled.

"They're clean, thank you! But wait, no...
nevermind still, haha!" she laughed hysterically.

"You are so goofy!" he said as he sat back down on the couch.

"I know, I know!" she giggled uncontrollably as she closed the dryer and pressed the start button. "Okay, I'm ready, we can go now."

"After you my lady..." Shane replied as he stood up.

The two walked down the sidewalk towards Shane's car. He quickly stepped ahead of her so that he could open her car door before she had the chance to do it herself. She thanked him as she sat down and buckled her seatbelt. As he walked around to the driver's side, his phone began to vibrate from the cup holder. Londyn couldn't help but to glance down at the phone, in which the name Man-Man was flashing across the screen.

"Somebody was just calling you..." Londyn stated as Shane sat down in the car and revved up the engine.

"Oh really?" he asked as he picked up his phone and intensely read the 3 new text messages in his inbox.

He was silent for a few seconds as his fingers swiftly typed away on the touchscreen keypad. From the look on his face, Londyn could tell that something serious was in those messages.

"Is everything okay?" Londyn asked, breaking the awkward silence.

"Oh. Yeah, yeah everything's cool." he replied as he shifted gears and reversed the car out of it's parking spot.

His eyes focused long and hard out the windshield as he made his way to the main road.

"Are you sure?" Londyn asked, "You look tense all of a sudden."

"Oh, nah... I'm good boo!" he said confidently as he turned on the radio to kill the awkward silence.

One of his favorite songs "Pretty" by Tahj began to play on one of Detroit's most popular radio stations, HOT 107.5, and Shane quickly turned up the volume.

"I see a pretty girl, and I want her to be mineeee. I can't stop staring cause she's oh so fine." he sang even louder as he looked over at Londyn and grinned.

She smiled and shook her head as she looked out the window. It was such a beautiful summer evening, and she couldn't help but wonder where Shane was taking her.

"Soooo, are you going to tell me where we're going?" she asked with a slight smile.

"Nope! You'll see! It's a test. If you can handle this then that'll tell me all I need to know. " he replied.

"I don't know if I can handle your surprise tests, Solo." she giggled.

"Aw man, we're real friends now if you're calling me Solo... I feel special."

"Whatever..." she giggled.

"I just have to head over to my neighborhood for a minute... needed a ride along partner, and I figured who better to hang with than Miss Londyn."

"You got me there... I can't think of anyone better to hang with than me either!" she laughed.

"Ha, ha, ha!" he chuckled.

They drove around for a while through Solo's old stomping grounds as they reminisced on their similar childhoods.

"...and that small building over there next to that field is my old elementary school. I got in so many fights in that front parking lot man... getting into it with dudes twice my size and then had to run my butt home..." he laughed as he shook his head. "I was a piece of work."

Londyn giggled as she wondered what lied behind the eyes of this complex man. Someone so gentle, sweet, and mature, yet with a mysterious past that she couldn't quite figure out.

"My Granny used to stay over here." Londyn began as she pointed out the window. "When Tony and I lived with her we used to walk to the candy store that used to be right there on that corner."

"Wow, really? Yeah that candy store burned to the ground in '07. I remember that day! So we grew up in the same hood. That's crazy."

"Right, who would've ever thought. My Granny always said they burned that place down for an insurance claim." she replied.

"I believe it... everybody has been saying that for years."

"Such a small world..."

"It really is." he stated.

They drove for about 10 minutes before approaching the Brightmoor neighborhood. Londyn looked out the window with a look of nostalgia as she thought back on her childhood.

"Wow, Lyndon. That's the street some of my cousins stayed on until they moved to the suburbs. Haven't been over here in ages. " Londyn stated.

Shane kept driving a few blocks, turning here and there, before making a left turn onto 7 Mile Road. He stopped at a stoplight next to a barbershop and liquor store, and then turned into the parking lot of New Hope Missionary Baptist Church. He quickly circled the parking lot until he found a spot close to the door.

"Wait, church... we're going in?" Londyn asked as she watched Shane unbuckle his seatbelt.

"If that's cool with you?"

"I mean, yeah of course, but look at me, I'm not dressed for church at all!" she replied as she looked down at her ripped jeans, tank top, and sandals.

"Neither am I! They say come as you are though right? Who cares... and we can sit in the back!"

"Oh God..." she replied. "You're really serious?"

"Yep!" he replied as quickly he got out of the car.

Londyn nervously shook her head and then followed Shane out of the car to the door.

"If my Granny knew I was walking into a church looking like this she'd wring my neck!" Londyn said as they approached the door.

"You look fine, Lo! Trust me!"

Londyn smiled inside and out at the fact that he called her Lo. For some reason, it always tickled her when guys called her that. They walked inside of the church building where Saturday night revival service had already begun. Shane shook hands with an usher outside the sanctuary before grabbing Londyn's hand and gently pulling her through the door with him. They selected a very back row of the sanctuary, carefully scooting down the pew to avoid obstructing anyone's view. The presiding Bishop Edward Thomas Booker III's voice echoed loudly from the front of the church.

"See what I want everyone here to realize is that relationships, both good and bad can affect, your destiny. You see the wrong relationship, can set you back. Just like the right relationship can propel you forward. The right relationships, will give you life. The wrong relationship, will suck you dry. Jesus had a circle. We know them as the disciples. It wasn't an outside enemy that betrayed Jesus, was it? No, it was one of his own: Judas. So my question is, who are you letting in, your circle? Can I get an amen?"

"Amen." Shane and Londyn replied in unison, along with the rest of the church.

They listened attentively as Bishop Booker held their undivided attention throughout the rest of the sermon. Just as the service was beginning to come to a close, Shane tapped Londyn's arm and motioned his head towards the door. The two of them quietly got up and headed towards the exit while Bishop Booker was still speaking. Shane nodded his head at a few people as they walked past, but quickly moved towards the door leading to the parking lot.

"Why'd you want to leave so early?" Londyn asked as they walked to the car.

"Oh... well, you know how people get when they haven't seen you in a long time. They want to talk, and ask all kind of questions about what's new in your life. I was just trying to dodge us a few nosey bullets." he stated as he unlocked and opened the passenger side door for Londyn.

"Mmmm hmmmm." she mumbled with a smirk.

He smiled back and winked right before

shutting the door.

"Have you ever been to The Beirut Stand?" Londyn asked as he put the key in the ignition.

"Beirut Stand... nah, never heard of it... what is it?"

"Aw man, it's the best place ever. Their chicken shawarmas are LIFE. We have to go. I'm starving..."

"Okay cool, I could eat... Where is it?"

"Not too far... It's over there on 9 mile and Woodward, in Ferndale."

"Alright bet, well you just direct the way lady." he stated as he began to pull out of the parking lot.

Shane took 7 Mile to Wyoming, and then hopped on 8 Mile. About 10 minutes later they turned onto Woodward, and arrived in Ferndale, a quaint, relatively small suburb of Detroit.

"Make this left right here." Londyn said as she pointed in the direction of a fancy food truck.

Shane quickly turned left and then parallel parked next to the curb. They got out of the car, and walked towards the food truck where a short line had already formed in front. Londyn smiled anxiously as they advanced closer to the sliding window.

"What can I get for you ma'am?" asked the gentlemen behind the other side of the sliding window counter.

"Two chicken shawarmas please, and two

Coke's." Londyn replied as she began to dig in her purse for cash.

Shane quickly reached his arm over her shoulder and handed the worker a $20 bill.

Londyn looked up at him and smiled. "You didn't have to do that, it was my idea, my treat."

"Hanging out with you is a treat in itself, the least I can do is pay for a meal." he chuckled.

The worker handed over two large chicken shawarmas wrapped in foil and two Cokes. As Londyn grabbed the food, Shane collected his change. He thanked the worker as the two of them began to unwrap their food and dig in.

"This is pretty good." Shane stated after about two bites.

"Told ya!" Londyn responded as she wiped the corner of her mouth with a napkin.

The two walked and talked down the quiet, calm streets of Ferndale. On any given weekend after about 11pm, those very streets would be filled with rowdy college students and young professionals bar hopping through the various restaurants that transition into quite an exciting nightlife after hours. However, on an early Saturday evening, the community was rather calm and peaceful.

After walking and talking down Woodward Avenue for about 10 minutes or so, they stopped at a small park, away from all the restaurants and bars.

151

Londyn walked towards a swing set and plopped down on a swing like a big kid. Shane followed closely behind and grabbed the metal chains. He pushed her swing slowly and gently.

"So what did you think of church? I meant to ask you that earlier." Shane asked.

"It was great. I loved it... I'll have to come back and visit. The Bishop seemed real cool and down to earth." Londyn asked as she pumped her legs back and forth. "Have you been going there a long time?"

"My whole life, really. But, I can't even lie though- I've been slacking recently. I hadn't been in some months, but I'm really going to try to get back to going. Ever since my aunt moved away about a year ago I haven't been going as much."

"Yeah, I need to do better too. I can't even remember the last time I've actually been to church. My Granny used to make me go every single Sunday until I got grown and out on my own. I mean, I still watch TD Jakes live stream every Sunday though." she giggled.

"Haha, that's a good start, but it's nothing like being there you know. I guess I kind of lost sight of that in the past few months. It's important for me to be spiritually in tune with God. He's my rock. My foundation. Without the man upstairs, I swear I wouldn't be here. I'd be lost...or dead."

"That's real... well let's make a pact. We'll make

an effort to spend more time working on ourselves and get back to our roots... back to church! Deal?" Londyn asked.

"Haha.. deal! See, that's why I like you girl." he laughed as he sat down on the swing next to her.

She smiled and continued to slowly swing back and forth.

"So, lemme ask you something..." Shane began as he sat still in the swing and looked right in Londyn's eyes.

"Ask away..." she replied as she brought her swing to a stop.

"Why are you single?"

"Ugh, I hate that question." Londyn giggled.

"Why is that?"

"Because.... whenever people ask someone that question, what they're really asking is 'What's wrong with you?' ...or, 'how come nobody wants you?'"

"Nah, I'm saying though, why hasn't anyone scooped up such a great girl like you?"

"I don't know..." she began, and then paused, "I guess you could say it's timing, or me being more focused on school, my job, and everything else in my life..."

"So nobody has ever stolen your heart?" he asked.

"I wouldn't say all that now..." she replied and

shook her head.

"Ohhhhh? What's the story?" he asked.

"Ohhhhh it's a long, long, long, story."

"Well, I have a long, long, long, time to listen."

"Okay..." she chuckled. "So, I had a boyfriend. We were together for two years, if that's what you want to call it. It wasn't a perfect relationship, but it was good, or so I thought. Come to find out, the last 6 months of our relationship before we officially broke up he was talking to a freshman at our school. Like legit dating her, basically he had two girlfriends... and I had no idea!"

"Wow, really...That's messed up!"

"Tell me about it..."

"So how did you find out about the other girl and everything?"

"Well... like I said the girl was a freshman and I was a junior... so we hung out with two totally different crowds. Plus, she was a little hoodrat." she giggled. "So, he never thought we'd cross paths. But, me being me, started getting suspicious when I thought he was acting a little weird. Like, he started disappearing for days at a time... got real defensive all of a sudden...you know, just signs of like, changing behavior..."

"Right..."

"So, my birthday comes around, right. My friends throw me this surprise birthday party... and he's not there. At the time, I'm lowkey upset because I'm thinking my friends just didn't invite him because they never really liked him much. But after the fact they let me know that they did extend the invite, and that he just chose not to come. Truth be told, I didn't see him at all on my birthday. He claimed he had to work. He sent me some little weak text like halfway through the day, but nothing special like what you'd expect your boyfriend of two years to do."

"I feel you."

"So over the next few days, I did a little investigating... snooping around... because I knew something just was not right, but I couldn't find anything. He hid his tracks pretty good, but then, I got on Facebook..."

"Aww man. The book tells all..." Shane replied, holding on to her every word.

"Right! So, I got on Facebook, and saw a younger girl I went to high school with tagged in a picture from a few days prior, on my birthday actually, at a house party. I looked on the picture, and low and behold, in the background of her selfie, there I see him kissing another girl."

"That sucks..." he sighed.

"Yup. He was slobbing another chick down, in a picture, on MY birthday. So of course the girl is tagged, and all the comments were in reference to them kissing in the background. So, I went to her page.

There's a picture of the two of them in her profile picture, and all of the comments were talking about how cute they looked, blah blah blah. She actually had tons of pictures with him, dating back to at least 6 months prior to that... and that's when it all made sense..."

"I'm sorry that had to happen to you. That's crazy."

"It's alright. I got over it. I mean, I had no choice to when a week or two later, in the midst of him trying to cover up his lies and apologize to me, homegirl announces to the world and the whole school that she was pregnant with his baby."

"What?" he asked as he threw his head back.

"Yup... talk about embarrassed! If I had a dollar for every time someone hit me up asking if Justin and I were together because they'd heard that a freshman was going around claiming to be the mother of his unborn seed, I'd be rich."

"Wow."

"It turned out not to be his baby I guess. But that's beside the point."

"That's crazy. Man, dude is wack. You deserve better."

"I do, but it happens to the best of us I guess."

"It doesn't have to..." he replied, staring deep into her eyes.

She was beginning to feel a little uncomfortable and uneasy so she decided to change the subject and focus on Shane.

"Sooo... enough about my sorry, sad relationship story. What's your story? Why are you single?"

"Commitment issues..." he replied bluntly.

"I've heard that one before."

"Nah, seriously. It's the truth. I'll be honest with you, I've had run-ins with girls that could've been potential girlfriends. I can't even lie and say that I haven't... just never seems to work out."

"Why is that though? You think it's because of what some girl did to you, or what?"

"I don't know... I can't really say it's a girl. I've never really had a real, real girlfriend."

"Wow, really? That's surprising."

"I know... I mean, I've talked to girls for a long time, had deep connections with a few, but never felt comfortable enough with one to actually go as far as making her my girlfriend, not unless you want to count like 9th grade, but I don't count that."

"Got it... that makes sense..."

"You feel me?"

"No," she giggled, "but it makes sense as to why people say what they say about you."

"What have you heard?" he asked with a

concerned expression on his face.

"Nothing too bad, just heard from a friend of mine that you're a ladies man, and that you break hearts."

"I don't do it intentionally. I mean, I'm a friendly guy. People always see me around a lot of women, but since they never see me committed to just one I guess that could look like a ladies man."

"Mmmmm hmmmmmmm." Londyn replied sarcastically.

"Haha. I'm serious, Lo! I'll admit I'm a flirt, and I'll admit that in the past I've hurt a girl or two, but if I'm anything, it's honest and real. I'm not out here purposely trying to lead anyone to believe that I'm their one and only if I'm not."

"I can respect that."

"Good, at least someone understands." he sighed.

"Yeah... I get it, sometimes people hold on to the slightest ounce of a hint that they have a chance of a relationship with a person. When you try to be nice, instead of outright cutting them off, they misunderstand it for hope for a future."

"You sound just like my Aunt Ryn." he laughed.

"She must be a wise woman."

"She is."

"So she gave you that advice huh? Must be

somebody you need to cut off." she giggled.

"Man... cut off isn't even the word."

"Seeeee! I knew it! I knew you had somebody... The people told me 'Solo is never actually solo.'" she giggled.

"The people huh. But, it's not even like that, I swear."

"Right... tell me anything!" she laughed and rolled her eyes.

"Everybody has a past right?" he asked.

"Yeah, but not everybody's past is really in their past. Sometimes the past is still lingering in the present."

"Yeah, well I'm trying to put my past all the way behind me. That's what I was talking to my Aunt Ryn about earlier."

"So who is the girl?" Londyn asked attentively as she got up from the swing set.

"Tuh..." Shane sighed, "This girl named Kyla that I used to mess around with. I met her when I first transferred to U.B.." Shane began as he quickly stood up and followed behind Londyn. "She was cool at first... but then, she started getting real territorial."

"Oh, I know how that goes."

"Yeah... it was wild. She wasn't really down for me when she needed to be, only when it was convenient for her. She was too busy trying to be somebody she wasn't, and she looked at me like a trophy I guess. So when I tried to get ghost, she was salty and has been playing the victim role ever since then."

"Are y'all still ...friendly?" she asked, insinuating more.

"Are we still intimate, is that what you're asking?"

"...Yeah, I guess it is." Londyn replied.

"Honestly... We did recently... it was a mistake that I'm paying for now."

"Oh...." Londyn replied as she looked away off into the distance.

"It was before I met you..." Shane quickly added, "... and I really regret it. Now she's back to that entitlement nonsense."

"Are you in love with her?"

"No. Not at all. I honestly can't stand her."

"Mmmmm hmmmm." Londyn replied.

"Londyn..." he began as he stopped dead in his tracks and looked directly in her eyes, "I don't want anything to do with that girl, I promise. To be completely honest with you, ever since June 30th, the only girl I can see or think about is you..."

Londyn smiled a bit as she realized she remembered the exact date they'd met. However, her guard was still sky high after the news he'd just given her.

"What if this girl is still around? What if she was at his house last night? What if he's lying to both me and her?" were just a few of the many questions that were racing through her brain.

"So what are you looking for now? You said it's never worked out for you in the past, so what do you want with me?"

"You just seem different. I've never met a girl like you."

"Yeah, there aren't too many like me." she chuckled.

"Ain't that the truth." he began. "I don't know Londyn, maybe I'm trippin'... but something just tells me that you and I could be something."

"So why should I believe you?" she blurted out without thinking.

"What do you mean?" he asked with a puzzled expression on his face.

"I mean, why should I believe that you and Miss Thang are really over if you just got it poppin' with her not too long ago? Don't get me wrong, I'm not trippin'. I'm not 'that' girl, but I'm saying, like why should I even take the risk of opening up to you when I know there's someone else in the picture?" she asked with her arms folded.

Shane gently grabbed both of her elbows, causing her to drop her folded arms. He grabbed both of her hands in his and looked deeply into her big brown eyes.

"Well for one, she's not in the picture. Man, she's not even in the frame." he giggled. "You can trust me on that. She knows it, and that's why she's upset about it... and I guess, I can't really say why you should believe me. You don't owe me anything, not even a chance, but I can say that I'm trying to be completely honest with you, which is why I even brought it up in the first place. I really like you Londyn... a lot... and I hope you'll see that and give me a chance to get to know the real you... the Londyn behind all the tough exterior."

Londyn paused for a moment before looking him in the eyes. She loosed her hands from his grip, and placed them on both of her hips.

"Well check this out..." she began, "I like you too... But Londyn Marie James doesn't play second to anyone. I'm not one of those lonely girls who will put up with somebody's bull for the sake of just having them, so if you want to get to know me, then all I ask is that you keep it 100. Don't have me out here looking stupid. Even if it is still early in the game..."

"I got you Lo... I promise, I won't let you down... You don't have to worry about a thing." he stated as he bent down and softly kissed her forehead. "Trust me."

Chapter 9

"Soooooooooooooo. Is he your boyfriend yet?" Reagan's mom, Brenda better known as "BeBe," asked as she cooked Sunday morning breakfast.

"Nooo, Mama BeBe! It's only been a couple of months since we first started hanging out. We're still trying to feel each other out!" Londyn replied as she sat in a bar stool with her elbows resting on the counter.

"Girl. What more is there to feel out? Either you like the guy or you don't, plain and simple, right?" BeBe asked as she flipped pancakes on the griddle.

"It's not that simple!" Londyn replied with a giggle.

"Child, yes it is, that's that young folk talk right there. If after a few months of hanging out, you can't tell whether or not you see potential in dating someone, then that's a problem. Y'all millennial folks want to talk for years before y'all claim each other. See my generation don't play that. We make decisions. You with me, or you ain't."

"You old, Ma!" Reagan stated as she walked into the kitchen in her pajamas, while wiping the morning crust out of her eyes.

"48 and proud, Reagan. I'm not old, I'm still in my prime baby." BeBe said as she swayed her hips from side to side.

"Whatever."   Reagan chuckled as she rolled her eyes. "So what are y'all in here talking about?" she asked.

"Your bestie still doesn't know if she likes ol' boy yet." BeBe giggled.

"Don't let her fool you, Mama. She definitely likes Solo. He's got her wide open." Reagan laughed.

"Stop it." Londyn said as she brushed her best friend's shoulder. "I never said I didn't know if I liked him or not. I just said he's not my boyfriend yet because we're still figuring each other out."

"Girl. That might as well be your boyfriend! As much time as y'all spend together! Shoot. You barely have 5 minutes for the kid these days!!!" Reagan chuckled as she stuck her finger in the cup of warm syrup BeBe has just pulled out of the microwave.

"Stop it!" BeBe snapped as she popped Reagan's hand.

"Dang, Ma! You trippin'!"

"Girl, gon' somewhere. Matter of fact, pull those biscuits out the oven."

Londyn giggled as she watched Reagan and her mom interact. They acted more like sisters than mother and daughter sometimes.

"Well have y'all at least talked about a relationship? Do you know if he wants one?" BeBe asked.

"Yeah. I mean sort of... He made it clear months ago that he was trying to get to know me and me only, and that he wanted to see where it could go. I know he's kind of scared of relationships though. I feel like he wants one, but he's unsure of himself and how to go about it or something."

"Well, you just make sure that you're not putting an unnecessary guard up or making it harder for him that it has to be," BeBe began, "it's hard enough for people to let their pride down, without the other making them second guess whether or not they should feel safe doing so. Men's egos are a trip honey..."

"They really are. It's like they'll be all into a girl, but will let her walk away because he's worrying the feeling isn't mutual, rather than admit he was really falling for her." Reagan sighed.

"So true babe. I've learned from experience that it's very important as a woman to have a healthy balance of independence and support. You have to be able to stand on your own, and let him be the man... but still provide that safe home for him to come to everyday." BeBe replied.

"I feel you..." Londyn replied

"... and I don't mean physical home either, I just meant a happy environment to be in. A peaceful relationship. They have to feel secure, like dogs, they gotta want to come home!" BeBe laughed as they all chuckled.

"Lo, tell my Mama what he did last weekend though, girl!" Reagan smiled as she pulled the buttermilk biscuits off of the baking sheet and placed them on a plate.

"Ohhhh, what did he do now?" BeBe asked.

Londyn smiled. "Okay... so I was kind of upset because I did horrible on one of my exams. He knew I wasn't happy so he drove all the way to my apartment with a Poetic Justice DVD... and everybody knows that's one of my favorite movies, but my DVD is all scratched up from playing it so many times. We set up a cozy little movie night picnic right on the floor of my living room. It was cute."

"....anndddddddd." Reagan exclaimed.

"and... he taught me how to cook a few things."

"Whaaattt, you done found you a cooking man! Haha, Londyn. He might be a match for you because we all know you can't cook for nothing."

"Stoooop Mama BeBe! I can cook a little, I just don't really know how to make a lot of different things." Londyn giggled. "We made macaroni and cheese, baked chicken, fried corn, and cabbage. It was soooo gooood!"

"Oweeeee, how'd he learn to cook all that?"

"His Aunt Ryn taught him. She used to work as a chef in a hotel back in the day. He said she worked the afternoon shift so much that sometimes she'd leave recipes out for him and told him if he wanted to eat, he had to cook."

"Aww, see that's sweet Londyn. You need to keep him around. That's a keeper." BeBe replied with googly eyes.

"Yeah, he's really amazing, too good to be true almost..."

"No, not too good to be true. Don't be one of those girls that's waiting on your relationship to fall apart just because you've been hurt before!" BeBe began. "Shoot, I never let an ex determine how I feel about my new man. If I did, I would've never been stable enough to marry my husband. Even though that man is crazy too."

"Don't talk about my daddy!!" Reagan chuckled.

"Well, don't act like it's not true Reagan. You know yo daddy is a fool!" she laughed.

Reagan rolled her eyes as she fed a forkful of

scrambled cheese eggs into her mouth. Londyn laughed hysterically as she tried not to choke on her orange juice.

After gaining her composure she said, "Well, Mama BeBe it's not so much that I'm expecting it to fall apart. I mean I really hope that it doesn't, and he hasn't given me a reason to think that it will. It's just that I'm a logical thinker, you know? Logically speaking, my track record with guys isn't the greatest."

"Londyn, you had one bad boyfriend. One. Not ten girl! You can't let one bad apple lead you to believe you have a bad track record with men." Reagan replied.

"Ok, right one bad boyfriend, but it hasn't necessarily been all kicks and giggles after Justin either." Londyn replied.... "Marcus?"

"Marcus was stupid. He wasn't on your level anyway."

"Okay, and what about TJ? That didn't work out either."

"TJ was too full of himself to even know how to date anyone other than himself."

"Okay, but you get my point though, right?"

"Nope! That's still only a few guys, Lo. You haven't dated a whole lot in college, and I think you're still letting a few bad experiences taint your idea of what relationships can be."

"Maybe you're right..."

"I know I am!" Reagan giggled.

"You see how she thinks she's the relationship guru because she and David broke the Guinness Book of World Records with a relationship that made it past high school?" BeBe joked.

"Mama. Don't hate, girl." Reagan laughed.

"Girrrrrrrrrllllllllllll. Bye. I love my man. No hating here." BeBe chuckled.

"Yeah I love him too. Speaking of my Daddy, I hope he comes through with these tickets to the Pistons season opener tomorrow night!" Reagan stated.

Reagan's dad was good friends with the team's assistant coach and often received many perks during the basketball season.

"You'd better call him now before he gets off work, and remind him. You know he's forgetful." BeBe stated as she finally sat down to enjoy her breakfast.

"Hey, you think he could get tickets for Shane and I too?" Londyn asked.

"Yeah probably so. I'll check and see." Reagan replied.

"Cool, thanks."

"Double Date!!! Lovebirds times twoooo!" Reagan joked.

"Yeah, yeah, whatever!" Londyn giggled, "Hey Mama BeBe, what time does your church start today?"

"Late service isn't until noon, boo. You want to come?"

"Yeah I do... I've been going to Shane's church lately, but service started already, at 9. He's not there anyway. He had to go out of town to interview for an engineering internship and won't be back until tonight." Londyn replied.

"Okay baby, well you know you are always welcome. You coming too Reagan?"

"Nah Ma, I gotta head up to the station in a few... You know I work every other Sunday."

"I forgot child." BeBe replied.

"I got you next week though, Mama. I'm bringing David too. Lord knows we all need to be in the house of the Lord."

"That's right...." BeBe smiled.

Chapter 10

Early the next morning Londyn awoke in her apartment to the sound of her phone vibrating on the dresser. She wiped the crust out of her eyes and slowly sat up with her phone to her ear.

"Wake up sleeping beauty!!!" yelled the loud voice on the other end.

"Dad, it's 8am. You know I don't have class until 1:00 on Monday's. This is my only day to sleep in." Londyn groaned.

"I'm sorry, Babygirl. I just haven't seen you, or heard from ya. You ain't been by the house lately... What's going on?"

"I'm sorry, just been busy with classes and work. I'm going to come home soon, I promise. What have you been up to?" she asked as she sat up in her bed.

"Working. Taking care of home. So you got a boyfriend now or something? Somebody named Solo? What kind of name is Solo?"

"I'm gonna kill Tony..." Londyn mumbled. "He's not my boyfriend Daddy. We've been dating, but we aren't officially together... it's still new."

"That's not what your brother said. Well, you should bring him by the house to watch the game tonight. I need to meet this dude."

"No can do, we might be going to the Palace to watch it with Reagan."

"Oh big shots... okay, okay don't let your old man ruin your fun. But seriously, I do need you to bring this kid by the house soon. I need to meet him and make sure he's good enough for my Babygirl."

"I got you Daddy... You just tell me when."

"Well, why don't you come by Wednesday night."

"Okay that should probably work..."

"Bring the boy."

"Okay Daddy. I hear you..."

"Okay, love you Londyn."

"Love you too." she said as she laid back down and hung up the call.

"He's so nosey." she mumbled.

She closed her eyes, only to feel her phone vibrate once again against her hand. She picked it up and answered it after seeing Reagan's picture flash across the screen.

"Hello?"

"Hey girl, what you doing?" Reagan asked cheerfully.

"I was sleep until my phone started doing numbers."

"Oh, you're so popular!" Reagan giggled. "Well I've been up since 4:30. It's practically lunch time for me."

"Why in the world have you been up since 4:30?"

"Girl. two-a-days... Coach Reid had us running laps at the crack of dawn."

"Oh yuck!" Londyn giggled.

"I know right, but anywho I was calling to tell you that my Dad came through in the clutchhhhh on these Pistons tickets for tonight. They're two rows up from courtside. He gave me 6 tickets so we're good to go! Call ya boyfriend!"

"He's not my boyfriend." Londyn giggled, "But okay cool. He'll be excited to hear that."

"Good, it's gonna be fun."

"Who are you giving the other tickets to?" Londyn asked.

"I don't know... Do you have anybody in mind?" Reagan asked.

"What about Bree?"

"Ugh... You sure, Lo? You know I think she's lowkey fake. Are you sure you want you, her, and Solo in the same room? She's gon' throw all types of shade." Reagan replied.

"I forgot about that," Londyn giggled, "but nah, she's cool. She just plays around, she doesn't mean any harm. Call her."

"Ooookay, if you say so. I'll call her now." Reagan replied.

"Okay, cool."

"Well I gotta get washed up and head to class. You wanna ride to the game together or...?"

"Umm, yeah that's probably cool. What time do you want to meet up?" Londyn asked.

"The game starts at 7:30 so I think we'll be good if we leave out about 6:30ish. Y'all can just meet me at David's apartment." Reagan stated.

"Okay cool, sounds good!"

"Okay girl, I'll see you later."

"Yep, bye Reagan." Londyn replied as the call ended.

Londyn immediately scrolled through her contacts until she landed on Shane's name, and began to send him a text to which he immediately responded.

Londyn: *Good Morning!! *heart eyes emoji**

Shane: Good Morning Babe

Londyn: Did ya sleep good? How was your flight home?

Shane: Yeah, can't complain. The flight was cool... but I didn't get in the bed until like 3am tho, working on homework. tired.

Londyn: Aww man, I'm sorry, did I wake u up?

Shane: Oh nah, not at all. I have class at 8:30, I'm actually on my way out the door now.

Londyn: Oh right, right, I forgot. Well, I have good news. I hope you're free tonight.

Shane: Yea my schedule is clear, Reagan came through on the Piston's tickets?

Londyn: Yep, sure did :-) Two rows up from courtside.

Shane: Bet! That's what's up. I'll just head that way after my last class gets out.

Londyn: Ok cool, see you then!

Shane: Thanks babe, have a good day.

Londyn: You too. TTYL.

At about 6:00pm Shane made his way down I-94 East from Ann Arbor to Detroit with his mother's younger brother, Brian, also known as Uncle Buck, riding along side him in the passenger seat. At only three years apart, Uncle Buck and Shane's mother were partners in mischief in their younger days. Uncle Buck took his sister's departure incredibly hard, and never really bounced back on his feet after she was gone. He worked odd jobs here and there, but was still heavily involved in the drug game. Although Shane constantly begged him to leave the hustling alone, his efforts were mostly in vain. Like most of the people in Shane's world back home, Uncle Buck wasn't completely opposed to making an honest living, but didn't know how to realistically make it happen. After all, Shane was just about the only person from their neighborhood who made it to college. Truth be told, he was accomplishing things that his family and friends wouldn't even dare dream of. However, just as much as Shane believed in himself, he also believed in others. He even went as far as to hook Uncle Buck up with a job interview at a manufacturing plant in Ann Arbor, and was determined to get him on his feet.

"Pistons game, mannnn I ain't been to a game at the Palace since Isiah Thomas was hooping." Uncle Buck said in reference to the legendary Piston's star that led the Bad Boy's to two back-to-back championships in the late 80's and early 90's.

"Aww man, you gotta get back up there and see some games, Unc! I try to go to at least 2 or 3 games every season. I'm gon' have to bring you with me one day."

"So you going with your girl, huh? You must really like her, since you've been keeping her around."

"Honestly man, I really am feeling her, Uncle B. Never thought I'd see the day where I could see myself really being with just one woman. But she's so loyal. I'd be a fool not to cuff her. Just ain't found the right words, or right time to ask her yet."

"That's what's up young blood. That's how I felt when I met Danielle. She was the realist female I had ever met in my life." Uncle Buck replied, in reference to his wife of 5 years. "I knew she was the one when I first had a conversation with her."

"Yeah that's how I felt too. We're so different, yet so much alike at the same time. We really balance each other out. It's like we're just meant to be."

"Yeah I know that feeling, I was young and foolish when I met Danielle though, so even though I knew she was the one, I didn't treat her like it. I was still fooling around on her... almost lost her a few times."

"I'm gonna do whatever I can not to mess this one up. She's too perfect for me." Shane replied.

"That's good."

"Yeah... So anyway, how did the interview go? You think you got it?" Shane asked in reference to the interview Uncle Buck had earlier that day.

"Man, neph... all them preppy dudes in their fancy suits ain't about to hire a street cat like me. I don't even know why I'm playing myself man. I need to just stick to what I know."

"Man, Unc. You just gotta think positively. You never know what good can come out of it... but I know one thing, the streets ain't where it's at."

"The streets made you who you are today too, am I wrong nephew... or you forgot?" Uncle Buck asked.

"No doubt. I'll never deny that. But I'm saying though, now that I've seen another side of things and other options, I know it's just so much more out here than drugs, gangs, fighting, and dodging bullets everyday. We all are capable of so much more, but you'll mess around and cut your life short playing around with these clowns who don't have anything to lose. You just gotta want better for yourself and go after it man..."

"It's just that simple for you, huh?"

"What you mean, Unc?"

"I mean it's just that easy... If you want better you just supposed to say it, and life just magically gets better, right? Do you know how many job interviews I have been on in the last two months, nephew? Too many to count, and you know what they say to me each and every time? 'Oh I'm sorry, you're not qualified sir.' Or, 'Oh I'm sorry Mr. Jackson, we can't offer you this position based on your criminal record.' They not even willing to give me a chance! I'm just doing the best I can to feed myself, and my family. Man, you think I wanna do this? You think I dreamt of being a 36-year-old dope dealer?"

"I get what you saying Unc. I hear you, but."

"Nah, nah you don't hear me Solo. You think you do, but you don't. I don't even want to talk about it no more man. Just drop me off at the crib."

"Alright Unc..." Shane replied as they drove the next 5 minutes in complete silence.

Uncle Buck was just like Man-Man and so many other people from their neighborhood. Hardheaded, and not confident enough in themselves or their potential. To them, people like Shane were the "chosen ones"... the special people who could make it out the hood and live successfully, unlike themselves. They underestimated the power they held inside to be just like Shane, or got discouraged when their attempts to do so failed initially. Shane would've been just like them had it not been for Aunt Ryn. Growing up, he and all his friends thought she was the meanest person ever, but what Shane and everyone else failed to realize back then was that she was molding Shane into the responsible, hard working, honorable man he'd grow up to be. She may not have been able to reach her younger brother Buck, but she made it her mission not to let her nephew fall victim to the system. She constantly spoke life and positivity to Shane every day, and as time would tell, it most definitely paid off.

About 5 minutes later, Shane pulled up to a

house near I-94 and Chalmers where Uncle Buck lived. Uncle Buck nodded his head as he got out and shut the door behind him. Before he turned to walk away, he bent down and looked through the open window at Shane.

"Good lookin' on the ride young nephew. My car should be out the shop next week... and I'll umm, I'll let you know if I hear anything about the job..." he stated as he reached in and dapped Shane's hand.

"No doubt..." Shane replied as he returned the handshake.

Although Uncle Buck didn't respond in the way Shane would have liked, he knew that he was slowly but surely beginning to get through to him. Had it been a year ago, Uncle Buck wouldn't have even applied to a job out in Ann Arbor, let alone agreed to go out to an interview. Getting this job could change Uncle Buck's entire life, and Shane could only hope and pray for the best, even if Uncle Buck couldn't see it for himself.

Shane made his way back to freeway to head to David's house so that he could meet up with Londyn and her crew. As he looked at the clock and the amount of heavy traffic on the freeway, he realized that he was cutting it close time-wise. So, he picked up his phone and texted Londyn, while still attempting to keep his eyes on the road.

Shane: *Hey Lo. Running late, I'll just meet y'all at the* *game instead of David's spot.*

Londyn: *Okay, that's cool. u driving now?*

Shane: *yeah, just dropped Uncle B off on the east.*

Londyn: *Ok, stop texting and driving... see u there.*

He smiled and put his phone down on his lap. Londyn was always looking out for him and he loved that about her. There was such a huge difference in the way that she treated him in comparison to the way Kyla had. He smiled the whole car ride just thinking about Londyn. He knew that he needed to shake things up soon and make it official between the two of them. Although Londyn was very patient, and was in no way pressuring him to give their relationship a title, he felt that it was time to seal the deal.

After sitting in stop and go traffic for more than most of the ride, Shane finally made it to the Palace of Auburn Hills, the arena that served as the home of the Detroit Pistons. He circled the lot and eventually found a space to park his car after paying the parking fee. He was dressed in a classic Ben Wallace #3 Piston's Tee, commemorating his favorite retired player. He joined the many excited, and fashionably late, fans in line at will call to obtain tickets to the game. Luckily the lines moved rather quickly, as the game had already well advanced into the first quarter. Once Shane retrieved his ticket, he began to make his way to an elevator that lead downstairs to the courtside level seating.

As he approached their seats he could see an energetic Londyn jumping up and down as Pistons star point guard Brandon Jennings nailed an epic 3-point shot. A girl he could watch the game with was a winner in his eyes. As he made his way to the row where his friends were sitting, the Pistons scored again and the crowd erupted in cheer. Londyn happened to turn to her right and smiled when she caught Shane coming down the aisle.

"What's good bro?" Shane said as he dapped David's fist.

"What up doe Solo!" David cheered.

"Heyyyy Solo!!! About time you made it!" Reagan exclaimed as Shane scooted past her towards Londyn.

He smiled and shook his head. "I know right, traffic was crazy!"

He reached in towards Londyn and greeted her with a hug and peck on the lips.

"Hey Baby." she replied with a huge smile.

"Awwwwwww!!!" Reagan giggled loudly, tapping David's shoulder.

"Ha! Cakes." David laughed.

"Shut up! I know y'all ain't talking!" Londyn giggled.

Reagan chuckled. "I know right, we're still the cakiest."

She puckered her lips towards David, who playfully responded by pushing her face away.

"Skiiiirrrtttt. Cakiest ain't even a word, bro!" David teased.

"Ugh, Whatever!!!" Reagan laughed.

Everyone jumped up from their seats when Andre Drummond dunked the ball, giving the Pistons a 2-point lead over the San Antonio Spurs.

"Ayyyyeeeeee!" Londyn yelled. "My boys are gonna get this W tonight!" she yelled before sitting back down in her seat.

"I should've been going to games with you all along, Lo. You too hype!" Shane said.

"I loveeeee the Pistons man." she replied.

Londyn was dressed in blue jeans, a retro Grant Hill Jersey, and classic Jordan's on her feet. Her curly hair was parted horizontally, with the front half in a bun, and the curls in the back half of her head flowing free.

"You look really nice today." he whispered in her ear after looking her up and down.

"Thanks Handsome." she replied as she leaned over and quickly kissed him again.

"I am sooo not used to seeing Londyn be this affectionate. Solo, what did you do to my girl?" Reagan giggled from two seats away.

Shane looked over and laughed.

"I thought you said y'all girl Bree was coming." David leant over and asked randomly.

"She is. She said she was running late, let me call her." Reagan stated.

Just as she picked up her phone to dial Bree's number, she looked up and saw Bree coming down the aisle. In typical over the top Breanna Martin fashion, she was dressed in high heels, a midriff shirt, a Piston's hat, and a full face of makeup. Everyone waved, before noticing another girl behind her. The other girl was naturally pretty and didn't wear much makeup at all. Her, long, natural slick ponytail stretched down her back, and her nails were perfectly manicured. She was dressed in a fitted white tee, floral jeans, and heels, like Reagan.

"What the..." Shane mumbled to himself.

"Wassup everybody?" Bree stated as she got close enough for them to hear.

She looked a tad bit uncomfortable, but sat down anyway.

"This is my homegirl Kyla." she announced. "Kyla, this is David, Reagan, Londyn, and umm...you know Solo."

"Hey y'all." Kyla said in a soft, sweet voice.

"Hey!" they replied in unison.

Londyn turned her head towards Shane and mouthed the word "Kyla?" with a puzzled look on her face.

Shane shook his head in disbelief, as his whole mood had suddenly changed. He tensed up and looked straight ahead at the game, refusing to look over at Kyla.

"Hi Shane." Kyla leaned forward with an attitude from her seat 5 spots away.

"What Up." he replied as dry as possible before turning his attention back to the game.

Kyla immediately rolled her eyes and folded her arms across her chest as she sat back against the chair. Reagan being Reagan quickly noticed the tension as she looked back and forth between the two.

"What y'all know each other or something?" she asked loudly.

"Hmmhaa." Kyla smirked while still staring ahead at the game.

"Umm... I have to go to the bathroom. Come with me... Please..." Londyn stated as she grabbed Reagan's arm.

Reluctantly, Reagan got up and followed Londyn down the opposite end of the row, away from Bree and Kyla. Londyn didn't say a word until they made it up the stairs, and into the hallway where the concession stands were located.

"What's going on?" Reagan asked.

"That's Kyla. The girl I told you about that Shane used to mess with. The one that keyed his car and tried to fight him at a party one time..."

"Mannnn, I knew that girl looked familiar. That's the same girl I saw staring at you and him at the party we went to during Greek Fest. Remember when we thought he had a girl?"

"Yup... that would be her... She's freaking psycho. I can't believe she's here right now."

"Man. Bree is 'bout to hear it from me. That's petty! She knew Solo would be here..."

"Yeah I thought she was bringing a date, so why the heck would she bring her instead is what I wanna know?" Londyn asked.

"Because she's being childish, and she wanted to prove a point. Now that I think about it. She did say that Solo broke her friend's heart. That must be who she was talking about all along."

"Yep... had to be." Londyn softly replied.

"Yeah, I mean... but she really ain't that cute though." Reagan laughed as she rolled her eyes.

Londyn giggled.

"I mean, for real... she's not. I think she might be kind of crossed eyed too." Reagan continued while pointing to her own two eyes.

Londyn giggled a little more and smiled, although still upset.

"So wait, how long were they together, or not together... or whatever?" Reagan asked.

"Umm, I guess a few years. Why?" Londyn

asked.

"Because... you really left your man down there alone with a chick that's been wanting him for years?" Reagan asked.

Londyn's eyes suddenly bulged as she quickly pivoted towards the arena.

"Uh oh." Reagan mumbled as she quickly followed behind.

About 45 seconds later Londyn arrived back in the row where the rest of the crew was sitting, only to find Kyla sitting right next to Shane.

"So you really just ain't gon answer none of my calls though?" is what Londyn heard Kyla say as she walked up.

Londyn immediately cut her eyes at Kyla, who then shrugged her shoulders and got up from Londyn's seat. Londyn rolled her eyes again, and sat down with her arms folded in disgust.

"Don't even trip off this broad man." Reagan said loudly as she sat down.

"Excuse me?" Kyla asked.

"Just chill Ky..." Bree said, realizing the drama she'd just started.

"I swear... let a trick try me..." Reagan mumbled.

All the while, Shane still hadn't said a word. Instead, he stared ahead at the court, only pausing to look at his phone every few seconds, send a text, and then focus back on the game. He continued this pattern for the next 15 minutes. Each time he looked at his phone, he seemed to tense up more and more. Londyn looked down the aisle at Kyla, to see if she was texting at the same time as Shane, but fortunately most times, she wasn't. Every time she tried to sneak a peek at Shane's phone, he quickly switched the screen. Instead of paying attention to the basketball game, she wondered what game Shane was possibly playing with her, and if Kyla was at all involved.

About two minutes into the 4th quarter, Shane's phone rang. He quickly answered it, but turned his head to the side so that nobody could overhear his conversation, or try to read his lips.

"What? Are you serious. Right now? Man... Okay... Okay... I'm coming..." were bits and pieces of the words Londyn could overhear him saying before he abruptly ended the call.

"Aye y'all... I gotta go... emergency..." Shane stated as he stood up fidgeted around in his pockets for his keys.

"Really? The game isn't even over yet!" Reagan exclaimed.

"Yeah I know. It's just that something came up, and I gotta go handle it." he replied as he bent down and gave a Londyn a one-armed hug.

"Aight be safe bro..." David replied.

"Bet..." Shane replied as he walked away, without much of an explanation.

"Where the heck is he going?" Reagan whispered to Londyn. "Why didn't you say bye?"

"He barely said bye to me... did you see that weak hug he gave me? He started acting funny the moment that girl walked in." Londyn said with a disappointed frown.

"Well, maybe it was something else going on. He didn't really seem to be paying her any mind. Just call and check on him when we leave here, okay?" Reagan said as she patted her best friend's leg.

"Yeah, okay..." Londyn quietly replied.

The rest of the game was a blur. While everyone else seemed to be having a great time, Londyn's mind was elsewhere. She wondered if Shane was ashamed to be there with her while Kyla was around, or if he was hiding something. All of it was too much for her to process, and all she really wanted to do at that point was go home and be alone.

Soon enough, the game ended with a Pistons win: 102-94. As everyone started to exit the arena, Reagan decided to "check" Bree.

"Hold Up..." Reagan began.

"Huh?" Bree replied, as she turned around while walking up the stairs.

"I have a bone to pick with you Breanna." Reagan replied with a straight face as they moved over to the side, allowing everyone else to continue up the stairs ahead of them.

"You good girl?" Kyla asked as she walked by.

"Yeah I'm good. I'll be up there in a second." Bree replied.

David and Londyn followed behind Kyla as she walked up the stairs, until Reagan grabbed David by the arm.

"Uh uh... you walking a little too close." she snapped.

Kyla, who chose to ignore her comment, kept walking while David laughed and plopped down in an empty seat. Oddly enough, that left Kyla and Londyn to walk almost side-by-side up the stairs. Once they reached the top, Kyla stood with her hands on her hips, and looked at Londyn.

"He's a good guy," Kyla began, "but... you better watch your back. He ain't nothing but a little player that doesn't even know what he wants half the time."

Londyn looked uncomfortable as she glared at Kyla.

"Y'all can talk and go on as many nice dates as you can imagine. He'll have you feeling like you're so important to him, but you won't be. He'll never make you his girlfriend. You'll just ride his roller coaster until the wheels fall off, and he runs and downgrades with the next chick." she continued with an attitude before rolling her eyes and walking away.

Londyn took a deep breath and cracked her knuckles as Kyla walked away. She didn't know if she wanted to slap her in the face, or ask her questions.

"Is she just jealous? Or is she being brutally honest?" Londyn wondered.

It was hard to tell, but the thought of it all made her head hurt. Meanwhile, down at the bottom of the stairs, Reagan was still demanding answers from Bree.

"Nobody tells me anything Reagan, how the heck was I supposed to know Solo and Londyn were still talking, let alone that he'd be here tonight." Bree said as Reagan walked away from her, up the stairs.

"Whatever." Reagan stated as she began to walk up the stairs, leaving Bree behind.

"I'm serious, Kyla and I have been hanging out all weekend, and she was with me when you called me about the tickets! I asked Corey if he wanted to go, but he said he couldn't make it so I asked her instead."

"Maybe Londyn will listen to your lies, but I don't wanna hear 'em."

Bree turned towards Lo and shrugged her shoulders. "I'm sorry Lo... you know you're my girl, and although I still don't think Solo is the right guy for you, I wouldn't try to sabotage or purposely start some drama... I'm sorry." she said as she reached over to give Londyn a hug.

Londyn quickly shifted her body weight to the side, as to let Bree know that she did not in fact plan on hugging her back. She didn't say anything back, she just sort of looked at her as if she could see straight through her.

"Okay, well... I'm gonna go..." Bree said.

"Mmm hmm. You do that." Reagan replied as Bree walked away. "She is such a liar." Reagan whispered, "She knew you and Shane would be here. I told her."

Londyn shook her head and pulled out her phone to see if Shane had texted her. After seeing no missed call or text notifications, she put the phone in her purse and walked away disappointed, with Reagan and David following closely behind.

The three friends rode home in silence, other than the radio and an occasional joke from David. The whole way home, Londyn did nothing but stare outside the backseat window, deep in her thoughts.

Meanwhile, on the other side of town, Shane sat in his parked car, staring out the window with his phone pressed to his ear.

"Man, pick up…" he mumbled.

"Aye Solo you here?" said the panicking voice on the other end.

"Yeah. I'm outside."

"Aight bet. Stay right there, I'm about to come out from the back." the voice stated as he hung up the phone.

Shane sighed and threw his head back on the headrest. It was obvious that this was not somewhere he necessarily wanted or needed to be. The street was dark, except for a few streetlights, with broken bottles surrounding the defaced property lining the residential street. Police sirens echoed through the night air, and a group of men stood huddled on the sidewalk.

Suddenly, a man knocked on the window, causing Shane to jump just a little. He quickly unlocked the door after recognizing the face outside.

"What's brackin' Solo." Shane's friend Man-Man exclaimed as he sat down in the passenger seat.

Man-Man was dressed in all black, with a red bandana sticking out of his back pocket. His eyes were red and hung low. As usual, he was high off marijuana, among other things.

"What's the emergency Man-Man?"

"Man! It's finna pop off on the Mile. I need to go over there and make sure my boys straight, grab my stuff, woo woo, and then leave, you feel me?"

"What? Man-Man you got me over here on some gangbanging nonsense. You know I left this street life behind me man, I have responsibilities." Shane replied frustratingly.

"Brooo. Chill, its gon' be smoove. What you want me to go over there by myself? I mean I ain't scared, but I thought I could at least count on my brother to have my back. You know I'm on probation. If the police see my car, it's O.V."

"You out of your mind"

"Mannn, you gon' drive, or not? I'm talking all of 10 minutes of your life dawg." Man-Man pleaded.

"You really don't get it, do you? This life you living, it can only end two ways bro. Behind bars or in a casket. Have you not learned anything in the past 5 years? Look where just about every single dude we grew up with is at now. You really want to end up like them?"

"Look Solo, I'm really not here for your motivational speeches right now, man. I get it, you done moved up in the world. You a college boy now. I'm proud of you, but the rest of us are still living in the real world, and out here you gotta fight to survive."

"Man, all I'm saying is..." Shane began before being interrupted by a loud voice outside of their car.

He looked up and was completely shocked to see a man aiming a gun right at his passenger window.

"Get down!" Shane yelled as the man outside

pulled the trigger, and shot a bullet right at the car.

Shane's survival instincts kicked in and he slammed on the accelerator. The sound of the bullet hitting the body side molding pierced his ears and nearly stopped his heart. With one hand on the wheel he reached over in panic towards Man-Man.

"You good?" he yelled.

"I think so." Man-Man replied as he patted himself down.

"Yo, what the..." Shane huffed as he clinched the steering wheel in frustration. He took a deep breath, and then glanced at Man-Man again, "Man-Man... what... what just happened?" he yelled as he swerved down another street.

"I don't even know man. It's so many haters out here that want my head. Jealous motha... Oh, wait turn right here. " Man-Man stated calmly as if it was no big deal.

He pointed towards a corner at the end of the alley before reaching down towards his ankle. Shane turned quickly and sped down the street, still in complete, utter shock.

"He lucky I ain't have a chance to pull out the nine." Man-Man mumbled as he sat straight up with a gun in his hand.

"Watch out." Shane snapped.

"Relax man. You act like you never seen a gun before. You been out in the 'burbs too long. I hate to say it bro, but you acting kind of soft." Man-Man chuckled as Shane stared out the windshield in disbelief.

"How did I end up right back in the middle of all of the mess I've been running from for so long? At what point is loyalty just not enough?" he thought.

Shane was so in shock as he listened to Man-Man instruct him to turn left, right, left, that it didn't even dawn on him that not only did he have a bullet hole in the middle of his car, but that they could possibly still be in danger. All he could think in that moment was... *how did I get here?"*

"Aye slow down, pull up right here..." Man-Man said as they approached a street corner populated with people.

"Hell nah! I'm not stopping here. We just got shot at."

"I'll pay to get your car fixed bro..."

"It's not even about that. I value my life, and you clearly don't."

"It's cool. I promise. This is my boy house, we good.... I'm just gon' make sure everybody straight, grab my stuff, and come right back out."

"I'm not staying here." Shane stated as he put the car back in gear.

"Bro... 5 minutes." Man-Man begged as he jumped out the car and ran across the street.

"Ughhhhhhh...." Shane grunted as he was forced to put the car back in park.

He looked out his window and watched in disbelief as Man-Man ran across the street towards the house. There were about 5 or 6 men, and 4 women posted on the porch. One of the men stood up with his arms folded once Man-Man made it onto the porch. Shane watched as Man-Man pleaded with him to be let inside. One of the men looked over to Shane's vehicle, then back at Man-Man, before nodding his head. A woman stood up and began to pat Man-Man down, and paused once she got to his ankle area. Man-Man looked her in her eyes as she retrieved the handgun, and tossed it to one of the other women. The man in front of the door stepped aside and finally let Man-Man go inside of the house.

"His boy's house... right." Shane thought.

He sat in the car in complete silence for about 5 minutes, hoping that Man-Man would come outside at any moment. He contemplated leaving him there, but decided against it. There was heavy traffic and activity on this block, so much so that he didn't feel right leaving him there with no way home but to walk. However, after about 10 minutes went by, he became suspicious. He quickly picked up his cell phone and dialed Man-Man's number.

"Brrrrrrrr." was the sound of Man-Man's black cell phone vibrating from the floor of the passenger seat.

"Man......" Shane whispered to himself as he hung up the phone and stared outside. "I am not trying to go in here and look for this fool."

He waited another 5 minutes or so, before deciding to get out and go after Man-Man. He looked at himself in the rearview mirror and thought long and hard before opening the door and stepping out of the vehicle. Once he started to walk, a black truck sped past, almost hitting him. Although Shane was no stranger to the street life, he was a tad bit nervous as he walked alone towards the house. Just as he stepped foot on the sidewalk, a gang load of police lights and sirens came out of nowhere.

"Everybody freeze. Hand's up." one of the officers yelled through a bullhorn.

Shane raised his hands in the air and dropped his head in shame. This had just turned into a horrible night.

Chapter 11

At approximately 1:15am, Shane and his line brothers walked outside of the Detroit Police Department's 12th Precinct on West 7 Mile Road. He was feeling tired and defeated as he walked towards Xavier's red Monte Carlo SS.

"Thanks a lot, Sands... for coming all the way out here to get me." Shane said as he sat down in the back seat.

"Oh no problem bro. You already know we got you." Xavier stated as he sat down in the driver's seat.

"Yeah, you already know, Sands." said Thomas, their other line brother.

Shane buried his face in his hands and held it there for a few seconds after Xavier pulled off.

"You sure you good man? What exactly happened?" Thomas asked as he looked over his shoulder into the backseat.

"Man... long story short, my mans called me and said it was an emergency, and that he needed me to come scoop. I pull up, and some dude shoots at my car as soon as he gets in. I pull off, to try and get away and make my way home, or anywhere really. We end up at some trap house. Then he gets out of the car, talking about he had to get something of his from inside. I wait for dude for like 15 minutes before I decided I needed to go inside and make sure he was straight. Walk up, soon as I hit the property, police run up and raid the whole place. They arrested everybody. Turns out they'd been staking it out for a while.

"That's crazyyyyy. I knew you were a hood guy, but I ain't know you was Stringer Bell." Xavier chuckled.

"Nah man. From the hood, but not a gangster. I'm off that now. I was just in the wrong place at the wrong time man. I'm so mad at myself."

"At least they let you out..." Xavier said.

"Yeah... I'm so glad I hadn't made it all the way up to the house yet. Cops ran my record and saw that it was clean. Plus, my boy Man-Man told them I had nothing to do with it, so I guess you can say I caught a break."

"Yeah man you really did. This night could have ended much, much worse." Xavier said.

"I know right, but my boy ain't getting out no

time soon. That's for sure." Shane stated.

"What you think your girl gon' say when she find out?" Thomas asked.

"I have no idea. I was too embarrassed to even call her from jail, that's why I called y'all instead. I don't know how I'm gon' tell her. Y'all know she don't play." Shane replied.

"Look, Sands. Londyn is a good girl. Everybody knows that, so don't mess it up. I know Man-Man has been your friend since y'all were kids, but look at how much of a cancer he is to your life bro. You just walked out of jail man, but even worse you got shot at, and could've been dead. You just gotta think things through bro, even if it means letting go of certain things and people. I wouldn't be your bro if I weren't being honest with you." Thomas stated.

"I know. Trust me man. I know..." Shane replied as they cruised down the freeway.

Xavier chuckled and attempted to lighten the mood. "Thomas, bro, I just had flashbacks to us pledging, when you gave all those pep talks saying we better not mess it up for you because you ain't take all that wood for nothing."

"I'm saying, man. Y'all fools would've never crossed if it hadn't been for me. Y'all were pretty terrible." Thomas chuckled.

"Man, whatever. I'm the best deuce to come through Delta Phi. Yoooooooooo." Xavier yelled.

The three of them laughed as Xavier blasted NWA's 1988's hit "Boyz In The Hood" through his speakers. A few minutes later they arrived on Mansfield Street where all the madness had occurred earlier that night. The neighborhood was extremely peaceful and quiet now, as everyone was either inside hiding, or had been hauled off to jail during the bust.

"Aye, thanks again for coming to get me. Appreciate y'all." Shane stated as he got out of the car.

"No problem at all bruh." Xavier replied. "You want to trail us back to campus right now or?"

"Nah... I think I'm gonna go swing by Londyn's. Gotta make sure she's good. I'll just crash there if she isn't too mad at me." he replied as he got into his car.

"Aight bet. Check you later, playboy." Xavier said.

"See you later, Sands." Thomas replied.

Shane shut his car door, and then looked at his reflection in the rearview mirror. He stared hard and deep as if he was looking through his eyes straight to his soul. Anger, disappointment, fear, and relief were all of the emotions running through his mind at that moment. After a few seconds of reflection, he started the car and drove off into the night towards Londyn's house.

Once he arrived on ELU's campus and pulled into Londyn's apartment complex he felt a great sense of comfort once seeing her car parked outside. He parked right next to hers and got out of the car. Before approaching her door, he walked over to the passenger side to finally look at the bullet damage. There was a small hole near the handle of the passenger seat door that he'd definitely need to get fixed immediately. Seeing that Man-Man was locked up, he knew he couldn't count on him to pay for the damages.

"Money down the drain." he whispered to himself.

He pulled out his cell phone and called Londyn as he walked up the walkway to her door.

"Hello?" she answered.

"Hey Lo... I'm outside your apartment."

"Okay." she stated in a dry monotone voice before hanging up the phone.

He wasn't sure if that was an "Okay, I'll open the door," or an "Okay, who cares. Go home." Fortunately, he didn't have to wonder for very long, because Londyn opened the door a few seconds later.

"Look who decided to finally pop up." Londyn said sarcastically.

She stepped to the side, making room for him to walk through the door. The glasses, oversized t-shirt, and pajamas pants she wore made her look like a little girl.

"Long story..." he replied as he walked through the door.

"Isn't it always." she replied as she walked away and plopped down on the couch.

She grabbed her remote off the end table and pressed play on the movie she was watching. Shane could tell that she was tired and uninterested in whatever it was he had to say, and he honestly couldn't blame her. This wasn't the first time he'd failed to communicate, and left her worried or confused.

"Look Londyn. I'm sorry for storming out the game like that. I'm sorry that Kyla was there, I'm sorry for going missing, and then showing up here in the middle of the night, I'm just sorry for everything, but I promise I can explain." he stated as he sat down on the couch next to her.

"I'm listening." she replied without so much as even turning her head away from the TV.

He took a deep breath before beginning his story.

"Kyla has been calling me nonstop ever since I told her that you and I had something going on. I haven't been answering, but she leaves voicemails. She calls my line brothers checking for me. It's ridiculous. I know she and Bree knew I was going to be there today, because they're both sneaky like that. Kyla sent me a text asking if I was going, but I ignored it. I didn't think she would really show up. I just figured she assumed I'd be there because that's my favorite team. And Bree and I have had a rocky relationship for the past year or so all because she feels like I've done Kyla wrong. So I'm sure she was trying to prove a point. But Kyla and I are over, and I don't want you to ever feel like you're in competition with her. There is no competition. I'm sorry if I made you feel that way at all." he stated.

She looked up slightly, but her facial expression didn't change much. He hadn't quite won her over. So he moved closer to her, and wrapped his arm around her shoulder.

They sat in silence for a few moments, until he decided to come clean. "I went to jail tonight." he blurted out.

"WHAT?" she exclaimed.

"I got arrested."

"Shane, what? Why?" she asked, as he now had her full, undivided attention.

"I left the game because Man-Man said it was an emergency and he needed me. I got to his crib. My car got shot at. We ended up around the corner. He ran into a trap house. I tried to go get him. Cops showed up and raided the place. Everybody went to jail." he responded in one breath.

Londyn stared at him with her big brown eyes without saying a word. Her silence scared him a little, so he continued on.

"I was only in there for a few hours. They didn't press any charges, and let me off on a warning. Xavier and Thomas came to pick me up."

Londyn stood up from her seat on the couch and paced back and forth. She ran her hands through her hair in frustration, and then paused.

"Shane... Have you lost your mind? You out here getting shot at, going to jail? What were you thinking?"

"It wasn't even my fault, I was really just trying to help my friend. Wrong, place wrong time..."

"Wrong place, wrong time could've gotten you killed Shane! Killed! Do you realize that?"

"Yes." he stated with his head held down in shame.

"You have to be more responsible."

"I know."

"You could've caught a case."

"I know." he replied again.

"I don't know what I would do if something would've happened to you." she said as she stared him right in the eyes.

"Really?" he asked as he lifted his head in surprise.

"Really, " she said as she sat down on the couch next to him, "I've lost too many people in my life to carelessness Shane. I don't want to lose you too."

"You won't... I'm done with that life, I promise."

"Then there are some things you just have to leave alone. Man-Man isn't good for you. I know that's your boy and all, shoot he's practically family to you, but he's bringing you down. You have so much going for you, so much potential. Bullets don't have names Shane... and if that's the life he's living then that's the life you're living as long as you stay in his company."

Shane paused for a moment and closed his eyes. "You know... when I was about 12 or 13... back when I was really going through it because of my mom and everything. I was mad at the world, always trying to fight this dude named Ronnie Byers, the biggest kid in school. He used to pick at me everyday and I was never having it. One day, I was walking home by myself, and Ronnie, he tried to step to me... he knocked me out actually." Shane chuckled. "Out of nowhere, here comes Man-Man on his bike. Jumped in before I could even get off the ground and beat Ronnie all by himself. I don't know how Man-Man was so strong to be so little. He was smaller than me, but he always protected me. Then when I was 16, and had just got my first car, the cops pulled us over and I had weed on me. Man-Man took it without asking and put it in his pocket, knowing the police were gonna search us. When I asked him why he covered for me, he said I was too soft to go to juvie." Shane chuckled. "And last year, when I came home from school to find out that my Aunt Ryn's ex boyfriend had beaten her half unconscious, Man-Man showed up and let me know that we'd never have to worry about him ever again, if you catch my drift. Man-Man has spent his whole life protecting my family and I. All while he's had it extremely rough himself. So yeah he might have put me in a complicated situation or two, and he might ask me to come have his back every now and again, but nothing compares to the risks he's taken for me...I owe him..." Shane replied as he buried his face in his hands.

Londyn wrapped her arm around his back and leaned in close. "What you owe him, babe... is to make the most of your life, and show him exactly why you were worth protecting all these years."

Shane suddenly looked up as if a light bulb had just been turned on in his head.

"Thank him for all he's done for you by becoming everything he knew you could be. He might be spiraling down a bad path now, but deep down I'm sure he doesn't really want to drag you down with him. Just keep on making something of yourself so that all the hard work he put into protecting you and your family doesn't go in vain. Sometimes you just have to love people from a distance."

"Wow.... That's deep Lo."

"It's the truth..."

"It's crazy how when you say things to me, it just clicks... it's like we speak the same language... you really get me..." he said. "You're really something special, you know that?"

He opened his arm and pulled her closer towards him. She leaned in and laid her head on his chest, as he twirled her hair in his fingers.

"You're special to me too..." she replied.

"How'd I end up with such a special girlfriend?" he asked, going out on a limb.

Londyn lifted her head a little so that she could look up and see his face. She smiled and laid back down.

"Girlfriend?" she asked with a grin.

"Yeah, I thought you knew." he replied jokingly.

"Nah, I don't remember being asked." she giggled.

Shane lightly pushed Londyn up from where she lay on his chest, and got up from the couch. He walked outside through her front door without saying a word. Londyn was confused and wasn't sure if he was mad, or what was going on.

A few seconds later, Shane returned with a single yellow rose.

"Oh my God," Londyn giggled, "did you just steal that from my neighbor's porch?"

"Maybe." he chuckled, as UGK's "International Player's Anthem" played through his phone's speakers.

"Whaaat?" she laughed.

"Okay, stand up." he said.

"What, why?" she giggled.

"Stand up!" he replied, grabbing her hand

politely.

He took two steps back and stood facing her with the rose in his hand.

"It's been a long 21 years, searching for the one. And tonight, I only have one rose." he chuckled.

"The Bachelor, reallyyyy babe?" Londyn giggled.

"Just let me do my thing, Londyn" he replied.

"Okay, okay my bad." she smiled.

"Like I was saying. All of you, all of you are amazing. I'm a lucky man to have gotten to know each of you, but this is about my future." he said looking around at the imaginary women in the room, as Londyn giggled. "I choose this cutie pie right here, and I don't really care if y'all get mad... but I only have one rose, for one special lady. One special lady, will continue on as my girlfriend... and as for the rest of you, you ain't gotta go home, but..."

"You are crazzzyyyy." Londyn laughed uncontrollably.

"Londyn, will you accept this rose?" he said dramatically as he stepped forward.

"Of course, baby." Londyn smiled as she walked forward and reached up, wrapping her arms around his neck.

"I knew you would." he replied, while pinching her on the butt.

"Whatever." she laughed before kissing him on the lips.

"I think I'm in like with you girl." he smiled.

"I think I'm in like with you too. So much for Mr. Solo never committing to just one girl." she chuckled.

Chapter 12

"Ding Dongggg..." was the sound of the doorbell ringing at Londyn's dad's house.

"Dang Daddy, how many people did you invite over here?" Londyn asked as she sat at the kitchen table with Shane seated beside her.

"You know I always go all out for the Mayweather fights." her dad, Gerald, stated as he hopped out of his chair and opened the door, welcoming in more guests.

It was Wednesday evening, and as promised, Londyn went to her father's house to catch up, as well as introduce him to Shane. In typical Gerald James fashion, he had invited all of his buddies, frat brothers, and their wives and girlfriends over for a full-out fight party.

"I thought you invited me over to spend time

with MEEEEE." Londyn giggled.

"I can do that and watch the fight." Gerald said as he reached down and kissed Londyn on the forehead before having a seat at the kitchen table.

"So what were we talking about again? Oh yeah. Shane Solomon, the Beta man... in a house full of Mu Psi men. You feeling alright bro? You good?" Gerald joked.

"Oh I'm always smooth." Shane chuckled.

"So tell me about yourself young man." Gerald began.

"Yeah what's your story brother?" Gerald's line brother and best friend Wallace asked as he sat down.

Wallace, also known as Big Wally, was 6'5, 300 pounds and looked like he should be someone's bodyguard. Londyn always joked that her dad kept Wally around because it made him look important.

"Dad..." Londyn whined.

"Nah its cool Lo." Shane began. "Well I'm 21 years old, going on 22 in December. Born and raised right here in Detroit. Attending the University of Boazer on a full ride scholarship. Engineering Major, Math Minor. No kids, don't want any trouble. Just trying to do right by your daughter, sir."

"Sir. Just trying to do right by your daughter sir." Wally stated, playfully mocking Shane.

"So are you a party animal?" Gerald asked.

"Not at all, Sir." Shane replied.

"Do you do drugs?" Wally asked.

"No sir, I don't drink either."

"Ohhhhhh look little Londyn done found herself a saint." Wally chucked.

"You ever been to jail?" Gerald asked.

Shane's eyes jumped.

"Nah I'm just messing with you!" Gerald said as he laughed hysterically. "My son Antonio already told me that you were a cool cat, so you're good with me homie." Gerald said as he reached over and squeezed Shane's hand tightly, "but if you break my Babygirl's heart I will break your neck."

"Dad, stop playing so much." Londyn said as she pulled her dad's hand from Shane's.

"I'm not playing. Do you think I'm playing, Shane?"

"Not at all, sir."

"Did Londyn tell you I'm a Veteran?"

"Yes, she did."

"Yeah, so I have access to a plethora of artillery. I just hope you and I can remain on good terms."

"Oh most definitely. I got you." Shane said with a smile.

"Nah, but I'm really a cool dad you know. I'm hip. I'm just overprotective of my Babygirl..."

"Understandable, she's special."

"That she is. So, who you got in this fight?"

"The Money Team of course." Shane chuckled.

"Okay just had to make sure. You know Floyd is from Michigan. Gotta root for the home squad... Ay Tammy, them wings done yet baby?" he asked as he looked over at his wife who stood over the stove preparing the fight party feast.

"Almost babe." she replied as she turned and walked over to the table.

"Y'all want some appetizers? Drinks? I made margaritas if you guys want something." Tammy asked.

"Yeah baby let me get a beer, please. Thank you baby. You so sexy." Gerald hissed.

Londyn rolled her eyes at the sight of her dad's flirtatious ways.

"Daddy, look at my picture. It's me and you." Little Sabrina exclaimed as she ran into the room with a coloring book.

"Oh wow little princess, it's beautiful. Great job." Gerald exclaimed.

"Tuh.." Londyn mumbled as she rolled her eyes at the sight of her dad being so affectionate with his stepdaughter.

Tony gently kicked Londyn's leg under the table and gave her a look that read "Stop." She straightened up her posture, and started to scroll through Twitter on her phone.

"So how was the game? Londyn told me y'all were heading out to the Palace yesterday." Gerald asked.

"It was cool, Dad." Londyn replied with little emotion.

"Yeah, it was fun. It's always cool to be there in the midst of all the action." Shane replied.

"You hoop?" Gerald asked.

"Yeah, I hoop." Shane replied. "I played Varsity back in high school, never played in college though."

"Oh okay, that's what's up. You know, I went to Eastern Michigan University when Londyn was a kid, to play basketball, but some situations came up. You know, life happens, and I had to leave campus, but I hoop still. We gon' have to check out your skills one day."

"Yeah you gotta come up to the rec and hoop with us one weekend." Wally said.

"Oh bet. I'm there for sure. Gotta see what the old school working with." Shane laughed.

"Old school. That's right. Better than y'all new school shenanigans. I don't know what's up with you 90's babies. This generation has no taste." Gerald laughed.

"No taste." Wally replied.

"The TV shows are trash." Gerald began.

"Trash." Wally echoed.

"The music is trash." Gerald continued.

"Trash." Wally echoed again.

"The ..." Gerald began

"Who are y'all Kenan & Kel?" Londyn interrupted in a burst of laughter.

"You know your daddy is a mess." Tammy laughed as she walked over to the table and stood near Gerald with a beer in her hand.

"What's that new song these kids listen to?" Gerald asked. "You know the one with the queen and the bands?"

"Trap Love. By Lil' Bunny!" answered one of his friends, Jeremiah from his seat on the couch in the living room.

"Young Rabbit!" Londyn corrected him.

"Yeah that's the one! Now that song makes about as much sense as putting sugar in grits." Gerald laughed.

"Lil' Bunny. Young Rabbit. Either way, these kids don't know real music." Jeremiah's wife Shawnie chuckled.

The group laughed and mocked the song as Tammy simultaneously turned on their iPod speakers.

"Now this is real music!" Tammy chuckled as Prince's 80's classic hit "Little Red Corvette" blasted through the speakers.

"Ayeeeeeee!" Shane jumped up, grabbing Londyn by the hand.

She stood up at his request and followed his lead as he began to ballroom hustle.

"Okay okay! I see y'all" Tammy said as she quickly joined in.

"Black folks in Detroit hustle to any and every song!" Gerald chuckled as he too began to get his hustle on.

Within a few moments just about everyone in the house, even Big Wally, had joined in on the family hustle session. An awkward moment turned into loads of fun, thanks to the two underdogs in the room, Tammy and Shane. Operation ease Shane into Londyn's crazy family was on its way.

Chapter 13

Snow flurries fell across the sky as the luxury charter bus traveled across the slick roads. It was early December, the week after Thanksgiving to be exact, and time for the annual Statewide Collegiate Ski Resort Weekend. Every holiday season, the greek chapters across a few of the larger campuses in the state of Michigan got together to plan a collaborative statewide trip to a ski resort up north. The resort was owned and operated by NFL Hall of Fame legend, and U.B. Alum, Sean Washington.

Londyn laid sound asleep with her head on Shane's shoulder as he listened to Outkast's classic Stankonia album through his Beats headphones. Everything was finally starting to fall into place in Shane's life. He and Londyn were in a really good space, Kyla had finally taken a hint and backed off, his 22nd birthday was a week away, and his Uncle Buck had gotten a new job. As far as his academic endeavors, he was excelling in his classes, and was in the running to win the 2015 National Society of Minority Engineers Award.

"Ay Solo, you think the freaks gon be D.T.F. this weekend?" asked Henry Gordon, one of his U.B. peers who was sitting in the seat in front of him.

"Huh?" Shane asked as he removed the Beats from his ears.

"I said, you think the freaks gon be feeling frisky this weekend?"

"Haa.. I'm chillin' man." Shane replied as he looked down at his sleeping beauty.

"Haha. I feel it. More for me!" he laughed as turned around and sat back in his seat.

"He's such a pig." Londyn mumbled.

"I thought you were sleep." Shane replied.

"I hear everything." Londyn replied as he sat up. "Are we there yet, it seems like we've been driving all day."

"I think so. You've been slobbing on my shoulder for two hours."

"My bad." Londyn chuckled as she wiped her mouth.

"It's okay, I don't mind your slobby sleep face." he said as he playfully smushed her face with his palm.

"Ugh. You two are so corny. Get a rooooom."

yelled Reagan from the seat behind.

"Hater." Londyn replied as she leaned over and gave Shane a peck on the lips.

"You know, she is right. It's still not too late for us to get a room at the resort." Shane stated as he tickled Londyn in her side.

"No... Stop... Stop Shane." she chuckled. "Now you already know that wouldn't be a good idea. I'll stick to rooming with Chanel."

"Yeah yeah..." he laughed sarcastically.

A few moments the later the charter bus came to a stop in front of the resort. After 4 long hours on the road, the seven charter buses full of anxious college students began to empty out onto the snowy pavement. Londyn wore a crème colored hat, scarf, and mitten set, purple Northface coat, and chocolate Ugg boots. Shane stood tall next to her in a crispy black pea coat, red scarf, and red Beta Kappa Epsilon skullcap.

"That's me right there." Shane yelled to the attendant when he spotted Londyn's bright pink Victoria Secret duffle bag.

After grabbing her bag and passing it to Londyn, he spotted his own duffle bag and quickly threw it over his shoulder. The two of them walked over to where Reagan, David, Chanel, Chris, and a few others were standing, when a short man wearing the same Beta skullcap approached Shane.

"Is that the young boy Solo?" the man hollered.

"Jamal, what up doe?" Shane exclaimed as he greeted him with a manly hug.

"What's good with you man? Long time no see!"

"I know man, it's been what, at least two years bro? How's that California life treating you?" Shane asked.

"It's amazing! I love it, never moving back to Michigan!"

"I hear that, I bet the weather is great too, huh?" Shane chuckled.

"Mannn. It's beautiful. So much opportunity there. I just started working at a big studio in Hollywood. Got a lot of big projects coming soon."

"That's what's up bro. I'm so proud of you. You're an inspiration to us all, real talk."

"I'm trying man. But I see all of y'all are out here doing big things too! Your Dean told me you got nominated for that big engineering award. That's what's up."

"Thanks, I'm just trying to get like you out here."

"Ahem." Londyn mumbled as she had patiently stood in silence unannounced until now.

"Ohhhh, my bad. I'm sorry. Londyn, this is my prophyte, Jamal. Jamal, this is my girlfriend Londyn."

he said with his arm rested on Londyn's middle back.

"Hi, nice to meet you." Londyn smiled with her arm extended for a handshake.

"Nice to meet you too girlfriend, Londyn," Jamal replied as he shook her hand, "my youngin' treating you like a queen I hope?"

"Haha. Yeah, he's aighttt." Londyn replied with a smirk.

"Good, Good. Well, I'm about to go find my bag and then head up to the chapter suite. I'll see you there?!"

"Aight, bet bro. Yep, I'll check you later on." Shane replied.

Shane and Londyn walked over to where their friends were waiting for them so that they could all head to check in together.

"Ohhhhh I am soooooo excited. I wonder if they have a hot tub here?" Reagan asked the group.

"Reagan, you've got to be the only person in the world that comes to a cold ski resort and wants to find a hot tub." David replied.

"Soooo? And your point is?" Reagan giggled.

"I was wondering the same thing too lowkey." Chanel giggled.

"Women!" David shook his head. "I'm trying to get on those slopes! Show these folks what a black man can do on some ice, you feel me!"

"Yeah, well just don't fall and bust your big, black head!" Reagan laughed.

"Y'all fooling, let's go check into these rooms though." Chris stated as he turned towards the main building entrance.

The group followed Chris through the double doors into the beautiful lodge entrance. The resort was very classy, and had been voted one of the best in the nation. People from all over the country often traveled to Michigan during the winter to visit the famous resort. Sean Washington was a proud member of his community, and always gave back by allowing student groups to visit his facilities for a fraction of the normal cost. For this weekend in particular, he'd even arranged for a popular rapper to come and perform, unbeknownst to the students.

As everyone began to crowd into the lobby, whispers began to spread as they all noticed the huge sign that hung from the balcony. "Welcome Michigan College Students to Sean Washington's Academic Appreciation Weekend, Feat. Special Musical Guest, Tahj!"

"Tahj is coming!! Chanel look!" Londyn screeched.

"Oh my God, Oh my God." Chanel screamed when she read the sign.

Tahj was her all time favorite rapper and celebrity crush.

"Aye this weekend is about to be lit!" David stated.

"Yassssss, I'm too excited!" Reagan exclaimed.

After waiting in line, the group was finally able to check in and get their room keys. They decided to split up and locate their separate rooms. Shane and Chris were in a big suite with a few other Beta's from U.B., Reagan and David had a room together, and Londyn and Chanel had agreed to bunk together for the weekend.

"Okay, so let's all get freshened up, and meet back here in the lobby in like what, 20 minutes? Cool?" Reagan asked the group.

"Yeah, yep, sounds cool." they all answered as they headed towards their various rooms.

Chanel picked up her huge suitcase on wheels and began to walk with Londyn.

"Thanks for rooming with me Nelly. You know Shane was trying to room together, and I was not having that..." Londyn giggled.

"Oh no problem, you're my girl. It'll be fun! How come you didn't want to room with him though? You think he'll try something slick?" she asked as they waited for the elevator.

"Girl. I'm scared that I will be the one trying something slick, you know what I mean?" Londyn laughed as she high fived Chanel. "It's been a long time girl... a longgg time. And I know me, a whole weekend together in one bed would be trouble. I'd leave here knocked up." Londyn laughed.

"Ohhhh lord!" Chanel giggled as they stepped onto the elevator.

"I'm serious. I mean, we haven't done it yet. We're not planning to either. We're both celibate. It was his idea actually. We've been going to these bible study groups at his church, and there's been a lot of lessons about Christian dating and how you have to know yourself and not place yourself or your partner in tempting situations. You have to know what your weak points are."

"That makes sense! That's impressive. So what do you do when he comes to visit and stuff?"

"Well, we make it a point not to do too many sleepovers, and in the event that he does stay over, girl, he sleeps on the couch if things get too heavy! Another one of his ideas."

"Wowww. That's good. I need a relationship like that." Chanel giggled.

"It ain't easy..." Londyn began to say as the elevator doors slid open.

She paused right in the middle of her sentence when she looked up and saw Kyla and her friends getting on the elevator. Kyla rolled her eyes as she stepped inside and turned her back to Londyn. She leaned over and whispered something in her friend's ear, who immediately turned her head to roll her eyes at Londyn as well. Londyn felt extremely uncomfortable, and looked up at the lights to see how close they were to the 5th floor. Luckily enough, she heard a ding and the number 5 lit up, meaning she and Chanel could get off the elevator, away from Kyla and her crew. As the doors opened they quickly scooted through the small crowd and out the door. Londyn could hear Kyla snickering as she walked off of the elevator.

"Soooo, what was all that about?" Chanel asked.

"Girl... that's just Shane's ex, or wanna be ex. I don't know what to call her. A chick Shane used to mess with."

"Oh wow. I should've known. She and her friends were clearly hating."

"Yeah that's pretty much all that girl is good for. Hating and trying to hold on to Shane. I'm not worried about her though," Londyn said as she swiped their room key in the door, "I'm not thinking about her and neither is my man. He really doesn't pay her any attention at all. Her loss." Londyn shrugged.

"I know that's right. That's a good attitude to have." Chanel giggled. "O.M.G. this room is gorgeous!" she exclaimed as she entered the room and plopped down on one of the beds.

"I know right, it's soooo pretty!" Londyn replied as she walked over towards the window that overlooked the slopes.

"Just so you know Lo. If I meet Tahj, this room is all yours because I will be somewhere singing sweet love songs to the best singin' rapper alive." Chanel laughed.

"Haaaaa. Crazy girl." Londyn replied as she plopped down on her bed and laid on her back. Neither of them said a word for a few moments, before Chanel interrupted the silence.

"So... are you in love Lo?" Chanel asked.

"Random!" Londyn chuckled as she sat straight up on the bed.

"Well you know I'm random like that! That's nothing new."

"Right... ummm... I don't know... like, part of me is still waiting for things to fall apart."

"Yeah, I feel you... that's how it usually goes... real love takes time. But, when it's there, you'll know! Don't be scared of it though... mess around and end up letting your own insecurities ruin what you have..."

"Yeah... I mean, don't get me wrong, I love him... but as far as actually being in love, in love... It's like I'm just scared to say it out loud and admit that to myself. Once you're in love, in love... things get real. It's a lot of pressure. I'm scared."

"Do you think Shane will hurt you?"

"All guys are dogs, Nelly."

"No they aren't"

"Well, they have the ability to be."

"Yeah, and all women have the ability to be scandalous heartbreakers too, but Shane doesn't seem to be letting that hold him back from trying to be open with you."

"Yeah you're right...He tries really hard. I don't know... I'm trying to let my guard down... I just don't do well with the whole love thing..."

"But love is a beautiful thing!! Well, not that I know personally or anything." Chanel laughed.

"Shut up Nelly, you've been in love before haven't you?"

"No, not real love. Puppy love maybe... but definitely not the real deal. I'm just waiting on the right guy to come along."

"And he certainly will! But enough of this love talk, I'm ready to have some fun! I need to see what clothes you packed Ms. Fashionista."

"Hahaha, you know I had to bring out my good stuff girl." Chanel giggled as she hauled her suitcase up onto the bed.

"Ahhhhh that is so cute!" Londyn exclaimed as Chanel pulled out a red halter style fitted dress. "Is that for the party?"

"I don't know... I brought like a million outfits. If you like it you can wear it to the party. Red isn't really my color anyway." she giggled.

"Oh right, Miss Pink & Green." Londyn said in reference to Chanel's sorority. "I'll try it on later, after we eat."

"Cool. Did you see an itinerary?" Chanel asked.

"Uhhh, yeah there's probably one on the back of the door." Londyn said as she got up off the bed.

Surely enough, there was a typed itinerary located on the back of the room door. She grabbed it and handed it over to Chanel.

"Okay, let's see... I'm just trying to see when my husband Tahj will be here."

"Haha, I know that's right."

"Okay, so this says that the concert is tonight. Tomorrow, outdoor snow activities all day, and then the party is tomorrow night. Sounds like a plan. I have to start beating my face now, only a few hours until I'm face to face with Tahj!"

"You are obsessed with him, Chanel." Londyn chuckled.

"Sure am! Haha. Let's go eat though." she said as she hopped up off of her bed.

They lined their luggage neatly against the wall and grabbed their purses off of the beds. Chanel opened the door and stepped outside into the hallway, with Londyn following right behind. As Londyn stepped through the doorway she paused as she noticed a tall curly haired guy walking out of the room directly across the hall.

"Oh, what's good Londyn... What up Chanel?" said Justin, Londyn's ex boyfriend.

"Hey." Chanel responded, alone.

"You can't speak?" Justin asked Londyn.

"Hello, Justin." Londyn replied as she walked past him.

"Ugh. What is my luck? Is everyone at this freaking resort?" Londyn whispered under her breath.

"Hush, just pretend he's not even here girl." Chanel said as she interlocked her arm in Londyn's.

They hopped on the elevator and headed down to the lobby to meet up with the rest of their friends. Once they arrived downstairs they noticed that their small group had expanded. Joining them now was Shane, Xavier, Thomas, Reagan, and David, David's cousin Quincy, a set of twins from ELU: Ashley and Allison, and Chanel's sorority sister Jasmine. The group walked through the lobby to the food-court style eatery area to get a bite to eat before the concert. Everyone dispersed to the various lines in front of the wide variety of restaurant options before all reconvening back at one large rectangular table.

"I'm so excited to see Tahj!" Allison exclaimed.

"I know right. He's the realist!" her twin sister Ashley chimed in.

"Mannnn. Tahj know he be in his feelings a little too much. He bout to have all these people pulling a Throwback Love tonight." David chuckled.

"Tell Makayla Jones she can pull that Throwback Love act if she want to. My fist will be introduced to her face!" Reagan said as she rolled her eyes.

"Yooo, I'm convinced Reagan is really crazy in real life!" Thomas said with a laugh.

"Ohhh. But she is though. Makayla Jones was David's girlfriend in the 9th grade." Londyn replied.

"Dawgggggggg...." Shane laughed. "Are you serious. You still remember her?"

"Sure do, and if she wants to try it, we can take it there." Reagan replied with a serious straight face, before she burst out laughing at her own silliness.

"Aye real talk though, why do people do that?" Quincy asked.

"Do what?" Londyn asked.

"That Throwback Love game. Like why do girls always want to come back and hate when they see you happy with your new girl. Talking about they miss what y'all used to have. If you missed it so much then why are you just now saying something about it?" Quincy continued.

"Because once you see your ex in a new relationship it brings up old feelings of what you two used to have. It's human nature to miss the good in them that you now see them giving to someone else," Chanel replied. "but that doesn't mean you have to act on it though... I wouldn't."

"I'm saying though, you can't break up with a dude, and then come back later telling him he downgraded. If you ain't break up with him in the first place then he wouldn't have had to downgrade, upgrade, nothing. Right?" Quincy asked.

"Okay, but then I have to ask why she broke up with you in the first place?" Allison asked.

"Because you cheated?" her sister continued.

"Mannnn." Quincy replied.

"Exactly. Case Closed," Allison began. "if you cheat on me, and we break up... then I see you with somebody new that's not doing better than me, I have a right to express that."

"Nah, you really don't because if you're over here reminiscing and telling me that I can do better, it's because you still care or feel that your opinion should still be relevant to my life. Meaning you shouldn't have ever dumped me in the first place if you were going to be all up in my business." Quincy stated as he bit into his hamburger.

"Quincy you sound so dumb!" Jasmine laughed.

"I'd have to agree." Londyn giggled.

"Nah, I get what he's saying though," Xavier began. "It's like girls love to act all big and bad, and claim they're cool with the relationship being over...

but the MINUTE she even thinks he's slightly happy with a new girl, all of a sudden she wants to start being all forgiving, texting his phone like "hey big head... whatever happened to what we had?"' Xavier stated.

"But guys do that too..." Jasmine said.

"Not me..." Xavier responded.

"Oh so you never went back to an ex all in your feelings?" Chanel asked sarcastically.

"Never, the past is the past for a reason." Xavier stated.

"Well I've definitely had guys pull that stunt on me!" Chanel began, "texting me late at night saying that they miss me and that the dude I'm talking to is weak and will never amount to him."

"Aye, real talk, I can't even hold y'all up. I definitely Throwback Loved a few in my day." Thomas chuckled.

"Seeeee! That's why I like you Thomas, you always keep it 100." Chanel replied.

"Sometimes you just can't see what you have until it's gone, and once you realize that and try to win her back, it comes off as you saying forget your new guy. Because you're looking at this new dude who seems to have popped up out of nowhere, and you're thinking- he couldn't possibly love you like I do, when in all actuality, you ain't really love her and treat her the way she deserved, or else you wouldn't have ever lost her." Thomas replied.

"Thank youuuuuu. Finally someone that is honest!" Allison giggled.

"It's a maturity factor that comes into play. A mature enough person can be happy for their ex having moved on to someone better if they can admit to themselves that they weren't man or woman enough to handle their business in the first place." Thomas continued.

"Yeah, I definitely have to agree with that. An immature girl will try that, but a real woman who is secure in her life, would never try to sabotage your new relationship. You just chalk it up as a loss and move on." Jasmine stated.

"Right..." everyone began to chime in.

"Whatever, if David ever tries to get a new girlfriend I'm sabotaging that whole thing!" Reagan stated plainly.

The whole group burst out in laughter, because they knew that crazy, Reagan was telling the absolute truth.

Chapter 14

"What upppp doe, Detroit?" Tahj sang live from the stage.

He had been going in for about 20 minutes so far and the crowd was absolutely loving it! Londyn stood in front of Shane, who had his arms wrapped around her as he rapped along with Tahj's every verse. The concert had been a great one so far, and Chanel even managed to finesse her way up onto stage for 15 seconds of fame with Tahj. The crowd was rocking as Tahj jumped back and forth from his earlier hits to his more recent ones. The memorable moment of the night came when he announced his special guest, Monica, who joined him onstage for a duet of his and her versions of none other than, "Throwback Love." Shane and Londyn were vibing to the song in their own world until she noticed Justin off to the side.

"Ugh..." Londyn mumbled.

"What's wrong?" Shane asked, as he looked over towards where Londyn was staring. "Who is that?" he asked.

"Nobody important... that's Justin. I can't stand him."

"Justin, as in, your ex Justin?" Shane asked as he stepped back, releasing her from his embrace.

Londyn turned around so that she was facing him and grabbed his hands in hers.

"Yeah, that's him. I'm so mad he's here."

"Don't even worry about him." Shane replied as he tried to regain her attention.

Londyn danced playfully, but still continued to look over at Justin.

"Ugh... is he pointing at me?" she mumbled.

Shane looked over at Justin and then back and Londyn in confusion.

A few seconds later, a jealous Justin walked past the two of them and mouthed the words of the song along with Tahj.

"You can do better, I know you miss my love..." he sang, shaking his finger at Londyn.

He was obviously intoxicated, and in the mood for drama.

"Ay man, you better watch who you talking to!" Shane stated calmly, yet firmly to Justin.

Justin immediately paused and turned back to

face Shane.

"You got a problem?" Justin asked, raising his voice substantially.

"Yeah I do, you need to watch what you saying around me and my girl." Shane said as he took a step closer towards Justin.

"Shane stop." Londyn said as she tugged on Shane's shirt.

A small crowd began to form as people noticed the commotion.

"I'll say whatever the hell I wanna say to you or your girl. How you enjoying my leftovers? She still do that one lil' thing she used to do for me?" Justin asked as he got in Shane's face.

Shane clinched his fist and swung swiftly and viciously in Justin's direction. Justin nearly lost his balance as Shane's fist sunk into his jaw. Just as Justin tried to swing back, Shane's line brothers quickly stepped in, forming a human barricade between the two of them.

"Shane, stop it. He's not even worth it!" Londyn pleaded.

"Ya boy needs to watch his mouth." Shane huffed.

"Do we have a problem here?" a security officer asked as he walked up towards the small crowd.

"No, no.... officer everything is fine ." Londyn

pleaded.

The officer looked over at Shane and stared him in the eyes.

"No problem here, sir." Shane replied sternly with anger in his eyes, as his fists were still balled.

The officer looked over at Justin and paused.

"I'm good." Justin replied as one of his line brothers gripped the back of his shirt.

The officer bobbed his head and turned to walk through the crowd. Londyn grabbed Shane by the hand, and pulled him a few feet away so they could talk privately. She pressed her stomach against his body and wrapped her arms around his lower back. Looking up at him, she stared deep in his eyes.

"Don't let him get to you... he's ignorant."

"Yeah well it would've been nice if I had a warning that your ignorant ex-boyfriend was gonna be here, all in my face. He's lucky I didn't knock that Jheri curl right out his head. You know that right?"

"Babe." Londyn chuckled.

"Just don't let me catch him again..."

"Mm hmm... I know." she giggled as she grabbed his muscles before laying her head on his chest.

A few seconds later the beat dropped and Tahj began singing Shane's favorite song, "Your Love."

"Ayeeeee." Londyn whispered softly.

Shane finally cracked a smile as he began to shimmy behind her. She turned around and laughed as he put on a full blown strolling performance just for her. Leave it to Londyn to take his mind off his problems, just by being herself.

Chapter 15

"Yo, I meant to ask you, what happened last night with Solo and Justin?" Reagan asked as she and Londyn huddled in line in front of the hot chocolate booth outside on the slopes.

The air was frigid and the gusting wind made it feel even colder.

"They got into it, to say the least... Justin started it... was being ignorant and disrespectful as usual... and you know Shane is so over protective. So he punched him in the jaw just like he deserved." Londyn stated as she rubbed her gloves together and then lifted her hands up to shield her mouth and nose from the cold air.

"Dang man. I bet you were happy to see that!" Reagan chuckled. "I would've paid good money to see Justin get a beat down. I can't stand him."

"No, I wasn't happy. I don't want my man out there fighting. Especially not Justin. He's not even worth it."

"Mmm hmmm."

"But I guess it did feel kind of good seeing Shane land that one punch though." Londyn laughed.

"Girl, I know it."

"Oh, so I forgot to tell you. Justin's freaking room is right directly across the hall from me and Chanel's." Londyn stated as she grabbed a cup of hot chocolate and passed it to Reagan.

"Shut up! Are you serious? What are the odds of that?" she exclaimed.

"Tell me about it."

"I bet Solo was mad when he found that out wasn't he?"

"Girl please, I did NOT tell him. He can barely handle him being at the resort, let alone the thought of him sleeping just feet away."

"I guess you're right," Reagan giggled, "but if he finds out that's gonna be a big mess, girlfriend. He'll sock Justin in both jaws this time."

"Who you telling." Londyn chuckled.

"What are y'all laughing about?" Shane asked as he stomped through the snow towards them.

"Oh, nothing much." Londyn giggled. "Are you ready for me to whoop your butt in this sled race though, baby?"

"You ain't bout that life Lo!"

"I am! Let's go!" Londyn stated as she took off running.

Shane and Reagan quickly followed behind Londyn as she headed towards the dock where the sleds were housed. As always, Reagan managed to summon David from afar, turning this race into a couple's activity. The foursome each individually picked out a blue sled and laid it on the ground of the snow covered hill. As they laid their stomachs down on their sled, Shane reached over and pinched Londyn's behind.

"Heyyy, stop it." she giggled.

"Just a pinch for good luck because you're going to need it." Shane chucked as he pushed off against the cold ground and started off down the hill.

"Cheater!!!" Londyn yelled as she too pushed off, followed by Reagan and David.

"Ahhhhhhhh." Londyn screamed as she quickly sped down the hill head first on the sled.

The four friends laughed as they collided with the soft piles of snow at the bottom of the hill.

"You cheated." Londyn stated as she got up and dusted the snow off of her snowsuit.

"Nah, you just lost!" Shane chuckled as he tossed he and Londyn's sled to the side and wrapped his arm around her shoulders.

"You definitely cheated, Solo!" Reagan laughed.

"Nope. The champ is here!" Shane laughed as he flexed his muscles. "Don't be mad Reagan!!"

"I'm tired, this has been such a long day. I think I need a nap." Londyn stated as she walked and cuddled under Shane's arms.

"Yeah I could use some rest too, lowkey. You want to eat first?" Shane asked.

"Yeah we can... that's cool."

"Y'all trying to go eat?" Shane asked Reagan and David who were walking just a few feet ahead of he and Londyn.

"Nah bro, we're good. We're about to hit these ski's up again one more time." David replied.

"Yeah, we'll catch up with y'all in a little bit though." Reagan stated.

"Alrighty." Londyn said as she and Shane pivoted and headed towards the main cabin.

Shane paused for a moment, bent forward slightly, and winked. Londyn immediately stood behind him, and jumped onto his back. He piggybacked her all the way to the main cabin.

"You're the real MVP." she giggled.

"That's all you, Babe..." he replied.

"Such a gentleman." she giggled as he let her

down onto her feet.

"What do you want to eat?" he asked.

"Let's get Chipotle."

"Bet. I can do that." he replied as they walked towards the Chipotle line.

As they stood in line, with his arm wrapped around her shoulder, Shane reached down and kissed Londyn on her forehead. She smiled as she wrapped her arm around his waist. Not a moment sooner, did they realize that Kyla was standing in the line right in front of them. She must have felt the tension, because she just so happened to turn her head and look back at them, like a deer in headlights. A look of shock and disappointment spread across her face. She quickly got out of line and walked over to Chick-Fil-A, where a few of her friends were standing. Her friends glanced over at Shane and Londyn, but quickly looked away when they caught them staring back.

"Wow... I'm surprised she didn't try to start some drama..." Londyn mumbled.

"Nah, we don't have to worry about that anymore..." Shane replied.

"What do you mean?" she asked.

"I mean. I handled it..."

"What did you do?"

"I just told her she doesn't stand a chance with me and that she shouldn't waste her time... because you're my girlfriend and she has to respect that fact or she's going to find herself with some problems."

"Oh lord, you threatened the girl?" Londyn asked.

"Nah, not at all. You know that's not even my style. I just told her that she needed to respect you... or else." he chuckled.

"Right, whatever that means..." Londyn giggled and shook her head. "Well, hey, whatever you said must have worked because I've never seen her be so passive."

"That's because your man knows how to lay down the law. Ain't nobody bout to come in and mess up this relationship."

"Mmmm hmm..." Londyn mumbled with a smile.

It pleasured her to know that her man was so committed to making sure they didn't have any form of interference in their relationship; a factor that seemed to destroy every attempt at a relationship she'd ever had in the past.

They decided to cut their losses and avoid an awkward stare down from Kyla and her friends in the dining hall, by eating upstairs in Londyn's room. As they rode the elevator up to the 5th floor alone, Londyn caught Shane staring at her.

"What?" she giggled.

"Nothing, you're just beautiful." he replied.

She smiled and winked at him as they walked off the elevator. Once they arrived in her room, they took off their snowsuits and sat down on Londyn's bed. Londyn grabbed the remote and flipped through the channels as they chowed down on their burrito bowls.

"Martin or The Wayans Brothers?" she asked.

"You already know..." he replied.

Londyn quickly flipped the channel back to BET where a "Martin" rerun was playing.

After finishing their food, Shane pulled Londyn by the waist as to hint to her to scoot back towards him. Londyn obliged and scooted back so that she was sitting between his legs with her back resting on his chest. They laughed together for a while at Martin and Gina's shenanigans.

"Tommy never had a job though man for real, that's so funny." Londyn giggled.

"I know right... reminds me of some of my family members to be honest. He was making money somehow..." Shane laughed.

"Yeah... speaking of Tommy's though, how's Uncle Buck?" Londyn giggled.

"Aye, chill out!" Shane chuckled. "He's doing really well, thanks to you. I really appreciate you plugging him with the hiring manager at the manufacturing plant... looks like he might finally be on the straight and narrow." Shane stated as he wrapped his arms tighter around her.

"No problem at all. It's the least I could do. Shoutout to my Dad. I'm just glad everything worked out after that Ann Arbor job fell through."

"Yeah, me too... he was really disappointed when he didn't get that job man. I'm glad somebody finally gave him a chance. Now let's just hope that he can maintain."

"Yeah I hope so too... for his family's sake." Londyn replied.

"Exactly. It's crazy how life plays out," Shane began as he scratched his head, "like, how people can come from the same neighborhood, same household... and end up on such different paths. My boys from home, my little cousins, Man-Man... and Uncle B too, even though he was a lot older... we all grew up together. We went to the same schools, hung with the same crew. Now, they're all locked up, or worse, dead. Then there's me. I don't know how I got to be the lucky one. I feel guilty sometimes like I messed up, and somehow didn't bring them up out the hood with me."

"You're not lucky, you're blessed Shane. You ended up this way because at the end of the day, you made good choices. Yes, you all grew up together, but that doesn't mean you all have the same values, morals, or determination. You wanted better for yourself and you made it happen. You got out. It's not your fault that they're still stuck in that cycle. Just do what you can to motivate and inspire them, but whatever you do, don't feel guilty for your success."

"Yeah you're right..." he replied.

"How is Man-Man anyway? Have you heard from him?"

"Yeah he's sent me a few letters. He said it's not too bad in there, but I know he's just saying that because he doesn't want me to worry about him..."

"You think he's learning his lesson by being in there?"

"I wish I could say yes... but I'd be lying if I did. Man-Man, his world is so small, he just doesn't see the bigger picture. To him, going to prison is just apart of normal life for a black man. Everybody else around us went. He's been in and out of the system his whole life. His dad caught a manslaughter charge, and got sentenced to life. His granddad is doing a 40 ball, and I think he has like 12 years left, so that's basically life, at his age. His older brother was murdered as a teenager. He just doesn't know any other way."

"That's so sad..." Londyn replied.

"Tell me about it...." he replied as he held her hands in his and focused his attention on the TV screen.

"I'm really proud of you Shane." Londyn began after a few moments of silence.

"I appreciate that babe," he said as he leaned over and kissed her on the cheek, "We're getting married one day babe."

"You think so?" she asked.

"I know so... why, you don't think so?"

"That's just a lot to think about... we're too young to think that far..."

"I'm not saying I want to get married tomorrow, I'm just saying it's me and you 'til the world blow. You're it for me..." he replied as he waited for her to agree with him.

Her silence disappointed him a little. Whenever he went out on a limb and tried to express his deep thoughts for Londyn, she shut him down every time. This time was no different than all the rest, as she avoided furthering the conversation about the future. Instead, she began to slowly rub her hand on his leg. He gave in to her distraction, and reached down and kissed her slowly, and passionately on her neck in return. Londyn's body cringed as she rolled her neck to the side. He knew her weak spots, and she couldn't necessarily say that she wanted him to stop either. One thing led to another and the couple found themselves in a passionate make-out session, their body's passionately grinding on each other, as hands slipped here and there, and articles of clothing slipped off.

"Alright, let's not do something we'll regret later." Shane said.

"I won't regret anything." she replied as she leaned in and kissed his neck.

Shane began to kiss on her stomach, until Londyn sat up on the bed.

"Okay, maybe you're right, let's just stop." she replied.

"Alright." he said as he rolled over shirtless, facing the window.

Londyn shook her head and put her sweater back on. Things were beginning to get too hot and heavy for what she could handle.

"Marriage..." she thought as she closed her eyes and reflected on the topic he'd brought up.

However, within a few minutes the both of them were sound asleep.

About an hour or so later Londyn and Shane were awakened by the loud laughter and chatter of Chanel and Reagan as they entered the room. Londyn rubbed her eyes and looked at her cell phone to see what time it was, as Shane sat up and started to put on his shirt.

"Ohhhh, what's going on in here?" Reagan chuckled.

Londyn playfully rolled her eyes and gave her the "leave me alone" look as she stretched and yawned.

"Mmmm hmmm... I'm on to y'all now!" Reagan laughed as she sat down on Chanel's bed with a small overnight bag sitting beneath her feet.

"Right? What's going on in here?" Chanel giggled.

"Nothing. We were taking a nap... geez..." Londyn replied as she rubbed her eyes.

"Don't lie now." Shane laughed as he playfully kissed her neck while she tried to crawl out the bed.

"Stop playing!" Londyn giggled as she hit him with a pillow.

"Mmmmm hmm... Well, not to break up this little freaknik or whatever... but, it's 8:00 y'all, we have to get ready for this party." Chanel stated as she walked into the bathroom.

"Yeah... I'ma go on and head back to my room. I'll come back this way after I get dressed." Shane said as he stood up and reached for his wallet on the dresser.

He slipped into his snow boots, grabbed his coat, and walked towards the door.

"Alright..." Londyn said as she got up and followed him.

"See ya Solo." Chanel hollered from the bathroom, where she stood in the mirror brushing her teeth with the door open.

After Shane backed through the doorway, he leaned in and passionately kissed Londyn once more, then smiled. Londyn quickly closed the door behind him and walked back over to her bed.

"Freaks." Reagan chuckled.

"Shut up." Londyn replied as she pulled her phone from underneath a blanket on the bed and plugged it into the speaker dock on the nightstand. Moments later, Rihanna's voice came blasting through the speakers.

"Alright, time to get ready for the turn up!" Londyn said with a smile.

"Ayeeee." Reagan replied as she jumped up and began to dance along to the beat of the music.

Chanel came out of the bathroom, toothbrush in hand, and began to twerk by her lonesome.

"Get it Nelly! Get it Nelly! Work, Work, Work, Work, Work." Londyn chanted.

The three of them laughed hysterically as they danced all over the room.

"Alright who's showering first?" Reagan asked.

"You can go ahead. I'm feeling lazy." Londyn replied as she fell backwards onto the bed and spread all four limbs apart.

"Get it together Lo." Reagan chuckled as she grabbed her small overnight bag and skipped barefoot into the bathroom.

"20 minutes tops Reagan!" Chanel yelled from her spot on the bed as Reagan closed the bathroom door. "You know that girl will take a 45 minute shower if you let her."

"Tell me about it... when we lived together last year, our water bill was through the roof every single month." Londyn giggled.

"Terrible." Chanel laughed as she got up and walked over to her suitcase. She opened it and quickly grabbed the red halter dress that she had shown Londyn earlier. "Here you go Lo." she said as she tossed the dress across the room to Londyn's bed.

"You're the best, thanks Nelly." Londyn replied.

"No problem. You can keep it actually. As you can see, I've never worn it."

"Awww, thanks! An early Merry Christmas to me!"

"Right!" Chanel replied as she rummaged through her suitcase to search for an outfit.

"So...did y'all have fun on the slopes after Shane and I left?" Londyn asked.

"Yeah. It was cool..." Chanel began. "I met a new guy..."

"Oh really?" Londyn asked as she sat upright on the bed.

"His name is Michael. He goes to Grand Valley. He was soooo nice... and cute."

"Ohhhh la la... new bae alert!" Londyn laughed.

"Nah, nothing like that!" Chanel giggled.

"Mmmmmm hmmm... we'll have to see about that. Is he going to the party tonight?"

"Yup he is... I'll point him out to you."

"You better!" Londyn replied.

★

Meanwhile, in the Beta suite, Shane and his fraternity brothers pregamed as they engaged in deep conversation.

"I can't even lie to y'all, getting with my girl was the best thing that could've happened to me." said Shane's prophyte, Jamal.

"That's what's up bro. We all hope to find that right one someday." Jalen, a Beta from Michigan State University chimed in.

"Shhiiiiii. Not me." Xavier chuckled.

"You silly bro. You gon' be a player forever?" Jalen asked.

"As long as these girls are still out here trapping dudes, keying cars, and overreacting at every moment of the day, then yes. My baby mama is enough drama for one lifetime. I'm straighttttt." Xavier said as he took another shot.

"You attract what's inside of you, bro." Thomas chimed in.

"Here you go, getting philosophical as always." Xavier replied.

"Nah, nah, just hear me out. I used to be a savage out here. Then I watched my sister get her heart broken by her dude, and I took it super personal. We can't be out here playing these women. It just perpetuates a never-ending cycle, and supports the stereotype that men are dogs. You gotta man up at some point." Thomas continued.

"Aye, I get what X is saying though. Some of these women ain't the type you commit to. They're just as scandalous as us low key." added Chris from ELU.

"Right, but that takes me back to my point. You attract who you are. If you're out here being reckless, then you're not going to attract a queen." Thomas replied.

"He's right." Jamal began. "Men have these super high expectations for women, but don't live up to the hype themselves. When you change who you are, you'll find the right girl."

"That's exactly what I'm saying. Tell them, bro." Thomas continued. "I mean, look at Solo! Soon as my mans bossed his life up, he got with Londyn... and y'all know he was out here doggin' em..."

"Aye, chill out bro... way to put me out there." Shane replied.

"My fault, no offense, but am I wrong?" Thomas asked.

"I made a lot of mistakes in the past. I was just like Xavier, didn't really think there was a girl worth committing to, but I at least started putting forth some effort to better myself, as a man, you know. If I would've met Londyn like a year earlier I know it wouldn't have worked, Timing is everything." Shane replied.

"I don't know how y'all do it bro. Every chick I meet is off her rocker once feelings are involved." Chris replied. "They'll be cool until a good 3 weeks in."

"Don't get me wrong, everybody has a little crazy in them... but with the right person, y'all will communicate and she'll be like a breath of fresh air. The right woman will change your life, and your perspective on all this love talk fam." Shane replied.

"Love... did I just hear Shane Solomon use the word love?" Xavier asked.

"Shut up fool. Yeah, I love my girl. I ain't ashamed. She made me a better man." Shane chuckled as he took a sip of his Red Bull.

"I'll toast to that." Thomas stated. "...to growing up, and finding out what's most important in life."

"Cheers..." everyone other than Xavier said in unison.

"Y'all too emotional for me. Cheers to the DM's I'm gon' slide in after this party." Xavier laughed.

★

As the guys chatted about life, Reagan, Londyn, and Chanel took turns running in and out of the bathroom, taking showers, doing their hair, and huddling over the vanity as they put on makeup. Finally, at about 10pm they were dressed and ready to go.

"Selfie!" Reagan yelled as she whipped out her cell phone to take a picture of she and the girls.

Chanel and Londyn smiled, as Reagan pursed her lips together, making a classic duck lips face.

"Snapchat!" Reagan squealed as she snapped the picture.

As Reagan posted the photo, Londyn walked over to the long mirror that hung from the back of the bathroom door. She shifted her body weight back and forth as she pulled and tugged at her new red dress.

"You look great Lo," Chanel stated as she too walked over to the mirror, "Shane is gonna be all over you tonight."

Londyn smiled as she stared long and hard at herself. The halter style neckline accentuated her petite, yet curvaceous frame, and the shimmery shine of the fabric made the dress all the more unique.

"I love it... I feel like I'm missing something though." Londyn said as she twirled one of her curls in her fingers.

"Hmm...I got it..." Chanel replied as she stepped into the bathroom and flipped through her makeup bag.

She pulled out her favorite red lipstick by Mac, and handed it to Londyn.

"Can never go wrong with this... it'll make your whole look pop!"

"But I never wear lipstick..." Londyn replied.

"Well... today is the day you will." she joked as she took the lipstick from Londyn's hand, opened it, and wiped it with makeup cleaner. She smirked and handed it back to Londyn. "Put it on..."

"Okay, okay..." Londyn replied as she began to apply the lipstick to her lips.

She puckered her lips and took another long look in the mirror before flashing a happy smile.

"Told ya... that did it! That's all you needed." Chanel replied.

"CAAA-UTE! Super hot!" Reagan said as she jumped up from the bed to get a closer look at Londyn's final look. "Now we have to take another picture!"

The three of them stepped back and posed in front of the mirror as Reagan snapped a full body shot of their reflection.

"Ayeeee we're about to turn some heads tonight!" Reagan screeched.

"Baddies!" Chanel giggled.

"Yep... killing the game with these outfits for sure!" Londyn replied.

Londyn was dressed in the red dress and cream-colored pumps. Reagan wore a tight black pencil skirt, leopard colored pumps, a tan blazer, with a black bandu bra underneath. Chanel, the fashionista, wore a forest green leather skater skirt, a pink and gold sleeveless button up shimmery top with a stiff black collar, and short black ankle boot heels. They posed for a few more pictures before they were interrupted by a knock on the door.

"I wonder who that is..." Londyn pondered aloud as she put her hand on the doorknob, and opened the door with Reagan and Chanel closely behind her.

"Who tryna drink though?" yelled Marquan, a Mu from ELU, who also happened to be Chanel's best friend.

"Ayeeee, best friend!" Chanel yelled as she reached past Londyn and opened the door.

In walked a long line of guys, mostly Mu's from ELU.

"Hey Darren, Hey James, Wassup Rick!" Londyn greeted their friends as they walked through the door.

They all exchanged hugs with Londyn, Chanel, and Reagan as they piled into the room.

"Y'all looking all scrumptious and what not!"

said, Timothy, one of Londyn's favorite Mu's.

"Awww thanks Timmy Timmy... we try..." Londyn giggled.

"About this bottle though! Everybody has to take a shot." Marquan stated as he opened the bottle of liquor he held in his hand.

He began to pour double shots into shot glasses and passed them all around the room.

"Dang y'all came prepared!" Reagan chuckled as she leaned up against the wall.

"Girllll don't act like you ain't know how the Bruh's get down. We stay prepared." Darren replied as he unplugged Londyn's phone from the speaker dock and hooked his own phone to it.

Within seconds his favorite song by Young Jeezy was blasting through the speakers.

"Ayeeee, I'm geeked up." everyone chanted as they danced and passed the shot glasses around the room.

As everyone joined together to take his or her first shot, Reagan, who was standing closest to the door, heard a knock. She opened it, and was excited to see the twins, Ashley and Allison had arrived.

"Heyyyyyyyy, I see y'all started the turn up already!" Ashley squealed as she ran in the room.

"Wassuuuup Bruh's!" Allison said as she walked in and greeted her fraternity brothers.

"Awwww snap... the Wilson twins are in the building. Wassup Soror? Wassup Ash?" Marquan yelled as he began to pour them both a shot.

"You already know!" Ashley replied.

"Turn up then!" Timothy stated.

A few moments later, Reagan heard another knock on the door. She opened it, and to her unpleasant surprise, she stood face to face with the infamous Justin. Without saying a word, she attempted to push the door back in his face. She was not at all fond of the guy who broke her best friend's heart.

"Chill out." Justin replied as he tried to gently push open the door.

Reagan stepped to the side to avoid getting hit by the door, but rolled her eyes as he walked past her.

"Justin, my son! Where you been at man?" Darren asked.

"What's good Dean? What up Bruh's?" he asked with a head nod. "I was just down there with the K's! Chanel, I'm surprised you're not down there with them."

"I know, I'm going down there in a minute." she replied.

"Bet... what's up Ashley. Allison. Londyn. How y'all doing?

"Heyyyyy." the twins replied in unison.

"Dang Londyn, I still can't get a hello, huh?" he

quickly asked before Londyn even had chance to speak.

Reagan who'd been rather quiet up until then immediately spoke up on her best friend's behalf. "Okay, he gotta go. You coming up in here like you cool with us." she said as she rolled her eyes and downed another shot.

"Reagan dawg. You always trippin'."

"I'll trip if I want to, but you gotta get out!"

"Dang Reagan, you just gon' go in on my neo like that? What he do to you?" Darren asked.

"He knows what he did." she replied as she looked over at Londyn, and then back at Justin.

"... always coppin' an attitude. You want me to leave too, Londyn?" he asked as he looked over to her for confirmation.

Londyn stood silently without uttering a sound.

"Oh, word... alright. Now that you got you a little boyfriend you wanna act fake. You still trippin' on something that happened over a year ago." he replied as he walked towards the door. "Bruhs, I'll catch y'all down at the party..."

"Aight J. We'll see you in a little bit, fam." Marquan stated as he began to drink straight from the bottle.

As Justin walked through the door, he began to

sing lyrics to a popular rap song loud enough for everyone to hear.

"Got rid of my old girl. She was never on my level." he rapped as the door shut behind him.

"I'm sick of him." Londyn said as she charged towards the door.

"Hold up!" she yelled as she ran into the hallway, ready to give him a piece of her mind.

As chance would have it, at that exact moment, Shane and two of his fraternity brothers were walking down the hallway and witnessed what appeared to be Londyn running out of her room towards her ex. As she turned and saw Shane's look of disappointment, Justin chuckled. As if things couldn't get anymore awkward, Justin grabbed Londyn's hand and kissed it quickly before she could even pull away, and then proceeded to stick his key in his door directly across the hall from Londyn's. Shane just shook his head and turned right back around, heading back towards the elevator. His fraternity brothers immediately followed behind.

"Shane, wait... " Londyn cried out as she watched her boyfriend walk away.

He threw his arm down as to say "Stop," and continued to walk away.

"Shane!" she yelled again.

"Girl... don't even trip, he'll get over it..." Allison said as she stood in the doorway.

A single tear ran down Londyn's face as she

walked back towards the room.

"Now don't even be crying now. Your face is beat! Don't ruin your makeup now!" Allison said as she grabbed a tissue from her purse and gently dabbed Londyn's face.

"What the heck happened?" Reagan asked as she, Chanel, and Ashley, joined them in the hallway.

"You okay Lo?" Chanel asked.

"No. Shane just walked up when I ran out here after Justin... and then Justin tried to be funny and kissed my hand in front of Shane. I already know it looked so bad..." Londyn replied.

"Awwww... he'll understand, you just have to tell him what happened!" Chanel replied as she placed her hand on Londyn's shoulder.

"He looked so pissed y'all... Like he could barely even look at me... just walked away. I gotta fix this..." she replied as she grabbed both sides of her face.

"Well for right now, don't even trip Babygirl. We're about to have a good time tonight!" Allison replied as she pulled a 5th of Hennessy out of her purse.

"For real twin?" Chanel laughed.

"What...?" she laughed.

"You just pulling bottles out your purse now?" Chanel asked.

"Don't judge! Come on Londyn. I'll pour you a shot... or two... or three..." Allison said as she pulled

Londyn towards the door.

Before Londyn could get all the way into the room, Reagan pulled her to the side. "Text him. Tell him it was a misunderstanding." Reagan stated. "Don't listen to Twin. The last thing you want to do is let pride keep you from squashing something so minor." she continued.

"Alright." Londyn replied.

As the crew enjoyed the next 15 minutes in the room, Londyn tried her best not to worry about Shane.

"*I didn't do anything wrong, so why should I feel guilty?*" she thought as she downed a few more shots of Hennessy.

Slowly but surely, the liquor started to settle in, and soon enough, Londyn had forgotten her troubles and was ready to party. The crowd finished their drinks, and began to pile out of the hotel room into the hallway.

"Ayeeeeeeeee I'm ready to party! Turn uppppp." Reagan yelled.

"Yeah, Reagan you already know it's about to get real!" Marquan replied.

"I know. Let me call my man and see where he is." Reagan said as she dialed David's number.

Chanel, who didn't drink at all giggled as she watched her drunken friends happily head towards the elevator.

"You good Lo?" Timothy asked Londyn as they lingered behind the rest of the crowd.

"Me? Yeah... I'm good... why do you ask?"

"Come on now girl, I've been knowing you since the 5th grade. You know I can tell when something is bothering you..." he said as he playfully pushed her shoulder.

"Haha... I'm good Timmy... got some things on my brain, but I'm not worried about it... I'm just ready to have a good time."

"Aight, well turn up then!" Timothy smiled.

"Let's get it..." Londyn chuckled as they quickly hustled towards the elevator.

The party was nothing shy of epic. Popular Hip Hop disk jockey, DJ Dramatic, flew in to spin for the occasion and brought a few of his celebrity friends along. Strobe lights flickered through the crowded dark club style room, as many people waited in line for drinks in front of the various glow in the dark bars. Partygoers stood around taking selfies with their friends, while most people danced their hearts out on the huge dance floor, surrounded by Greeks strolling around the outskirts.

Londyn stood in a corner with Reagan sipping

a cranberry and vodka as her eyes scanned the room in search of Shane. They'd already been in the party for about an hour and he hadn't said one word to her, let alone come anywhere near her. She knew he was upset, because he didn't even respond to the text she'd sent him upstairs. While she was mad at him for storming away like he did, she couldn't blame him. After all, it did look pretty bad, her running after Justin, and then him kissing her hand. Had the shoe been on the other foot, she knew she wouldn't be too particularly happy with him either. Nonetheless, she tried to make the most of the night. She stood tensely tapping her foot as she sipped her drink through a glow in the dark straw.

"You ok, Lo?"   Reagan asked as she stared at her friend.

"Not really..." Londyn replied. "I'm just worried that Shane is going to do something stupid you know... to get back at me..."

"Now you know Shane isn't cut like that at all, Lo. Just give him a little minute to calm down, and then talk to him. It'll be alright. He'll understand."

"I hope so. He's probably gonna dump me though." Londyn replied as she sat her now empty cup down on the bar counter behind her. "Well, might as well have some fun while I'm here right?"

"He's not going to dump you. But that's right, have some fun girl. You sent the text and apologized right? I know Shane, he'll let it go!" Reagan said as she grabbed Londyn's arm.

They headed over towards the dance floor and joined their friends who were happily dancing and having a blast. Londyn tried to join in, but she couldn't really fool herself into having fun. All she wanted to do was find Shane and explain things to him.

"I'll be right back," she said to Reagan as she tapped her on the shoulder.

"Okay girl." Reagan responded as she looked over her shoulder, mid dance move.

Londyn walked around the party in search of Shane. He wasn't in the stroll line with his frat brothers, and she didn't see him on the dance floor either. She continued to walk around the outskirts of the party hoping she'd see him, but as her luck would have it, he was nowhere to be found. She pulled her phone out of her purse to see if he'd called or texted her, knowing that the chances of that happening were slim to none. She shook her head and put her phone back in her purse as she walked over towards a chair near a wall and sat down. She sat with her arms folded, mouth turned down, all while a million thoughts ran through her mind.

"Where is he? Is he somewhere with another girl trying to get back at me? Is he with Kyla? Is it over? Will he forgive me? Does he really think something went down between Justin and I? Am I overreacting?"

She quickly decided that she was over the party

scene and wanted to just call it a night. She pulled her phone out again and texted Reagan & Chanel letting them know that she was heading back upstairs to her room. With the most pitiful look on her face, she got up and left the party.

As she stood waiting for the elevator, she heard soothing melodies coming from the lobby area. Intrigued, she glanced over and smiled, as she was pleasantly surprised at who the pianist just so happened to be. Seconds later, the elevator doors opened, but instead of going inside, she pivoted and headed towards the black grand piano. As she approached, the pianist noticed her, and abruptly stopped playing.

"Can I sit down...?" she asked.

"Free country..." Shane replied with little emotion.

"Listen... baby," Londyn began, placing her hand gently on his back, "I promise it wasn't what it looked like at all. I didn't invite him over there, he just walked in, said some rude things and then ran out. I was just trying to..."

"Just save it, Londyn..." Shane replied nonchalantly, cutting her off mid-sentence.

"But..." she began with a confused look on her face.

"You don't get it. You wouldn't dare catch me in a hotel room with Kyla. Let alone, running after her.

It's not that I don't trust myself, or that I even think anything would happen. But I care about you too much Londyn to put you in a situation where you'll be left feeling embarrassed. Do you know how that made me feel? Man, I was just telling my boys how much being in a relationship with you has changed everything about my life. About how much better of a man I've become because I don't ever want to let you down. Then I turn the corner and see you running after him, of all people? And I know he was just trying to get to me by randomly kissing your hand, but my question is, why was my girl even in a position where that could go down? Nah man... not cool."

"I'm sorry babe. I..."

"Do you know how hard you make things sometimes Londyn? I mean I'm out here really trying to be the best boyfriend I can be to you, but I really can't tell if you're all in like I am. I'm really trying to make us work, but I think you're too stuck on Justin to see that."

"Now wait a minute, you know I don't want Justin..."

"I didn't say you wanted him. But either way you're still giving him so much control in your life. You gotta let go, babe. When I see Kyla, I feel nothing. She's old news and quite frankly it doesn't matter to me if she's in the room or not because she doesn't mean anything to me anymore. When you see Justin you can't even think straight, you get so angry and worked up."

"Excuse me, but weren't you the one punching him in the face?"

"I was defending YOU!"

"I didn't ask you too."

"You've never had to."

Londyn froze and thought in silence.

"Londyn, You won't even open up to me because of the things he did to you. You can't be in a relationship when your guard is all the way up Lo, it just doesn't work like that. I'm not him. I'm not going to hurt you. I've asked myself over and over what more do I have to do to show you that, but I've realized I can't force you to trust me. I'm doing everything in my power to reassure you that I'm here for you and you only. I'm in love with you Londyn, but if you can't let go of your past then I just don't know how you'll ever see it."

Londyn sat in silence, completely at a lost for words. He looked at her, expecting a response, but as always, he got nothing. He shook his head, stood up, and began to walk away as she wiped tears from her eyes.

"What do you want from me Shane?" she said as she stood up from the piano bench.

He turned around and looked at her wet face, stopping dead in his tracks.

"I just want to know that you're as invested in this relationship as I am. I just want to know that you care, and that I'm not in this by myself."

Londyn looked around and then climbed up onto the piano bench.

"What are you doing?" he asked.

"To whoever is listening, I, Londyn Marie James am in love with this man right here." she stated aloud for the empty room. "Are you still going to break up with me?"

"Who said anything about breaking up with you?"

"Well I just figured..." she began.

"See that's the thing I want you to understand Londyn. When I say I'm in this for the long run, I truly mean it. I'm not here to abandon you when times get tough. My feelings for you are real, and they aren't going to change." he said as he lifted her down off of the piano bench and sat her down next to him. "So, my aunt took me to counseling when I was younger right, at church... The pastor, he had me sort through a lot of my issues and I was able to realize that I struggled with the fear of abandonment. Because of how things went down in my family as a child, not having either parent... It's like I always pushed people away because I was trying to beat them to the punch. You know, get rid of them before they could get rid of me. It was counterproductive, and not a good way to live. But, once I was able to realize that about myself, I was able to work on it and get through it. I don't want to ever push the people that I truly care about away, because I know how it feels. Now, I'm not trying to speak that over your life, or tell you what issues you have, but it's something to think about, ya know. It's like you just gotta...."

"You're right...." she interrupted.

"Huh?"

"You're right... all my life, I've, I've pushed people away. I'm scared to get close to people because in the back of my mind I'm just expecting them to one day leave and take a huge part of my heart with them. You know, I guess I never really told anyone this, but I've been so angry for so long, and held so much resentment towards my father for leaving me and Tony the way he did." she stated with tears in her eyes. "As if what we were going through wasn't enough, two little kids, to tragically lose our mother like that... and then, to basically lose our dad at the same time... all because he wanted to be immature. I mean and now here he is married to Tammy and raising Sabrina as his own. He didn't even raise me as his own." she sniffled.

Shane reached over and squeezed Londyn tight as a few tears fell down her cheek onto his sleeve.

"I'm sorry." he said while holding her chin as she looked up at him, staring deeply in his eyes.

"I've never felt a love like this before, and it

freaks me out." she began. "You challenge me in ways no one ever has, and you're constantly pushing me to be the best version of myself. I never knew love could come so strong and so fast, but it did and it just scares me. I just don't want to get hurt again..."

"I love you Londyn, with all my heart. The moment I met you was the moment I started living. You speak to the King inside of me, and so for that I promise to always treat you like the Queen that you are. I don't care that it's only been 6 months, if I wasn't broke I swear I'd marry you right now." he chuckled.

Londyn smiled and laughed as she reached in and kissed him on the cheek.

"I love you..." he said as he smiled and laid her head on his chest.

"I love you too." she replied.

Chapter 16

"Happy Birthdayyyyyyy!!!" Londyn screamed into the phone as Shane in the bed, phone in hand, on FaceTime.

"Thank you!" he replied with a smile.

"I luhhh you!"

"I love you more babe."

"What do you have to do today again?"

"Just one class and then I have to turn in a final project."

"Well, don't work too hard today, and remember I need you to be ready at 8:00 tonight, okay? Dress nice. I'm picking you up." she said as she playfully stuck her tongue out at him.

"Ahh man, so you're really not gonna tell me what you've got planned, boo?"

"Nope. It's a surprise, just wait and see."

"Okay, okay... I can't wait." he said with a huge smile.

"I have to go get ready for class, but I'll see you later, baby!" Londyn replied.

"Okay bet, see you." Shane replied before hanging up the call.

It was Shane's 22nd birthday, and Londyn was determined to make it one to remember. Shane had been under a lot of pressure over the past month as he competed for the prestigious National Society of Minority Engineers Award. After an extensive application and interview process, Shane could do nothing but await the hopefully positive news. In an attempt to ease the stress of it all, Londyn put together a surprise birthday dinner for him at Ruth Chris' Steakhouse.

At around 7:55pm Londyn arrived at Shane's apartment. As she pulled into a parking spot near the door, she pulled out her phone and dialed his number. It rang for a few seconds before she heard his voice on the other end.

"Hello?" he answered.

"Hey birthday boy, I'm outside. You ready?"

"Yeah, here I come now."

Londyn pulled her window visor down and checked her makeup in the mirror. She tucked one of her long natural curls behind her ear before flipping the visor back to its upright position. She'd put a lot of work into Shane's surprise dinner, and couldn't wait to see his reaction. Within a few minutes, Shane came walking through the door of his apartment in an unbuttoned navy pea coat, showing off a classic all black suit and tie.

"Mmm hmmm hmmm." Londyn mumbled.

Instead of walking towards the passenger side of Londyn's car, she noticed that Shane was heading straight for the driver's side. Puzzled, she quickly rolled down her window and waited for him.

"What's wrong?" she asked.

"Nothing, but let's take my car." he replied with his arm bent slightly, so he could lean through the window.

"No, I'm treating you, you don't have to use your gas on your own birthday." she implored.

"You know I don't mind."

"Well, I do." she replied.

"Well, at least let me drive your car, I'm not about to make you drive in all of this ice and snow when I'm right here." he responded.

"Alright." she replied as she opened the door.

Before her feet could even fully touch the ground, Shane grabbed her hand and helped her out of the car. He escorted her around to the passenger side, and politely opened and closed her door. A few seconds later, Londyn looked at him with "googly eyes" as he buckled his seatbelt.

"What?" he chuckled.

"You're just such a gentlemen, how'd I get to be so blessed? It's your birthday, but here you are, putting me first."

"I put you first everyday," he said as he leaned over and kissed her on the cheek before starting the ignition, "just guide the way."

About 15 minutes later they arrived at Shane's favorite restaurant, Ruth Chris' Steakhouse in Ann Arbor. Shane smiled from ear to ear as he maneuvered his way into a parking spot on 4th Avenue.

"You're the best." he smiled.

"I know." she giggled as she flipped her hair to the side.

The two walked hand in hand down the street towards the restaurant. Londyn was glad to see Shane so happy, but she couldn't help but to wonder if the night would play out as planned. Her worries were quickly displaced when they walked into the restaurant and were greeted by an energetic hostess.

"Wow! You two look absolutely amazing!" the hostess exclaimed as she marveled at their attire.

"Thank you." they replied in unison.

"I mean seriously, you all are beautiful!"

Shane's suit complemented Londyn's sleek,

cocktail dress and black heels perfectly.

"How stunning, and that dress! Turn around, let me see it!" the waitress squealed modestly.

Londyn smiled as Shane helped her remove her unbuttoned black peacoat. As the peacoat fell from her body into his arms, he couldn't help but to marvel at how beautiful she was. Londyn grinned and spun slowly to show off her fitted, navy cocktail dress.

"Gorgeous, and that embellished waistline is to die for! Sorry, I'm a fashionista at heart." the hostess chuckled. "Oh, and I love your hair too." she added as she admired Londyn's big natural curls.

"I'm just trying to look half as good as her." Shane chuckled as he wrapped his arm around Londyn's lower waist.

"Will it just be the two of you today?" she asked.

"Yes, we're here for his birthday. I made reservations, under my name, Londyn."

The waitress nodded her head and replied, "Right this way."

Londyn gently grabbed Shane's hand as they followed the hostess towards a private back room. As the hostess pushed against the heavy doors, Londyn quickly reached up and covered Shane's eyes.

"SURPRISE!!!" a crowd yelled.

Londyn moved her hands, so that he could see

the room full of smiling faces and clapping hands! He smiled from ear to ear as he dropped his head and laughed. Londyn giggled and clapped as he reached down and gave her a warm hug.

"You got me" he whispered.

"Happy Birthday Shane!!!" everyone yelled from their seats around the long rectangular table in the center of the small room.

"Wow!" Shane exclaimed as he circled the table and exchanged loving hugs with his loved ones.

He was pleasantly surprised to see those who came out to celebrate including, Uncle Buck and his wife and kids, his frat brothers, Xavier, Thomas, Chris, and Jamal, as well as Reagan, David, the twins Allison and Ashley, Londyn's brother Tony, and even his singer-cousin, Tanisha AKA Melody Rain.

"Jamal! You're still here." Shane chuckled.

"Yeah, Londyn tracked me down and I couldn't miss it for the world. I don't head back to California until tomorrow."

"What's good nephew?" Uncle Buck asked as he gave Shane a hug and handed him a thick birthday card filled with cash, "Just a little something for my favorite nephew. The new gig is paying me well so you know I had to spread the love."

"Good looking out Uncle B, I appreciate it man!" Shane replied with a firm handshake.

"So how does it feel to be 22?" Allison asked.

"It feels great! Better than ever." Shane smiled as he sat down at the head of the table.

For the next two hours he indulged in great food, laughs, and tons of crazy stories with the people that meant the most to him. It was the best way he could've imagined spending his 22nd birthday. The only person that was missing was his Aunt Ryn, but she made her presence known by way of a huge birthday gift wrapped and delivered to him by Uncle Buck.

"Big sis is proud of you and she wishes she could've made it down for your G-day boy. She mailed this to my house to give to you, but she made me promise to tell you that you can't open it until you get home."

"Awww man I'm scared to open it now..." he laughed.

Towards the end of the night, the waitress brought out a candle lit cupcake on a plate that read "Happy Birthday Solo" in chocolate drizzle.

"Okay let's sing Happy Birthday y'all!" Londyn exclaimed.

"Hold up," Uncle Buck exclaimed as he stood to his feet, "now, I don't know how y'all do it out here in Ann Arbor, but in Motown we sing the Stevie Wonder version."

"That's right!" Uncle Buck's wife, Danielle chimed in.

"1, 2, 3...." Uncle Buck counted.

"Ha-ppy Birthday to ya. Ha-ppy Birthday to ya. Haaaa-ppyyyyyyy Birrrrrth-dayy. Ha-ppy Birthday to ya." Shane's family and friends sang with pure joy.

As the song came to an end, Shane stood up and tapped his glass with a fork to get everyone's attention. Everyone's voices fell silent as they looked towards Shane.

"I just want to thank each and every one of you for coming out tonight. It truly means so much to me to be able to spend this day with you guys. If I had tear ducts, I'd cry right now. But y'all know I don't cry!" he chuckled. "You know, I never really felt like a family man. Growing up I didn't have anyone, besides Aunt Ryn, Uncle Buck, and Man-Man really. It's crazy because now I look out and realize that I do have family. Man, y'all came out here in all of this ice and snow so I know y'all love me!" he laughed as everyone chuckled. "My U.B. and ELU family, my frat brothers, Uncle Buck, Aunt D, lil' cousins, Tanisha, man, I love all y'all for real. And mostly, I just want to thank you Londyn for setting this up for me. I appreciate you Beautiful." he said as he winked at Londyn, who smiled back at him.

"Awwww." the whole tabled cooed in unison.

Before Shane could get out another word, his phone began to vibrate on the table. He looked down and could tell from the area code that it was an important call.

"This might be the call." Shane said as he

looked at Londyn.

"Take it. You got this." Londyn replied as she lightly grabbed his hand.

"Excuse me for just one second everyone, I have to take this!" he stated as he quickly got up from the table and walked out of the room.

"Hello?" he asked as he put the phone to his ear.

"Good Evening, is this Mr. Solomon?"

"Yes, this is he..." he replied confidently.

"Hi Shane, My name is Derrick Robinson, from the National Society of Minority Engineers. I'm sorry to call you so late, I'm out on the west coast and totally forgot about the time difference."

"Oh, no, it's no problem at all!" Shane replied, now a bit more nervous as he realized this was indeed the call he'd been waiting on for so long.

"Okay great, well I don't want to keep you long at all. I'm calling to congratulate you for being selected as one of our five 2015 award recipients!"

"Wow! Thank you so much Mr. Robinson. Wow, I'm honored."

"No problem Shane, you earned it. You should receive official notice via e-mail tomorrow, but I wanted to give you a personal phone call, because you do have to respond and confirm your top site locations for your internship. They'll be assigned on a first come, first serve basis. As you were told in your interview, the internship is paid and runs from June until September of next year, with a $10,000 stipend. You'll have your choice to work with various engineering based companies in either San Francisco, NYC, St. Paul, Salt Lake City, or Denver. The reception in which you'll receive your actual award and meet your future internship employers will be held at our headquarters in Chicago at our annual conference on December 28th –31st, but the email will have all of those details laid out for you!"

"Thank you so very much Mr. Robinson. I'm speechless. Thank you so much." Shane replied with a huge smile on his face.

"The pleasure is all mine. Shane, I personally reviewed your file and can say I was quite impressed. Like I said, you definitely earned this!"

"Thank You!"

"No problem, we'll be in touch."

"Okay sir! You have a great evening."

"You too, oh and unofficial word of advice, from one Beta brother to another, take the Denver site. Blackmond Hill is the best of the best when it comes to Environmental Engineering. You impress them while you're interning, and you're a shoo in for a permanent position."

"I will definitely keep that in mind, frat. I can't thank you enough."

"No problem. Now you have a great rest of your night!"

"You too sir!" Shane replied as he hung up the phone and sighed the biggest sigh of relief of his life.

"What a birthday." he thought.

Chapter 17

A few weeks later, on the day after Christmas, Shane stood in his bedroom shirtless, packing his suitcase for his business trip to Chicago. Londyn laid across his bed, as the movie "ATL" played on his flat screen TV.

"You nervous?" she asked.

"A little. There's gonna be a lot of important people there so I just want to make sure I make a good impression."

"You will, I'm sure of it. Just be yourself." Londyn replied.

"Thanks Lo." he replied as he neatly folded a pair of black dress pants and laid them in his suitcase.

"Do you need a ride to the airport tomorrow?"

"Nah, I'm cool. Xavier is gonna drop me off. No sense in you driving all the way out here, when U.B. is only 20 minutes away from the airport." he replied.

"Alright." Londyn said as she glanced back at the TV. She stopped for a moment and then looked up again at him. "So what are you going to do for New Years Eve... in Chicago... man, that's going to be so live." she asked.

"I don't know, you know me, I'll probably just be chilling... maybe link up with some Beta's out there, see what they got up." he replied as he reached up towards the top of his closet and grabbed a pair of dress shoes.

Londyn licked her lips at the sight of Shane's muscles glistening with light sweat. She cringed at the thought of all of the beautiful girls he'd potentially be around on New Year's Eve. In a moment of panic, she hopped up from her spot on the bed, and walked over to Shane. She lightly grabbed his face, and then kissed him on the lips.

"What was that for?" he chuckled, taken aback by her spontaneity.

"Just had to give you something to remember when you're down there with those pretty Chicago girls."

"Them girls ain't got nothing on you babe." he replied as he leaned in and kissed her again.

"Mmmmm hmmm... don't you forget it either. You better be curving those chicks left and right." she chuckled as she plopped back down on his bed.

"Yeah, same goes for you." he replied.

"Mmm hmmm... So, I know this is a few weeks out, but Granny's 90th birthday celebration is next month on the 15th. I know she would love to see you, and it would be nice to have you on my arm. I have to give a speech, and for some reason I'm low-key kind of nervous."

"Oh no doubt I'll definitely be there. I wouldn't miss it for the world." he replied with a grin.

"Yay! You can finally meet the rest of my family too."

"Sounds good to me. Aunt Ryn is finally coming home that weekend, so I'll already be out in the city." he replied.

"Cool." Londyn replied as she laid back on his bed. "My stomach hurts. I feel like I have to throw up." she said as rubbed her hands on her stomach.

"You're not pregnant are you?" Shane asked.

"Really babe, how?"

"You let somebody else get the cutty, but I can't get none?" he joked.

"You're irritating." she replied as she closed her eyes and grasped her stomach.

Shane stopped packing and laid down on the bed next to her.

"Does this make it better?" he asked as he leaned in and kissed her forehead.

"Maybe a little." she replied with a slight smile.

"How about this?" he asked before leaning in and kissing her slowly on the lips.

"Mmm hmm." Londyn hummed quietly.

"Well, you know what would make it all the way better?" Shane asked with a devious smile.

"What?" Londyn asked as she gazed into his eyes.

Shane leaned in towards her slowly, and paused when his nose lightly touched hers.

"A can of Vernors. I'm gonna go grab you one out the fridge." he chuckled.

Londyn couldn't help but to laugh as Shane quickly hopped off of the bed.

"You want me. I know it." Shane teased from the doorway.

"Shut up." Londyn laughed.

"Too bad, girl. You can't touch this!" Shane laughed as he "M.C. Hammer" danced out of the room.

The next morning Shane arrived in Chicago, Illinois for the engineering conference. Of over 1,000 applicants, only 5 winners were chosen. Throughout the week Shane's schedule was jam packed, so by the conference's end he was exhausted and ready to party hard for New Year's Eve.

"FaceTime is so clear on this new laptop your Aunt Ryn bought you. That was a good birthday gift." Londyn asked as she video chatted with Shane.

"I know right. It's dope." Shane replied from his hotel room where he sat on the bed.

"How has your trip been so far? You've been so busy I haven't even really talked to you." she whined.

"Yeah, I know. I'm sorry. Everything has been super busy, but I can't complain it's been a really great experience."

"That's good. What did they have you doing?" she asked.

"A lot of workshops, meetings, and interview with their local media outlets... met a bunch of big shot engineers and business owners, oh and I got to meet the Mayor of Chicago too."

"Wow! That's so awesome. Did you meet your new boss?"

"Yeah I met him the very first day. His name is Arnold Haywood. Real cool dude! He said he's looking forward to working with me."

"As he should be." Londyn replied.

"Thanks Beautiful."

"Sooo, did you find some people to hang with tonight?" Londyn asked.

"Yeah. I'm going to meet up with some of the Beta's from the University of Illinois at Chicago. Hit up a few parties or whatever. What about you?"

"I don't know yet for sure. Reagan wants to go downtown. Chanel wants to chill, so we'll see."

"Go out and have a good time."

"Yeah, I should...."

"Okay well, I'm tired Lo so I'm gonna try to get a quick nap in. I'll talk to you later baby. Be safe out here in these streets."

"Alrighty... call me later."

"Yup." he replied as he ended the FaceTime call.

After hanging up, Londyn decided to text Reagan and Chanel in a group message.

Londyn: So what's the word on plans?

Reagan: Well it's looking like a wrap on partying downtown. I heard they're taxing on the parking. I'm not trying to pay $50, plus pay to get in the club.

Chanel: Yeah nah, that's why I didn't want to go down there at all.

Londyn: So what are we going to do?

Chanel: The Alpha's are throwing a pajama party. A lot of my Sorors are going.

Reagan: Ok, cool that sounds like a plan to me.

Londyn: Yeah sounds fun. So is it like a real pajama party or?

Chanel: 90's theme so yeah. Sweats and leggings, you know.

Reagan: awwww that's hot. Ok I'm excited now.

Londyn: Me tooooo. :)

Later on that night, Londyn, Reagan, and Chanel partied the night away at the Alpha's House Party. They looked super cute in their impromptu 90's influenced outfits that consisted of leggings, thick tube socks, and cutoff sweatshirts. As midnight approached, everyone came together to get ready for a countdown and toast to the New Year.

"Hey girls!" they heard a drunken, excited voice screech from nearby.

They turned around to see the infamous Bree, whom Reagan and Londyn hadn't spoken to since the Piston's Game incident.

"Hey Bree!!!" Chanel squealed as she greeted her with a hug. "... and who is this?" she asked pointing to the handsome man next to her.

"Oh, this is my boo Devin. Devin this is Chanel, Reagan, and Londyn. We all go way back, to like freshman year." she smiled.

"Nice to meet y'all." Devin replied as he shook each of their hands.

"So where's David? And Solo?" Bree asked.

"David's at home sick with the flu." Reagan stated.

"Awwww poor baby. I'm surprised you're not at home taking care of him." Bree said.

"He got a mama." Reagan replied with an attitude.

"Ohhhhhkay... and what about Solo, where's the homie?" Bree asked Londyn.

"He's out of town in Chicago." Londyn replied.

"My city! You better watch him, you know us Chi-town girls don't play around. Don't let one of them take your man." she snickered.

"Girl..." Reagan stated as she rolled her eyes.

"Dang, chill out Reagan. I'm just playing. You know I'm playing, right Londyn?"

Londyn laughed sarcastically and grabbed a champagne glass from one of the Alpha's.

"Alright y'all ready?" The host of the party shouted over the microphone, "10, 9...."

"...8...7...6...5...4...3...2...1... HAPPY NEW YEARRRRRRR!" everyone hollered in unison!

"201666666! What upppppppppp doe!" the host yelled.

"Happy New Year!!!!" Chanel squealed as she hugged Reagan and Londyn.

"Happy New Year! I love y'all! 2016 is going to be epic." Reagan screeched.

"Happy New Year to my favorite girls!!!" Londyn replied with a huge smile.

"Let me call my sick boyfriend." Reagan stated as she grabbed her phone and called David.

Londyn picked up her phone and dialed Shane's number too. Even though it was only 11pm in Chicago, she still wanted to be the first to wish him a Happy New Year. Unfortunately, to her disappointment he didn't pick up the phone. Normally, she wouldn't have worried much about him not picking up, but at the back of her mind she couldn't help but think about Bree's comments.

"Nope, not even going to go there." she thought as she put her phone back in her purse.

"Dun dun dun dun..." was the sound that interrupted her thoughts as Bel Biv Devoe's hit song "Poison" began to blast from the speakers.

Everyone's excitement skyrocketed as they began to dance and sing in unison.

"This is going to be our year y'all! 2016, here we come!" Londyn cheered.

Chapter 18

On Monday afternoon, Shane hopped off the bus after an intense workout session at the gym. As he jogged up the concrete hill to his apartment, the light breeze felt refreshing against his face.

"Hey Solo! Wait up!" Shane's friend Desiree yelled from a few feet behind.

He'd had a longtime crush on Desiree back in the day, but she was one of the few women at U.B. who never seemed to pay him much attention.

"Oh what's up Desiree. What are you doing over here?" he asked as he waited for her to catch up.

She smiled and slowed down as she approached him.

"My friend lives over here. Just coming over to study for a while. How have you been?"

"I'm great, everything is cool. How about you?

How's life?"

"Life is good. I'm finishing up these last few classes, and graduating this semester." she replied.

"Wow! Congrats! I'm proud of you." he said as they walked up the stairs to his building.

"Thanks. It's been a long 5 years, but I did it!"

"I feel you... I can't wait to be done myself. One more year!"

"It'll fly by. For real."

"Yeah, that's what they say." Shane smiled as he stuck his key in his mailbox.

"So what's been up with you? My sister said she saw you on the news back home in Chicago! You're out here working hard, I see! What's that about?" Desiree exclaimed as she playfully brushed his shoulder.

"Oh, I didn't tell you? I won the Engineering Internship. I'll be in Denver all summer at a really dope firm."

"Whatttt. No, you didn't tell me! Not that I ever see you anyway! I'm proud of you!" she screeched.

"Thanks! Yeah, everything is really coming together, finally." he replied while casually shuffling through the huge stack of mail.

"I'm glad..." she began. "Do you still have my number?"

"Nope, I don't think I do... new phone."

"Here let me put it in your phone for you." she

replied as she took his phone from his hand. "So.. Solo, I have a question for you." she asked as she typed away.

"Yeah, what's up?" he asked.

"Okay, so I don't mean to come off too forward or anything... but, this girlfriend of yours. Are you happy?"

He paused for a second, before looking up at Desiree. He chucked inside at the thought of her finally showing interest after all this time. Nonetheless, he thought of Londyn and smiled.

"Yeah, I am. I really am..." he replied.

Desiree smiled and shook her head. "Good. You're a great catch, Solo. It's about time someone noticed the real you." she smiled as she handed him his phone. "I'll catch you around, okay? If you need anything... and I do mean anything, just hit me up." she said as she stroked his shoulder, and then walked away towards her friend's unit.

"See ya." Shane replied as he stood there and reflected on how much his life had changed over the past few months.

While he was flattered by Desiree's remarks, he was content. He had the girl of his dreams, a job lined up, and finally some peace and order in his world. As he jogged up the short flight of stairs to his unit, an envelope from his stack of mail fell to the ground. He leaned down to pick it up, and paused when he caught a glimpse of the return address label. "Chicago State

Penitentiary." He quickly unlocked his unit door and walked inside, tossing all of the other pieces of mail onto the kitchen counter. He leaned against the fridge, and quickly tore open the crisp white envelope.

"Dear Shane...." he read slowly and carefully.

As his eyes scanned the letter, the veins in his neck bulged as if they were going to pop right out of his body. Huge balls of sweat formed on his forehead, and a look of helplessness swept across his face, as he read each and every word. In a state of shock, he released the letter from his grasp, and a million thoughts ran through his mind. Within seconds, his vision blurred, and he felt dizzy as he paced back and forth through the kitchen. He grabbed a clean glass from the dish rack on the counter, and filled it with ice-cold water from the faucet. He drank only a sip before pouring it down the drain. He paced around the kitchen again, and then banged his fist on the countertop. Just when everything seemed picture perfect, life took a sudden turn for the worse for Shane Solomon.

Meanwhile, at Fairlane Mall in Dearborn, a suburb of Detroit, Londyn and Reagan were shopping in Forever 21 when Reagan's cell phone rang.

"Hey, David." Reagan answered.

"Hey Reagan, y'all trying to go to Punchbowl Social tonight? My cousin Quincy and his friends are going." David asked in reference to a popular billiards bar in the heart of downtown Detroit.

"Londyn, David said do we want to go to Punchbowl tonight?" Reagan asked.

"Yeah that's cool, I haven't been there in a long time." Londyn replied as she picked up a sweater from the rack and held it up against her body.

"Okay cool, we'll be there David." Reagan replied with a pile of clothes hanging from arm.

"Bet. Don't spend all your money at the mall." David laughed.

"Shut up." Reagan replied.

"I'm just trying to help you. Oh, tell Londyn to pass the word to Solo too. We can celebrate him getting that award."

"Okay, she will."

"Bet. See y'all later then."

"Bye babycakes." Reagan replied as she hung up the call.

She picked up another pair of jeans and added it to her already humongous pile.

"David said to invite Shane tonight. We can celebrate his award." Reagan said as she walked into the dressing room.

"Okay," Londyn replied as she reached for her

cell phone, "and hurry up Reagan, don't be in there all day."

Londyn hated shopping with Reagan, and was already more than ready to leave the mall. Knowing Reagan, she'd be in the dressing room for quite some time considering her normal routine consisted of trying on every outfit, taking pictures, and sending them to her mother to get her fashion stamp of approval, all before deciding whether or not to make a purchase. She walked over to a chair and sat down as she dialed Shane's number. The phone rang longer than usual, before he finally picked up.

"Hello?" he asked.

"Hey Baby. What are you doing?" she asked sweetly.

"On my way to Uncle Buck's." he replied.

"Ohhh yay, you're coming to the city! Well, do you want to go out with Reagan, David, and I tonight? We're going to Punchbowl with Quincy and them." she replied excitedly.

"Nah, I'm straight." he replied without much emotion.

"Oh... do you have other plans?"

"Nah." he replied without explanation.

"Oh... okay, well is everything alright?" she asked as she scrunched her face and scratched her head.

"Yep."

"You sure? Do you want me to come over?"

"Nah Londyn, I'm not really feeling it tonight."

"Okay.. you sound so dry. I'm worried about you."

"I just need to be alone."

"But I thought you said you were going to be with your Uncle Buck..."

"I gotta go, Londyn... I'll talk to you later..." he said before hanging up the phone.

"Rude..." Londyn mumbled aloud. "I wonder what's gotten into him."

As she sat confused, she decided to call her wise Grandma Hattie.

"Hey Granny." she exclaimed after her grandmother greeted her.

"Hey, how's my Babygirl doing?"

"I'm doing alright Granny. Just at the mall with Reagan, and I thought about you so I decided to give you a call."

"Well thank you baby, you know it's always good to hear your voice. How are you?

"I'm okay, just got off the phone with Shane."

"How's my future son-in-law, didn't he go on his trip last week?"

"Yeah, he did. He's acting really weird now...

like he doesn't want to be bothered with me. I hate when people do that."

"Oh don't you worry too much about it Londyn, the man is probably just exhausted or has a lot on his brain. Try not to be so sensitive, always thinking everything is about you child." Grandma Hattie giggled.

"I know, I know."

"Really Londyn. Especially in a relationship. You'll drive yourself crazy if you start overanalyzing every bad mood the other has. Don't do it. Just give him his space if that's what he needs today. He'll come around."

"You're right Granny. I'm working on it. He always tells me that he loves me no matter what, so I don't know why I wake up some days wondering if today is the day he'll stop."

"That's self sabotage dear. You can't live your life that way. You know your granddad and I were married for 49 years before he passed? 49 years of love, friendship, and a lot of bad moods." she giggled. "You and Shane remind me a lot of he and I when we were young."

"Really?" Londyn asked.

"Yes. You two still have a lot to learn about each other and yourselves. Every day won't be peachy, but you have to make sure you remember why you two are together in the first place. Emotions can change by the day, but love is forever the same."

"You're right. Relationships are hard Granny. But I'll remember that..."

"Good... if there ever comes a time where he doesn't treat you the way you deserve then that's a whole different story... then you gotta let him go... and you know you can call your Grandma Hattie whenever you need to talk, you hear me?"

"Yes Granny."

"Okay now, well let me go, I've got a lemon meringue pie in the oven."

"Okay Granny. Love you so much."

"Love you too dear."

Chapter 19

Over the next two weeks Shane and Londyn barely spoke. Londyn tried to take Grandma Hattie's advice, but after a week of avoided phone calls, dry texts, and no activity on his social media accounts, she began to worry. She even called Xavier, who informed her that Shane seemed to be just fine. This caught her by surprise, and led her to believe that he was actually just mad at her for some odd reason. She replayed the last two weeks in her mind, and couldn't recall anything that could have lead to Shane's bad attitude. By week two, she'd had enough of his shenanigans and made it up in her mind that she was going to get to the bottom of things whether he felt like talking or not.

On the Friday night before Grandma Hattie's birthday party, she picked up her cell phone and called Shane for the umpteenth day in a row. As in the past few days, he ignored her call. While Londyn would've normally given up, this time she immediately sent him a text.

"Call me NOW!"

Within seconds, he sent a message in return.

"I'm busy. I'll call you back."

"Nah. Ain't nobody waiting for later." she said aloud as she dialed his number and raised the phone to her ear. To her surprise, he finally answered.

"Hey Londyn." he answered.

"Shane what is wrong with you? Why have you been ignoring me for 2 whole weeks?"

"Why are you yelling? It's been too much, going, on, I just need to be alone. I still love you." he said as he stumbled over his words.

"Why do you sound like that? Have you been drinking?" she asked with concern.

"Since 1pm." he replied with little emotion.

"Shane, what? You don't even drink. Where are you? I'm coming to wherever you are right now."

"No, it's snowing."

"I don't care about the freakin' snow. We live in Michigan, it's always snowing. Where are you?"

Silence.

"Hello? Where are you?" she asked again, before realizing that either the signal had faded, or he hung up.

"What the heck...." she mumbled as she sat in her bedroom alone.

She stared off into space for a minute before it dawned on her to call Shane's line brother, Thomas, the most sensible of the bunch. After just a few rings, Thomas answered the phone.

"Hello?" he answered.

"Hey Thomas, have you talked to Shane today? I just called him and I'm 99% sure he's drunk."

"Yeah, he's here with me now. We're at Xavier's crib. Both of them dudes are pilt, but Shane is on some other stuff."

"Is he alright?"

"I don't know what's wrong with him, but he keeps saying he doesn't wanna talk about it."

"He's been acting so weird ever since he got back from Chicago... I'm worried about him, and now he's drunk? He NEVER drinks..."

"Tell me about it. We can barely ever get this guy to drink a beer, and now he's over here taking shots left and right..."

"Oh my goodness..."

"Yeah, don't worry too much though, I'm here and I won't let him drive or get too messed up. I already hid the rest of the bottles from them. I have his keys too. But, you might want to consider coming out here tomorrow after he sobers up, you're the only person that he listens to."

"Put him on the phone."

"Alright hold on a second... Shane! Yo! Your girl is on the line." Thomas stated as he passed his phone to a very drunken Shane.

"What uuup?" Shane slurred.

"Did you hang up on me?" she asked.

"No."

"Yes you did, what is wrong with you? Why are you drinking?"

"I'm grown as hell."

"So what. YOU don't drink. And YOU also don't ignore my calls for two weeks straight, so what's going on?"

"Man, if you were really worried about me Londyn then you would have been pulled up to check on me, rather than poppin' off over the phone like this." Shane said with an attitude that caught Londyn by surprise.

"Shane chill. You clearly just told me you didn't want me to come because it's snowing."

"So."

"So..."

"So if you really wanted to come you would've. I shouldn't have to beg you. If you can tell something ain't right the least you could do is come up here. But that's alright. I got other ways to stay warm at night."

"Oh, so you sleeping with other girls now?"

"Man, you tripping. Nobody said nothing about no other girls."

"What is wrong with you?"

"I don't have to listen to this. Bye." he replied as he passed the phone to Thomas.

"I'm sorry Londyn, he's tripping... don't drive out here tonight though, it's snowing pretty bad. He'll be alright, at this rate he'll be knocked out soon anyway."

"I can't believe this. Let me talk to him again."

"Solo...." Thomas said as he attempted to hand the phone over to Shane.

"Nah man." she could hear him replying in the background.

"Man, who all is over there?" she asked.

"Just me, him, Xavier, and my girl." he replied.

"Okay, can you put me on speaker please?"

"Yup," he said as he adjusted his phone accordingly, "okay go ahead Londyn."

"Shane. Are you still coming to my Granny's birthday dinner tomorrow?" she asked for the whole room to hear.

"Yeah, I gave you my word, didn't I?" he yelled as he laid on the couch.

"Yeah, but you've also been MIA, so I just

needed to know. I'm not telling my family you're going to be there just for you to stand me up Shane."

"Ughhhhhh, Londyn have I ever stood you up?" he grumbled.

"No, but."

"Okkkay, so leave it alone."

"Whatever, you're drunk. I'll see you tomorrow at 6. Don't even think about being late." she said as she hung up the phone in anger.

"Y'all are crazy..." Thomas' girlfriend Asia said as she and Thomas both shook their heads.

"Yeah, you really do need to chill on her Shane. She ain't doing nothing but trying to look out for you bro." Thomas replied.

"I told him these girls ain't nothing but a headache." Xavier slurred with his empty red cup in hand.

"You don't look too good." Asia stated as she walked over to Shane and handed him a trash bucket.

"Blahhhhhrtitfghj..." was the sound Shane made as he lowered his head into the bucket and threw up.

"I knew that was about to happen. Here you go," Asia replied as she handed him a paper towel, "are you sure you're okay?"

"I'm alright..." Shane replied as he wiped his mouth.

In that moment he knew good and well that he was far from alright.

Chapter 20

The next evening at about 6pm, Londyn and her family arrived at the historic Charles H. Wright Museum in Downtown Detroit, for Grandma Hattie's 90th birthday celebration. Londyn had been working tirelessly all day with a host of cousins and aunts to prepare a feast fit for their queen. While Londyn was eager to relax and enjoy the night, at the back of her mind she couldn't help but wonder if Shane would stand her up after their argument the night before. This would be the first time Shane would meet a majority of her extended family, and she was upset that they weren't on the best of terms with one another. She walked around the beautifully decorated room in awe, snapping pictures on her cell phone of everything in sight.

"Well look-a-here, little Miss Londyn. You look so pretty, and so grown up!" Grandma Hattie's cousin,

Leroy remarked as he leaned in for a hug and kiss.

"Thank you so much!" she replied.

"I love this little black dress! And those shoes! Oh man, I don't know how you young people walk in those things!" his wife, Elizabeth chucked.

"Awww they're actually really comfortable!" Londyn giggled.

"Well we just wanted to say that we're so proud of you, Londyn. Hattie talks about you kids all the time, and keeps us updated on all your accomplishments." Leroy replied.

"She sure does! You'll have to come visit us down in Tuscaloosa one day soon, ya hear?"

"Yes ma'am, I sure will." Londyn smiled.

She walked over to the front of the room and hugged her sweet grandmother.

"Happy Birthday Granny!"

"Hey Babygirl. I'm glad to see you."

"I'm glad to see you too Granny. You look so pretty in this white dress!"

"Thank you honey. You don't think it's too much?"

"No, no not at all. It's perfect for a young lady like you." Londyn giggled.

"Oh, stop it!" Grandma Hattie chuckled, "You ain't let your great aunts work your nerves this morning in that kitchen, did you? I know how my younger sisters can be. A real pain in the toosh."

"It was fine, Granny. We had a great time. As long as you enjoy yourself and the food tonight, then everything is everything."

"Everything is everything. Everything is on fleek!" she giggled.

"Granny! You've been watching too much TV? Talking about on fleek!"

"You know I'm hip!"

"Yes, yes you are Granny."

"Look there's your special guy." Grandma Hattie replied, as she pointed her finger towards the tall handsome man who just walked in the door.

Shane and Londyn's eyes connected immediately, and Shane smiled as he approached them.

"Hey Londyn. You look nice." he said as he embraced her in a hug.

"Um, thank you. I didn't know if you were going to make it, you know after your wild night and all." she said with a "smart alec" look on her face.

"Oh nah, you know I wouldn't miss Granny's birthday!" he said as he bent down and hugged Londyn's grandmother.

"That's right!" Grandma Hattie replied.

"Ooooh kay....." a very confused Londyn mumbled quietly.

Once the party kicked into full swing, Londyn and Shane sat down next to one another at Grandma Hattie's table. While Shane had a pleasant disposition, he was still a tad bit distant compared to his normal temperament.

"So are you feeling better today?" Londyn whispered.

"Yeah, I'm smooth, but my stomach is still a little queasy. I got to spend the day with Aunt Ryn, so that was cool. I'm gonna head back over to her house after I leave here."

"Oh okay. So, how long is she here for?" Londyn asked.

"3 whole weeks. Long overdue too." he replied as one of Londyn's great aunts stood up at the microphone to bless the food.

"Bow your heads. Dear Heavenly Father, We thank you for this time of fellowship and the opportunity for us to come together to celebrate the birthday of the matriarch of our family, my sister, Hattie Jo Ann James. Let us all enjoy one another's company, and may the food be of nourishment to our bodies. Bless those hands that prepared it, in Christ's name, amen."

"Amen." the crowd stated in unison.

"Amen." Shane echoed quietly.

"So, are we just going to act like last night didn't happen?" Londyn whispered.

"I'd rather forget last night."

"Shane. We talk every single day, but you haven't talked to me in over two weeks. I've never once seen you sip even a drop of alcohol, and now all of a sudden you're getting pissy drunk..."

"Shhh," he replied.

"I'm not even loud." she stated angrily.

"Listen, Lo. I'm really sorry. I was wrong. I've just had a crazy past couple of weeks, and last night I cracked. I promise we'll talk about it, just not here."

"Fine." Londyn stated as she swiftly got up from the table and headed over to the buffet line.

She was annoyed and didn't want to let her foul mood ruin her grandmother's dinner, so while everyone around her was having a grand ol' time, she faked her happiness. However, on the inside she was burning with anger, and needed answers from Shane. As she and Shane fixed their plates, she didn't say one word to him. Even still, he nodded politely at her family members and followed her back to their table.

"So when y'all getting married?" Londyn's cousin Shakira asked as she sat her plate on the table.

"Chill Kira. Can we at least graduate first?" Londyn asked as she took a sip of her glass of punch.

Shane laughed off the question and smiled as he shook his head.

"Shane, have you been saving for a ring?"

Shakira pried.

Shane coughed and his eyes bulged from embarrassment. "Since the day I met her." he chuckled, hoping his remarks would lighten Londyn's mood.

"Awww, too cute. Let me stop messing with y'all, I can already see Londyn is getting mad at me, per usual." Shakira giggled.

"Umm... can you excuse us, for just a minute?" Londyn asked as she stood up and grabbed Shane by the hand.

Shane apologized to the rest of the table as he dropped his fork and followed Londyn's lead. As they walked into the hallway, Shane contemplated how he could make things right.

"What's wrong?" he asked as soon as they were out of her family's sight.

"Listen, I know you said we would talk about it later. But I can't sit here and front like I'm not mad at you, Shane. I really have been going through it these past few weeks and now I just need you to give me an explanation. You've put me on an emotional rollercoaster, and I deserve answers. We're best friends, right? You always say that we'll talk about everything? That we won't hold things in... So... "

"You're right..." he began, "and I'm sorry. I shouldn't have treated you the way I've treated you these past few weeks. I don't know how I can make it up to you, but I'll do whatever it is I can to show you that I'm truly sorry. My world has literally been turned upside down, and I just didn't know how to tell you. But, you're right, I do owe you an explanation."

"You don't have to hide things from me. We're a team. If you're going through a rough patch, then I want to always be right here by your side. You don't have to do it alone." she replied as she reached up and briefly touched his shoulder.

"I know. Well, Londyn there's no easy way to say this, but... after I got back from Chicago I got a letter in the mail from my..."

"Babygirl? Babygirl, where are you?" Gerald hollered into the microphone.

All heads turned around the room in search of Londyn, as her dad continuously yelled into the microphone. Londyn quickly shuffled two steps to the right into the doorway so that all could see her.

"I'm right here!" she said loudly.

"Londyn, come up here girl," Gerald stated as he waved his hands excitedly. "...and, what in the world were y'all back there doing?" he asked over the microphone as Shane followed quickly behind and took his seat.

Londyn shook her head in embarrassment as she joined her dad and brother Tony at the front of the room.

"Now as I was saying," Gerald began, "I just

want to say that I love you, Mama! I owe you my life for how you stepped in and acted as a parent to my kids when I wasn't man enough to do it myself. You are truly a beautiful soul and I am so blessed to be your *favorite* son."

"Yeah right!" Gerald's older brother Frankie yelled from the audience.

"Most difficult son, maybe." his sister Rosalyn cosigned.

"You see how my siblings hate on me y'all? It's because half of them are over 60, and I'm just a young cat daddy in my prime out here." he chuckled as he danced and laughed, "I'm sure y'all are tired of my big mouth, so I'm going to go ahead and let my kids take it from here. These are my Mama's youngest grandchildren, and she asked specifically to hear from them tonight. Family, please show them a little love." he said as he clapped and stepped to the side.

"Mhhmm." Tony cleared his throat. "How is everyone doing tonight. You all look real nice! Umm but yeah, I just want to say Happy Birthday to the original gangsta, the OG, my Granny. Y'all all think she's sweet and nice, but I just want to know where were y'all when she was whooping me back in the day? Y'all ain't seen that side of her, huh?" he laughed.

Grandma Hattie chuckled and threw her hand at him, mouthing the words "boy quit."

"No, but on a serious note like Pops said, I just

really thank you so much for stepping in and doing more than you ever had to do to make sure me and my sister turned out alright. I love you so much Granny, and I can't thank you enough for everything you've done for me. You're the rock of this family, always holding us together, keeping us strong... and, I highly doubt we would've ever made it this far without your love and support. You know people, truth be told, the reason I'm so muscular today is because she had me out there pulling weeds and doing yard work at 6 years old." Tony laughed. "You're the real MVP Granny." he shouted as he tapped his chest with a balled up fist.

The crowd laughed and clapped as Tony passed the microphone to Londyn.

"My dad and Tony are clearly the comedians of the family." she chuckled. "Granny. I adore you. You saved my life, my brother's life, and my father's life simply by giving us your love. You taught me how to believe in myself, you taught me to always keep God first in my life, and you taught me how to be a good person. Everything I do is to make you, my dad... and my mom, proud." she stated as she looked up towards the ceiling. "From the moment you took us in, you held us to a standard that nobody else ever has. You set expectations for us that we may not have thought we could ever reach, like going to college, preparing for a career, and going after our dreams. Because of you, we're reaching those expectations. I love you so much with every bone in my body... and I don't know where

I'd be without you..."

Londyn, her brother, and her father took turns giving Grandma Hattie big hugs and kisses.

"I'm so proud of you, Babygirl." Grandma Hattie whispered in Londyn's ear.

Londyn and Tony walked back to their seats, while Gerald escorted Grandma Hattie up to the microphone. The crowd of family and friends stood in applause as the matriarch of their family stood before them with love and pride.

"Please, take your seats." she asked.

The room fell silent once she spoke into the microphone. Her soft, yet stern voice captured the attention of every single ear in the room.

"Well, I'm 90 years old today... and I have got to thank the good Lord, because I only look 65!" she giggled.

"I was born January 15, 1926. I've seen quite a lot in my lifetime, from Hitler, to World War II, Vietnam, and others. Dr. Martin Luther King Jr., Malcolm X, and segregation. I have seen Motown, Tupac Shakur, and President Barack Obama. My point is, I have lived a long time... and quite frankly, I've still got more to see. I must again give thanks to the Lord, for it is by His grace and mercy that I am still here standing strong. My children told you all how much I mean to them, but the truth is, I love them even more. They keep me young and they keep me wise. Especially that Antonio, I still have to give him a good whooping every now and again when he gets out of line." she joked with a balled up fist. "I am so glad to share this moment with you all, my sisters, cousins, all my children, my grandchildren, great grandchildren, my nieces, and nephews, and friends. Life without someone to share it with is not life at all. So appreciate your loved ones while you have them, and make peace when you get into an argument. Be kind to one another. Let people know that you care for them and that you are there for them when they need you most."

Londyn smiled as she felt Shane lightly place his hand on hers underneath the table.

"Love, is what life is all about." Grandma Hattie continued. "I am so overjoyed right now. This night is just perfect, the food was great, and I'm here with all of you beautiful people. My only wish is that my dear daughter-in-law, Charlotte, could be here to share in this moment with us, her family.

"Here she goes..." Tony said as he looked at Londyn and shook his head.

"Leave it to Granny to turn a nice moment into a tearjerker." Londyn mumbled as she nervously squeezed Shane's hand.

"As you all know," Grandma Hattie began. "this summer will mark 15 years since Charlotte passed away. Over time, although God's peace drowns out some of the sharp pain, it is still just as hard to accept as it was on June 26, 2001. God rest her soul. But, if I know anything, I know that my Charlotte would be so proud of her two babies, Londyn and Antonio, for growing into such fine adults. She'd be proud of my son, Gerald, for doing what he had to do... for growing up, and providing a good life for their children. She'd be proud of everyone here for the hand they played in supporting this family after her death. Most of you know this, but I'm going to tell it anyway, because it's my birthday, and they told me I can talk as much as I want. Charlotte Jean was like another daughter to me, the daughter of my dear friend Evelyn Carter, God rest her soul also. Charlotte spent so much time at my house growing up, that she became like one of my own children. I told Gerald he couldn't date her because she was more like a sister or cousin to him than anything, but oh no, he never looked at her as kin. No, he looked at her as a future wife from the time they were children, just 11 years old. Gerald married her the summer after she graduated high school, when he was only 19 and she was 18. They were the true definition of soulmates."

"Well this is awkward." Tony whispered aloud as he glanced over at their stepmother, Tammy, who instead of taking offense, smiled pleasantly.

"Londyn, I see so much of you in her. You have her heart, her strength, and her spirit. I want you to hold on to that, stay true to who you are. Because as you stay true to who you are, you're keeping her alive. Her legacy lives on through you."

Londyn mouthed the words "Thank You" and blew a kiss at her grandmother while Shane rubbed her back.

"Well here I go rambling on, but I just do really miss my Charlotte, you all know that. But she's in a better place, and we will see her again in eternity. I just want to thank each and every one of you again for coming here today. It has truly been a pleasure. I'm just so happy and thankful for 90 years. If I have any wisdom to offer, it is to simply live and love! Now let's enjoy the rest of the night. The DJ is charging us by the hour." she laughed as everyone chuckled. "I'm just playing. My great-nephew, Nathaniel is the DJ for the night. Nathaniel what's your DJ name again?"

"DJ Hot Sauce." he yelled

"That's right. DJ Hot Sauce." she chucked. "Oh, and my little great-grandbabies Keenan, Alexis, and Sean, oh and little Aaliyah too. They all taught me how to do the whip and the nay-nay so I'm ready to turn up." she yelled boldly as she dropped the microphone and walked away from the podium.

Everyone laughed and clapped as she walked back to her seat.

"Well you heard what Mama said, let's get this party started!" Gerald yelled as he hopped out of his seat.

DJ Hot Sauce played the "Cupid Shuffle," causing everyone in the room to rush to the dance floor. The family danced the rest of the night away, doing every hustle and popular dance imaginable. As promised, Grandma Hattie even got up to do the "whip and the nay-nay" with her great-grandchildren.

As the party wound down, Shane sat alone at a table while Londyn was taking family photos. They'd had a good night, but he knew that he still needed to talk to Londyn in private before the night was over. While he sat there attempting to mind his own business, he couldn't help but overhear the conversation at the table to the left. Grandma Hattie's sister, Aunt Ruthie, sat with two family friends, Mrs. Woods and Mrs. Randolph, discussing details of Londyn's mother's death. Seeing that Londyn never liked to talk about her mother's death, he couldn't help but to eavesdrop.

"It's just so sad what happened to Gerald's wife. To be killed so suddenly like that. She was a good woman. She didn't deserve that." Aunt Ruthie stated as she shook her head.

"I remember reading about that in the paper before I met you all. Car accident right?" Mrs. Woods asked.

"Yes. The poor girl was hit by some insane, devil of a woman... right over there near 94 and Grand River. That drunken, drug addict ran Charlotte right off the road into a pole. It really was a terrible sight to see." Aunt Ruthie replied.

"So, so sad..." Mrs. Woods cooed.

Shane's eyes bulged, and his throat suddenly went dry as he held on to their every last word.

"It sure is, and to make matters worse, the woman had two children in the car with her at the time. I just don't understand it. How are you driving drunk and high with your babies in the car? The nerve? That's why she's rotting in prison now, right where she deserves." Mrs. Randolph added.

"What a shame. Do you know what happened to the kids?" Mrs. Woods asked.

"They survived. I can imagine they probably ended up in the system, foster care. A woman like her doesn't strike me as someone who'd be married, or even know who her baby daddy is." Mrs. Randolph replied.

"Mmmm hmmmm." Aunt Ruthie replied.

Suddenly, Shane felt the room spin, and his body grew hotter by the second. In that moment, he didn't know whether to scream, cry, pass out, throw up, or all of the above. His hands were shaking, and his heart was beating rapidly as he gazed straight ahead into space.

"You okay baby?" Mrs. Woods asked as she reached over and touched his shoulder, awakening him from his entrancement.

"Sorry." he quickly stuttered as he grabbed his coat and scurried off towards the door.

"You know that's Londyn's little friend." Aunt

Ruthie stated as she watched Shane run off. "She always did like 'em a little weird."

"Hush, woman, he's probably sick from this food y'all cooked." Mrs. Randolph snickered.

"Oh hush."

Meanwhile, Shane had just about made it out the door when Londyn spotted him as she walked out of the bathroom.

"You're leaving?" she asked.

"Yeah... I gotta go." he replied, with a lifeless expression on his face.

"You weren't gonna say bye? What's wrong?"

"I just have to go."

"Wow... Here we go again. I mean what's up, Shane? What's really going on?" she asked with her arms folded across her chest.

"Goodbye Londyn." he replied as he turned his back and walked right out of the door, leaving Londyn alone and confused.

Brisk winds pierced Shane's face as he pressed his feet against the cold, slippery ground. He quickly got into his car and drove off before anyone, especially Londyn, could come after him.

Snow flurries tapped his windshield as he drove swiftly through the dark, Detroit streets. A million images flashed through his mind, as his brain continued to playback the conversation he'd just overheard, like a broken record that just wouldn't stop.

"That drunken, drug addict ran Charlotte right off the road into a pole. It really was a terrible sight to see." he thought.

Although his body was in the present, his mind was back in the summer of 2001, where he laid asleep in the backseat of that rundown, black 1991 coupe. Awakened by his frightened sister's screams, he sat up straight and looked around in confusion.

"Slow down Mommy!!! Slow down." is what he remembered hearing as the car flew at rapid speeds down the residential street.

His mother turned around briefly, looking at him. His eyes were filled with tears, silently pleading for her to stop whatever it was she was doing. However, she ignored his cries, and turned around facing the windshield, without saying a single word. Although he was only 7 years old, he could sense that something was terribly, terribly wrong.

"It's okay Shane..." his sister said as she grabbed his hand in hers.

"Beeeeeeeeppppp" was the sound of a horn blowing as headlights flashed in his eyes, snapping him out of his daze.

"Watch where you're going jerk!" a man in a shiny, new 2016 truck yelled as he flicked his middle finger at Shane.

With his mind now back to reality, Shane made

a sharp left turn onto Normile Street, and swiftly pulled into the driveway of a nice looking house with tan shutters. He hopped out of the car, and barely shut the door before rushing up the driveway. He jumped over all three steps to the get to top of the porch as quickly as possible. As his heavy breathing began to overtake his body, he banged his fists violently on the door. Within seconds, a tall, middle-aged woman with natural sandy brown dreadlocks opened the door. Before she could even open her mouth to speak, Shane fell into her arms, hyperventilating, and weak in the knees.

"It's okay baby... Aunt Ryn is here...it's okay..." she replied as she hugged him tightly. "It's okay..."

Chapter 21

"Knock Knock... Shane are you awake?" Aunt Ryn whispered as she opened the door to Shane's childhood bedroom, where he lay fast asleep in his old twin bed. His long legs draped over the edge of the mattress.

"My baby is knocked out." she whispered as she placed a plate of steamy hot breakfast on the nightstand.

Just as she was about to gently wake him, his phone started ringing loudly. He opened his eyes suddenly and began to feel around under the covers for his phone. He rubbed his eye with one hand and picked up the phone with another. Without hesitation, he clicked the "end" button, and sent his early morning caller straight to voicemail.

"Londyn again?" Aunt Ryn asked.

"Yeah..." he replied in a sleepy, dry, muffled tone.

"You know, you're not going to be able to ignore her forever, nephew. You're going to have to talk to her."

"I can't..." he replied as he sat up in the bed and yawned.

Aunt Ryn looked at Shane and shook her head. She tapped the bed with her hands, and he quickly scooted over so that she could sit down next to him. She placed both hands firmly on his shoulders, and looked deeply into his eyes.

"Now, I know haven't had the pleasure of meeting Miss Londyn yet, but from all you've told me about her, she's a keeper... right?"

"Yeah, she's the one..." he replied.

"Well, if she's anything like most women, then she won't take too kindly to being ignored."

"I know. She hates it when I do that..." he replied as he shook his head and reached his long arms over the bed frame.

He picked up the plate of eggs, bacon, grits, and honey biscuits from the nightstand and took a bite.

"Then why didn't you answer? She has to have called you at least 7 times since last night. She's probably just trying to make sure you're alive, boy."

"Nah... she knows I'm alive..." he chuckled. "I

texted her and told her I was okay."

"Then why won't you answer her calls?"

He paused for a moment, and then looked down at his plate. "Honestly... I'm scared, Aunt Ryn. Answering the phone means opening up a can of worms that I'm not prepared to clean up. It's literally going to change everything about our relationship." he replied as he stuffed his mouth with grits and bacon.

"Londyn is your girlfriend Shane, and a darn good one at that. She loves you and you love her, but without communication you two will never be able to get through this."

"None of that matters..." he said as his head hung low.

"What do you mean?"

"I love that girl. I want to marry her one day," he began as he lifted his head and looked at his aunt, "she's my best friend, my breath of fresh air, but absolutely none of that matters now. All that matters is that my mother is the reason that her mother is dead, and once she finds out the truth, it'll never work. She'll never be able to accept that. I mean who would? I can't blame her."

"You don't know what she'll be able to accept Shane. You don't know until you talk to her. It wasn't your fault. What your mother did was terrible. She stole someone's life, but it wasn't you that did it. You can't hold yourself responsible for that. You can't live your life that way, but if you keep blowing Londyn off, neglecting her, you're going to lose her."

"I'm going to lose her anyway..." he mumbled.

"How are you so sure of that?" she asked.

Shane paused and closed his eyes to avoid seeing Aunt Ryn's initial reaction. "I told her my mother was dead too." he said coldly with zero emotion.

"You did what?" Aunt Ryn asked sternly.

"I told her she was dead. I've been telling people that for years." he replied as he looked at her directly in the eyes.

"Why in the world would you do that?" she questioned, in a concerned, yet confused voice.

"It's the truth."

"No, it's not... it's not..." Aunt Ryn replied as she shook her head.

"She is dead, Aunt Ryn. She's dead to me!" he yelled angrily. "That's what she told me... at 10 years old, she looked me, her own child, in the face and told me that I didn't have a mother anymore... and that she didn't have a son... She told me to never come see her again." he continued with his face scrunched up in anger.

His fists were balled as he rocked back and forth. The veins in his forehead bulged again, and he felt his body temperature rising as the unpleasant memories flooded his mind. Aunt Ryn gently grabbed his fists, and held them tightly.

"Why did she hate me so much? Why wasn't I good enough for her? What did I do?" he asked as his bottom lip quivered violently.

"Come here baby, come here." Aunt Ryn replied as she embraced her nephew in a hug and rocked him like she did when he was a little boy.

"My younger sister had a lot of issues..." she began as she patted and rubbed his back, "She dealt with a lot of demons from a young age. It had nothing to do with you, or your sister. She was lost, baby. She was hurting. I don't quite understand it myself, but I know that she didn't do it to hurt you. All she ever wanted to do was protect her children. She just didn't know how."

Shane's anger subdued as he laid in her arms. This was a battle he'd been fighting silently for over 10 years, and one that only Aunt Ryn and Uncle Buck truly understood.

"My world literally shattered the day that she told me to never come back. The look in her eyes before she turned her back and walked away... I'll never ever forget that pain." Shane replied.

"CJ was in a bad space, mentally, physically, emotionally, and most of all, spiritually. She hung with the wrong crowd and got caught up in a whole lot of mess. By the time she was 16 she was so out of control that my parents felt they had no choice but to kick her out. I tried to convince Mama to let her come back home, and remind her that she was just a kid, but she couldn't see that. And Daddy, he gave up long before my mother did. They didn't understand. But see me, I could always see straight through my sister's rough exterior. Through the drugs, the gang activity, and the acting out, I always knew she was just a little girl in pain. A little girl who was constantly crying out for help, but felt like nobody was ever paying attention. She was abused numerous times by a family member, but Mama and Daddy never believed her. They didn't mean any harm, but they didn't handle it correctly either. So she rebelled. She looked for love in all the wrong places, including with your father. And as crooked of a situation as that was, finding out that she was pregnant with you is what saved her... so to speak. I mean, I know things ended up turning out badly anyway, but Shane, I promise when she found out she was pregnant with you she tried as hard as she could to turn her life around."

Shane sat back against the wall, as the anger in his eyes slowly dissipated even more. His aunt had never once gone into such specific details about his mother's life.

"She told me one day, she said 'Sis... I'm about to have a son, and I promise you my son ain't gon' end up like these jokers in these streets, not my baby. I'm gonna raise him the right way. He's going to be a strong black man. A successful black man.' She was determined to do things the right way. So, she started waitressing, bought herself a car, got an apartment, and got sober. Then she had your sister, and we thought things were finally coming together. She worked so hard to make a decent life for the three of y'all, and she honestly did do the best that she could for a long time. But, addiction is a strong drug in and of itself, and eventually she lost herself again. She got caught up with the wrong crowd and ended up getting set up by her so called friends who made it look like she stole thousands of dollars from some guy. Even though she didn't steal anything, she worked overtime to make extra money so that she could pay him back and hopefully start fresh again. Long story short, things just sort of spiraled out of control from there."

Shane was silent for a moment, just staring off into space in deep thought.

His face wrinkled a bit. "I just don't understand why after 3 years of me visiting her in prison, she cut me off the way she did. I mean, I know it wasn't an ideal situation, having mother-son visits through glass and bars, but we did what we had to do. As awkward as it was, I looked forward to seeing her, and hearing her voice every single time. I thought everything was okay, until that day when she just stopped looking at me the same. She just looked at me like I was a stranger. I could tell from that moment, from that lifeless look that she gave me after she told me that I wasn't her son anymore, that everything was going to change. She didn't have to say it with her mouth, because her eyes yelled it loud and clear... she didn't love me. I didn't matter to her anymore, not at all."

"You mattered to her, Shane. You mattered. You still do. She is your mother and you are her son. Nothing can ever change that. CJ spent a lot of time in solitary confinement for insubordination around the time that you last saw her. It was like she was literally losing her mind in there. I'm sure at the time, she couldn't comprehend what she was saying..."

"That's still no excuse..."

"I'm not making excuses for her, by any means. And I know this is a conversation we really should've had years ago, and I'm sorry for that, I dropped the ball. What she did was wrong and completely unacceptable. I've prayed for my sister for all of these years and could only hope that the Lord would one day heal and deliver her. Now I know I could never take away the pain that she has caused you, but I just wanted to put things into perspective and help you to see that her actions were a direct result of her own issues, and not at all because of you, or anything that you did."

Shane didn't say a word as Aunt Ryn leaned over and kissed him on the forehead.

"I just don't want you to do the same thing to Londyn..." she replied as she walked towards the door.

"Thanks Aunt Ryn...Thanks for breakfast...."

"Anytime..." she smiled, knowing in her heart that his thank you was more so directed towards the conversation than the food.

As Aunt Ryn closed the door behind her Shane picked up his cell phone and stared at it in deep thought. He cracked his knuckles, and then pressed Londyn's name with his thumb. His heart pounded violently through his chest as he waited for her to pick up.

"I don't know how to tell her this." he thought.

"Hello." Londyn answered.

"Hey Lo," he replied nervously. "How are you?"

"So you really just gon' hey Lo me like everything is cool? I called you 10 times, Shane. 10! I've been worried sick about you. You just ran out of the party last night looking like you'd seen a ghost or something, and then ignored me for 12 hours. You know I'm not even the clingy, needy type of chick, but c'mon man, you gotta work with me!"

"I'm sorry..." he replied, a bit shaken up and unsure of how to break the life shattering news to her.

"Yeah, well sorry is getting kind of old, Shane."

"I know... I just... I don't know." he replied stumbling over his words.

"Were you with another girl?"

"What? No! I can't believe you're still asking me

that."

"Well, I don't know... I mean, I don't know what to expect. I've barely talked to you in the last month, it's like you're a stranger to me now. Like you're not even my boyfriend anymore or something..." she replied sarcastically.

At that moment Shane paused, his brain frozen in time, and suddenly all of the feelings he'd felt that day when his mother turned his back on him came rushing back, stabbing him in the heart like knives.

"Like a stranger... like you're not my boyfriend anymore... you're not my son anymore... not my son anymore...not my son anymore..." echoed loudly through his thoughts.

"I need a break, Londyn. From us. I can't do this." he blurted out.

"Are you serious? Really... What did I ever do to you?" Londyn asked.

"I just can't do this."

"Whatever it is, we can fix it Shane... please, don't give up." Londyn pleaded.

"I gotta go..." Shane replied as he hung up the phone.

Chapter 22

"Let's go to the movies." Reagan stated as she sat on the corner of Londyn's bed.

"Nah, not really feeling that." Londyn replied.

"Shopping?" Reagan asked.

"Nope." Londyn replied as she laid down next to her on the bed.

"Canada?" Reagan joked.

"No."

"C'mon Londyn... you've been in a funk ever since you and Shane got into it. You've got to do something to get your mind off of him."

"We didn't just get into it, Reagan. We broke up."

"Lo, you know how many times me and David 'broke up'? Y'all are just on a little break. Things will get better. That man loves you girl."

"Well he definitely hasn't been acting like it."

"I really think he's just going through something right now. Men act out when something is bothering them that they don't know how to handle. I know he shouldn't take it out on you, but they do that sometimes. He'll come around."

"Whatever..."

"Knock, knock, knock." Reagan and Londyn heard as someone knocked on Londyn's front door. Londyn didn't budge, but instead just stared up at the ceiling.

"So, are you going to get the door, or?" Reagan asked.

"Nope." Londyn replied without lifting her head off the pillow.

"Ohhhh Kay." Reagan replied as she shook her head and got up from her spot on Londyn's bed.

She walked barefoot down the hallway towards the front door.

"Got me answering doors and what not. I may be your best friend, but I'm not your butler!" Reagan yelled from the living room.

"Knock, knock."

"I'm cominggggg." Reagan yelled.

She quickly opened the door and was shocked to see Bree standing before her.

"Oh you must have the wrong house." Reagan stated with her face wrinkled and nose turned up.

"Hey Reagan." Bree giggled.

"No, I'm serious. What are you doing here?"

"I came to see Londyn... obviously, seeing that this is her apartment." Bree replied with a little bit of an attitude.

"What makes you think she wants to see you? Y'all friends now? Because last time I checked you were trying to sabotage her relationship at the Piston's game, and then telling her to keep her man away from Chicago girls like you..." Reagan stated with her arms folded across her chest and her feet planted firmly.

"Girl... you need to find some chill." Bree replied as she attempted to brush past Reagan into the apartment.

"No, I don't actually. " Reagan replied as she stepped up, stopping her from entering.

"Seriously?" Bree sighed.

"Let her in Reagan." Londyn stated from her position in the hallway. She was dressed in sweatpants, mix matched socks, a baggy B2K concert tee, with her hair in a messy ponytail.

Bree walked in rolling her eyes at Reagan, while Reagan looked back at her with disgust.

"Why does she always have on freakin' heels. This is campus, not the club." Reagan snickered under her breath.

Londyn plopped down on her couch, as Bree sat on the loveseat across from her.

"Sorry Bree. I didn't realize it was 2:00 already... This morning just flew by I guess."

"Okay. Did I miss something here?" Reagan asked as she sucked her teeth and stood with one hand on her hip.

"I invited her over." Londyn replied.

"Why?" Reagan asked as she looked at Bree with the stank face.

"Because I need to talk to her. About Shane." Londyn replied with little energy.

Reagan smacked her lips and huffed as she walked over to the loveseat where Bree was sitting.

"That's usually my seat." she snickered, staring at Bree in the eyes.

"I'm not even about to do this with you today." Bree stated as she stood up and moved to the opposite end of the couch where Londyn sat.

"So, Bree. I know we haven't been on the best of terms ever since I started dating Shane."

"Because she's a fake trick." Reagan mumbled under her breath.

"REAGAN. Just stop. Please." Londyn snapped.

Bree cut her eyes at Reagan before turning to look back at Londyn.

"Like I was saying... I know we've had our issues, but I need to talk to you about Shane. I need to know if he's been messing with Kyla again. Or talking to her, or anything like that."

"No, not at all. Why do you say that?" Bree asked.

"Don't tell her..." Reagan said in an "I told you so" kind of way.

"What did you say?" Bree asked as she looked at Reagan.

"I SAID, Londyn shouldn't tell your ol' fake, disloyal butt nothing... so you can run back and tell who knows who? Kyla probably. You've been plotting on Londyn and Shane's relationship from jump."

"If you have that much of a problem with me Reagan then why were we ever friends?" Bree asked as she stood up from her seat on the couch and took off her earrings.

"Key word Breanna, WERE, past tense. You're an English major right? You know better. WERE friends. Used to be. As in no longer. Comprende?"

"What is your problem?" Bree asked as she stepped closer to Reagan.

"I don't have a problem. I JUST DON'T LIKE YOU. You're fake. You think you're slick, and you do things to get drama going. Londyn is the nice one, not me. I can see straight through you, boo. You brought your girl Kyla to the game because you were trying to prove a point, and you did. You proved one about yourself. I don't have time for basic bitties like you. Be gone." Reagan replied as she dismissed Bree with a wave.

Bree stepped up and threw her hands violently towards Reagan, but Londyn jumped in between, blocking her hit just in time.

"If you gon' swing trick, then don't miss!" Reagan yelled as she swung her arm around Londyn, punching Bree in the shoulder.

"Y'all are NOT about to fight. Not in this house." Londyn yelled as she held Bree back from retaliating.

"Alright, that's fine. You want to play with fire Londyn, just don't get burned." Reagan said calmly as she shook her head and walked over to the closet near the front door.

"Reagan, don't let me catch you outside." Bree yelled.

"Girl boom, worry about them eyebrows first. Looking like a permanent marker bled across your forehead..." Reagan snapped as she put on her boots, grabbed her coat, and stormed out of the apartment.

Londyn shook her head and sat back down on the couch, covering her face.

"Ughhhhhhhhhhhh." she grumbled.

"You should've let me hit her." Bree replied.

Londyn looked up and rolled her eyes.

"Reagan has been a hot-head since freshman year. She'll get over it. She's just trying to look out for you. I get it. She's wrong, but I get it." Bree said as she sat down next to Londyn on the couch.

"I'm so stressed out." she replied.

"So what's going on? What happened with you and Shane?"

"We haven't spoken in like a week."

"A week? Well that's not that long."

"It is when you add the three more weeks we hadn't spoken before that..."

"Oh... yeah... why is that?"

"I honestly don't know. I have no idea what's gotten into him. Everything was great between us before he left for Chicago. Then as soon as he got back it was like he was a whole new person. I've never seen this side of him before. He drinks, ignores my calls, doesn't bother to check on me, and then out of nowhere he broke up with me..."

"Did he say why he was breaking up with you?"

"Nope, just said he needed a break. It's so weird. I don't know if he's talking to someone else, or if he did something in Chicago, and is trying to push me away from him because of it. I just don't know."

"Hmmm....."

"That's why I wanted to talk to you to see if he'd

been messing with Kyla again. I know that's your girl, so I figured you'd know."

"Nah, not that I know of. I mean, if she was I'm not even so sure that she'd tell me since she knows that I know you."

"Yeah...you're probably right." Londyn replied. "Reagan thinks he's just going through something right now, and that's why he's acting out."

"I don't know... I don't think so because he used to pull this card with Kyla sometimes too. And I mean, what could he be going through though? He just got that award, his career is like, set. Family issues maybe?" Bree asked.

"I don't know. He doesn't have much family. Just an aunt and an uncle... a few cousins."

"No parents?"

"Nope. He doesn't talk to his dad, and his mom passed away. His Aunt Ryn raised him."

".... And you've met her?"

"Nah, she lives in Texas."

"Oh okay, got it... Well has he ever introduced you to her? Like on the phone?"

"No... but I mean... that's not really a big deal though, is it?"

"I don't know Londyn. Usually when a man is into you, you meet his mother, or in this case, his aunt. My boyfriend and his family are from Tennessee, but I talk to his mom on the phone all the time."

"Hmm...." Londyn replied.

"...and I wasn't going to say anything, but I did notice that this girl from U.B. named Desiree has been liking all his Instagram pictures lately... I mean, I wasn't trying to lurk or anything, but it showed up all over my news feed. I think she's plotting to make a move on Shane. I went to high school with her back home in Chicago."

"Wow...."

"Yeah. But she doesn't seem like his type though. Listen, I do think Shane is into you. I mean, he treats you wayyyyy better than he ever treated Kyla. But I do think something is up. Maybe Kyla. Maybe another girl. But something is definitely up, and you need to get to the bottom of it."

"...and how do I do that?"

"You've gotta do a drive by. Catch him when he's not expecting you. That's how you'll know."

"I'm not a stalker."

"I didn't say you had to be. I'm not saying go sneak and watch him from some bushes. I'm saying go to his house unannounced, knock on the door, and confront him when he has no time to get a lie together."

"Sounds pretty psycho to me."

"Sometimes you have to be a psycho girlfriend.

I mean, I'll go with you! You don't have to do it alone."

"I guess it couldn't hurt to just pop up and see."

"I know I shouldn't do this, because Kyla is my girl, but I mean... if he isn't home, we can ride past her place too and see if his car is there. Normally I wouldn't do that, but I know you're not some crazy girl who will go back to her house and kill her in her sleep or something." Bree giggled.

"Nah... that's not how I roll. I just want to know if Shane is cheating on me."

"Well, let's roll. You think he'll be home?"

"He should be. He doesn't work on Thursday's, and usually stays home to study all day."

"Alright well, let's go." Bree said as she stood up and walked towards the door.

"Let me grab my stuff." Londyn replied as she walked to her room.

A few minutes later she returned to the living room with a Detroit Vs. Everybody skullcap, her Northface jacket, purse, and boots. She grabbed her keys off of the kitchen counter and opened the front door.

"Let's get this over with." Londyn huffed.

They walked outside through the slushy rain-snow mixture towards Londyn's car, when Reagan suddenly hopped out of her own car and yelled at them.

"Where are y'all going?" she asked.

"I thought you left." Londyn said as she stopped in her tracks.

"No, Londyn, I was waiting til 'your friend' left so I could undo whatever damage she did. But it looks like I'm too late, where are y'all going?" she asked again.

"We're going to U.B." Londyn replied confidently.

"You talked to Shane?"

"No. But I'm about to go fix things with him, or end it forever. I need to see if he's cheating on me."

"Girl. These are the things you do with your best friend, not her." Reagan replied, "I'm coming with you."

"Umm I don't think that would..." Bree began.

"Save it." Reagan replied as she walked past Bree and stood at the front passenger seat door of Londyn's car.

Bree shook her head and silently opened the back seat passenger door, as Londyn walked over to the driver's side and got inside.

"Here goes nothing." Londyn mumbled as she stuck the keys in the ignition.

★

After a long, silent, 40 minute ride, the three of them arrived at U.B.'s campus. As Londyn turned into Shane's apartment complex her stomach began to turn in knots.

"Well, at least I know he's home." Londyn said as she parked next to his car, and turned off the ignition.

Bree looked outside her window and paused. "Ummm... Londyn." she said nervously.

"What's up?" Londyn asked, as she turned her head towards the back seat to look at Bree.

"Kyla's car is over there, yeah, that's definitely hers." Bree stated in reference to the little blue car parked a few spots over.

"Man..." Londyn sighed as she shook her head and took off her seatbelt.

"You sure you want to do this?" Reagan asked with her hand on Londyn's shoulder.

"Looks like I have no choice now, do I?" Londyn replied as she got out the car and slammed it shut.

Reagan quickly opened her door and looked over the back seat at Bree who sat there like a deer in headlights.

"I'm just going to stay in the car... conflict of interest... you know." Bree replied.

"Typical." Reagan responded as she hopped out the car and closed the door behind her, following Londyn as she quickly approached Shane's building.

Things were about to get real.

Chapter 23

Shane sat at his kitchen table, which was covered in paperwork, eating a bowl of chicken fried rice, when his phone rang.

"Hey Desi." he answered. "You outside? Alright. Front or back door? Back. Alright, here I come now."

He quickly got up from the table and walked into the hallway, closing the door behind him. As he hustled down the hallway towards the back staircase to the back door, Londyn and Reagan were walking up the front staircase.

"Whatever happens, you know I got you..." Reagan stated confidently as they paused in front of his door.

Londyn took a huge breath and knocked on the door. They waited for a little while, but no one answered. She knocked again. Still no answer. She turned the door handle, which to her surprise was unlocked. Her eyes bulged a little, but without hesitation, she opened the door and walked right into Shane's apartment.

"Wait, are you for real?" Reagan whispered as she stood in the hallway.

Londyn didn't respond, but the fact that she was now well into Shane's apartment, let Reagan know that her best friend was indeed, for real. While Londyn carefully tiptoed around the apartment, searching for Shane, Reagan moseyed around the kitchen, shuffling through the paperwork on his table. When she noticed an envelope from Chicago State Penitentiary, her curiosity wouldn't allow her to leave it untouched.

"He's not here. Must have taken the bus somewhere." Londyn replied as she walked around the corner.

"Hey Lo. Shane is getting letters from prison. Thug life." she laughed as threw up a mock gang sign with her hand.

"Probably his friend Man-Man." Londyn stated from the hallway leading back to the living room.

Reagan carefully pulled the handwritten letter from the already opened envelope. As she unfolded it, she glanced at the opened apartment door.

"Yeah I sure hope he took the bus somewhere far, because if he catches us we might be headed to jail too." Reagan chuckled.

She focused her eyes back on the letter. After reading the first couple of lines, her head cocked to the side, and a look of confusion swept across her face. She turned the letter over, and read all the way to the bottom where it was signed, "Sincerely, your mother, Carmen Jackson."

"Ummmmmmmm... Londyn!" she yelled.

"What?" Londyn replied as she walked over to Reagan.

"I thought you said Shane's mom passed away." Reagan asked.

"She did, why?"

"Well if she's dead, then Shane is getting letters from a ghost in prison." Reagan replied while re-reading the letter.

"Give me that." Londyn replied as she grabbed the letter from Reagan's hand.

Her jaw nearly dropped to the floor as she read each and every word. She couldn't believe her eyes.

"Yo, What the hell are y'all doing in here?" Shane yelled as he stormed through the door.

"So your mom is alive?" Londyn immediately yelled back.

Shane walked over to her and snatched his mother's letter from her hand.

"So you're breaking into my apartment now,

Londyn?" he yelled. "Who do you think you are going through my mail?"

"I thought I was your GIRLFRIEND." she yelled.

"I told you, I needed a break." Shane said calmly.

Londyn was at a loss for words as tears began to fill her eyes. She looked past him and saw a pretty pregnant girl, who looked about their age, standing in the doorway.

"So this is why you broke up with me, huh Shane? This is why you've been acting funny? This bi..." she began as she pointed at the pregnant girl.

"Uh uh... Girl you better chill the..." Desi interrupted with an attitude.

"Destiny... not now." Shane yelled, cutting them both off.

Londyn looked at the both of them and shook her head.

"Well, consider your little break over. You don't have to worry about me ever again in your life, cause we are through." she hollered as she marched towards the door.

Desi quickly moved out of her way to avoid any accidental contact as Londyn charged past.

From the doorway, Londyn paused and looked back with tears streaming down her face. "I should've listened to everything people said about you. I should've never given you a chance." she stated calmly as she shook her head and headed down the stairway.

Reagan quickly followed behind without saying a word. Shane threw his hands in the air as he stared at the empty doorway. He paced back and forth through his living room, as he processed what had just transpired. Within a few seconds, he turned towards the door and ran down the stairs after Londyn.

"Londyn! Wait!" he yelled as Londyn was unlocking her car door. He ran over and tried to lightly grab her shoulder.

"Don't touch me." she snapped as she opened the door and sat down inside.

He raised both of his hands in surrender to reassure her that he was not trying to touch her again. Nonetheless, she still couldn't close her car door because his body was in the way.

"Move." she stated plainly.

"Just let me explain." he pleaded.

"I said, move." she replied sternly.

He stepped back and put his hands in his pockets, as she slammed the door and reversed. With no way to stop her, Shane watched in despair as she pulled out of the parking lot.

"Ughhhhhhh." Shane grunted as he watched her car drive away.

He looked to his left and saw Desi standing on

the curb, near Uncle Buck, who showed up just in time to witness the action.

"Well that was awkward..." Desi stated.

"Dammit!!!" Shane yelled.

"So... are we still on for dinner tonight?" Uncle Buck chuckled, attempting to relieve the tension in the air.

Shane punched the air with his fist and walked back up the path to his apartment building, with Desi and Uncle Buck following not too far behind.

On the car ride home Londyn was completely silent. Tears streamed down her face, but she only wiped them occasionally. Her mind was running a mile a minute, as her hands gripped the steering wheel in anger. She didn't know how to feel, as her emotions wrestled back and forth between feeling angry and feeling devastated. Reagan was rather quiet, with little words to say to console her best friend. She never expected to find out that Shane was cheating on Londyn, and felt a tad bit responsible in a way for not catching him sooner. Reagan had felt the need to protect Londyn ever since they met in the 9th grade. When Londyn first moved in with her dad, after staying with her grandmother for so long, she befriended the awkward and shy young Londyn, and remained at her side ever since. She had always been there to fight the bullies, or speak up for Londyn when people did her wrong, so this news hurt her too. She just couldn't believe that Shane did the exact same thing that Justin had done. She'd had a lot of faith in Shane, and deep down was in denial that it could even be true.

"Are you okay?" she asked about 15 minutes into the ride.

"Yep." Londyn replied without taking her eyes off of the road.

Reagan knew her best friend better than anyone. She knew that "yep" really meant "absolutely not," as well as "don't ask me any more questions." Needless to say the rest of the ride was absolutely silent, other than The Weeknd's voice crooning through the radio speakers.

Once they finally arrived back on ELU's campus, Londyn pulled into a parking space in front of her apartment, and sat still staring out the windshield. A single tear rolled down her cheek as she shook her head back and forth slowly.

"You want me to stay here with you?" Reagan asked.

"Nah," Londyn replied as she wiped her face, "I just need to be alone."

She slowly unbuckled her seatbelt and opened the driver's side door.

"Alright mama, well if you change your mind, call me. I'll check on you later." Reagan replied with her hand on Londyn's shoulder.

"Bye Londyn..." Bree said as she and Reagan got out of Londyn's car and walked over to their own vehicles.

Londyn slowly walked to her front door and unlocked it without looking back. Once she made it inside, she took off her coat, and laid face down on her couch. As she cried softly, she drowned in her feelings of embarrassment, betrayal, and numbness all in one. As if she hadn't been hurt enough in one lifetime, this just added further insult to injury. She thought back to all of the times Shane tried to make it seem like she was the one holding back, or all of the occasions he'd accused her of not being true to her own feelings. She thought back to each and every time Shane had whispered, "trust me" in her ear. With those thoughts floating through her mind, it didn't take long at all for her pity party to evolve into rage.

She hopped up off the couch as if her pants had suddenly caught on fire and stormed down the hallway into her bedroom. She picked up the glass-framed photo of she and Shane that sat on her dresser and threw it violently in the trashcan next to her bed, shattering it to pieces. Next, she looked around in despair until her eyes settled on the charm bracelet he'd given her a few weeks after they officially started dating. She picked it up off of her nightstand and clutched it tightly in her fist. She marched over to her window and grabbed the ledge with both hands. To her disappointment, the old window barely budged even with her using all of her strength against it. So, she took a breath and tried again, this time with enough force to open it just a few inches. There was just enough space between the window and the windowsill for her to stick her hand through, as she dropped the bracelet outside in the pouring rain. On a mission to destroy anything that reminded her of the false love Shane had given her, she walked over to her desk chair, where Shane's favorite Red Wings hoodie draped over the oak chair's arms. She shook her head and stared at it for a moment, as she pondered how exactly to dispose of it. As she was thinking, she noticed Shane had left one of his prized possessions, a Burberry watch in her room also. She grabbed the watch and the hoodie, and walked out of her room towards the front door of her apartment. Without any care for what the rain would do to her clothes or hair, she ran outside with no coat or umbrella towards the dumpster.

She stood facing the dumpster, and then looked down at the items in her hands.

"*He played himself.*" she thought as she jumped up to reach the huge lid, and flipped it upright with all of her might.

"Ughhh." she groaned as she flung his watch and hoodie over her shoulders into the dumpster, and walked away.

When she heard the "thump" noise of the objects hitting the metal bottom of the dumpster, she patted her hands as to say, job well done. Although she knew that wouldn't solve all her problems, it made her feel a whole lot better.

Meanwhile, Shane sat in the front seat of his car, speeding down the I-94 freeway through the rain. While his face lacked emotion, his mind was running rampant. He could barely focus on the road as his thoughts drifted over the memorous ups and downs of he and Londyn's relationship. He reminisced on everything from when they first met, to when they fell in love, to when she pushed him towards greatness, and supported him like no one else had ever done. The thought of losing her sent painful chills down his spine, and made his heart sink further into his chest. He snapped out of his daze when Desi put her hand on his shoulder from her seat on the passenger side.

"You okay?" she asked.

"I don't know..." he replied as his eyes stayed focused on the road.

After about 20 minutes passed, Shane pulled into the parking lot of Londyn's apartment complex and parked his car. Rain poured violently against his windows, making it hard to see anything at all. His heart was beating rapidly as he pulled the keys from the ignition.

"Wait here a minute, alright?" he said to Desi as he opened his car door.

She nodded and rested her head against the window. Shane hopped out of the vehicle, and pulled the hood of his Northface hoodie over his head. He looked around at his surroundings, and then jogged towards Londyn's door. Once he reached the door, he clinched his fist, raised it slowly, and then dropped it down at his side again. A deep breath was followed by a quick and swift knock on the door. He waited a few seconds before knocking again. Still no answer. At this point, his clothes were drenched by the rain, and monstrous sounds of thunder vibrated through the sky. His knock quickly turned to pounding on the door, until Londyn cracked it open.

"Londyn, please just let me in." he begged.

"No, why are you here?" she asked through the small space between the doorframe and the open door.

"Because I love you." he stated plainly before she closed the door right in his face.

"Just leave..." she yelled from inside, as her bloodshot eyes were still wet with tears.

Between the loud thunder, thumping rain, and thick wooden door, her attempts to yell went unnoticed by Shane. Once she realized that he was not going to stop banging on her door, she opened it, reluctantly.

"Why won't you just leave me alone?" she asked softly, with little mental energy left in her body to argue.

"Because I have to explain this to you. You're jumping to conclusions and I just need to talk to you. I just need 10 minutes of your time, Londyn."

"We don't have anything to talk about."

"Just trust me, Londyn."

"Trust you? Yeah right." she replied as she pushed the door.

This time, Shane stuck his foot in the doorway, preventing her from closing it in his face again.

"10 minutes?" he asked, as he moved his foot out of the way.

She looked at him and grabbed her ponytail in distress, and then dropped both of her arms loosely to her side.

"5 minutes." she replied as she opened the door fully.

Before stepping into the house Shane turned and signaled towards his parked car. Seconds later, out came Desi, hustling through the rain with a black umbrella over her head.

"You have got to be kidding me. Did you seriously just bring your other woman to my house,

Shane?" Londyn yelled.

"Londyn, calm down." Shane yelled back.

"No! No! I won't calm down, because what you're not going to do is disrespect me in my own house. Nah, that's what you not gon' to do. Deja Vu. I've been there and done that. So you, and your lil babymama, can take your unborn child, and get out my house." Londyn yelled as Desi waddled into the apartment.

"Just have a seat right there." Shane said to Desi, as he pointed towards one of the loveseats.

"Tuh, this fool just told her to have a seat." Londyn whispered to herself with a sarcastic giggle as she paced back and forth across the living room.

"Londyn, if you would just calm down I could explain to you what's going on."

"Explain what, Shane? Explain to me how you're a liar? Explain how you've been punking me this whole time as if you know how it feels to lose a mother? Or explain to me how you're a cheater?"

"Stop."

"NO! Does she know how long you've been dating me? How do youuuu feel about that?" she asked, directing her attention to Desi.

"LONDYN! STOP! This is my sister. I have never, and will never cheat on you. If you would just listen for two seconds you would know that."

"Your sister?" Londyn asked as her face dropped in embarrassment.

"My sister." he replied, relieved that she had finally called down.

Londyn's eyes bulged and she scratched her head in disbelief.

"My bad girl." Londyn said as she looked at Desi.

"You good." Desi replied. "I'm Destiny, but everyone calls me Desi for short."

"Nice to meet you Desi... and again, I'm sorry."

"Don't even trip, hun." Desi replied.

"Londyn," Shane began as he looked directly in her eyes, "I love you. I promise I do. I would never, ever cheat on you, but you're right, I haven't been completely honest with you about me, and my life... especially when it comes to my mother, but that doesn't change how I feel about you."

"I just want to know why you lied, Shane? Why say your mother is dead, if she's not? I would do anything to have my mom back, man. Anything. So the fact that you have yours, but choose to say she's dead blows my mind." Londyn replied with her arms folded across her chest.

"Listen, what I have to tell you is going to change everything, so I can understand if after today you never want to see me again." he stated.

"What is it? Just say it." Londyn replied.

"Umm... you might want to sit down, boo boo." Desi butted in, in a dry, comedic tone.

Londyn looked at Shane and questioned him with her eyes, to which he responded with a nod of the head. So Londyn took a step back and sat down on the couch. Shane paced back and forth for a while, before finally opening his mouth to speak.

"Okay... obviously you know that my mom is not dead. She's very much alive, and has been in prison since I was 7 years old. We had an okay relationship for the first few years she was locked up, until I was about 10 when she basically denounced me as her son and told me to never come back to see her ever again. She refused to see me, write me, talk to me, or acknowledge me at all. She broke my heart, and she's been dead to me ever since. I always found it easier to tell people she had a brain disease, you know, because I guess, to me, it made me feel better to think of it that way. To say that her brain just didn't work the way it was supposed to is easier to live with than the reality of her just not loving me. None of my family kept in contact with her. Desi was already living with her father part time when our mother got locked up. So after that, he never brought her around. Even to this day, everybody pretty much speaks of my mother in past tense, or not at all. She's been moved around from state to state and nobody's ever really known where she was at any given moment. I don't know how or when she ended up in Chicago, but she read about me in the newspaper when I was there getting my award. From there she tracked me down for the first time in over 12 years." Shane said with a stern face that suddenly began to turn soft.

His nose wrinkled, and he gulped saliva as he mentally tried to prevent himself from crying in front of Londyn.

His voice cracked a little as he continued, "In the letter, she said she knows that I'll probably never forgive her or anything, but that she's a changed woman. She gave me Desi's number and said that all she wanted was for me to reconnect with my sister." he said as he looked over at Desi.

Desi cracked a loving smile and then looked over at Londyn. "So over the past few weeks, Shane, Uncle Buck, Aunt Ryn, and I have been meeting up to sort things out, the best we can at least. That was what you walked in on earlier today. He's not cheating on you. This baby has a daddy, that I am happily married to." Desi giggled as she flashed her wedding ring.

"I am so, so, sorry. I owe you an apology." Londyn replied. "I'm so embarrassed, I'm sorry. I shouldn't have jumped to conclusions." she said as she looked over at Shane.

"This has been a lot to deal with, all at once. That's why I've been so distant and unlike myself. I'm not saying it's right, but it's the truth. For half of my life, I've told myself that my mother was dead, and struggled to suppress the pain of abandonment, neglect, and sorrow... but as soon as I opened that letter, reality hit me in the face like a pile of bricks." Shane stated as he sat down next to Londyn on the couch.

Londyn stared at the ground for a minute before lifting her head to look at Shane.

"Why did your mom go to prison?" she asked, reluctantly.

Desi closed her eyes and looked the other way, as Shane turned and looked at Londyn. This was the moment he'd been dreading. The moment he felt would change absolutely everything.

"My mother was high on heroin, and extremely drunk, when she was involved in a fatal accident with Desi and I in the backseat." he stated quickly and plainly.

Londyn gasped and covered her mouth with both hands as she shook her head. She was shocked to hear a story repeated that she already knew far too well. She didn't want to believe what he'd just said.

She slowly removed her hands from her mouth. "When did you say this happened again?"

Shane hesitated for a moment, and then answered. "June 26th, 2001."

"No... No... No..." Londyn cried as she broke down in hysterics.

"I'm sorry... I'm so, so sorry." Shane replied as

he wrapped his arms around her shaking body.

"I can't believe this..." she cooed as Shane rocked her in his arms.

She breathed heavily and began pounding her hands onto his back. He had just broken the worst news possible to the one person he loved most. While he prided himself on being her protector, he knew this time there was nothing he could say to mend her broken heart.

Chapter 24

Over the next couple of months, things were extremely awkward between Shane and Londyn. As to be expected, Londyn needed time to process the situation, as well as break the disheartening news to her family. Shane began to adapt to the new family dynamic of having a sister again, as their family attended group therapy at their church. In lieu of all that was going on, Aunt Ryn transferred her job back to Detroit. With all of the emotions Londyn and Shane were dealing with respectively, there was little time or energy to work on their relationship. The unfortunate chain of events resulted in a mutual decision to let their relationship go. Shane spent all of his newfound free time studying harder than ever before, and preparing for his summer internship. Meanwhile, Londyn poured all of her time and energy into her upcoming graduation, focusing solely on classes, and interviewing for jobs at various broadcast networks.

"Any word on a job yet, Babygirl?" Gerald asked from the driver's seat of his 2016 Cadillac CTS-V.

"Not yet. Hopefully soon." she replied as she stared out the window.

"It'll come. Just be patient." he said with a head nod.

"Yeah..." she replied quietly.

"Is something else bothering you?" he asked as he glanced over at his unusually quiet daughter.

"I'm okay..."

"C'mon, you know you can always talk to your old man."

Londyn sat still for a moment, before turning to look at her father.

"Why did you have to marry Tammy?" Londyn asked very calmly.

"Whoa, where is that coming from?"

"I mean, I understand it's been a long time since Mommy died, and you have the right to move on with your life, but why her?"

"Why not her?"

Londyn shifted her weight and took a deep breath. She didn't want to offend her dad, but at the same time she was tired of holding her feelings inside.

"She looks JUST like Mommy. I can't even look

at her without wanting to cry. Of all the women in the world....you had to pick her... and I mean, do you really have to raise her daughter as your own. You go to Sabrina's dance recitals. You watch movies with her. What about me, Daddy? I had dance competitions that you never showed up to. I wanted to go to the movies with you. I needed you, Daddy... but you weren't there." Londyn replied dry-eyed and stiff faced.

Gerald pulled into the driveway of their house and put the gear in park. He thought long and hard before he opened his mouth to speak.

"Londyn, I was 21 years old when I became a father. Now I'm not making excuses, I'm just being honest. Mentally, I was still just a child. I thought I was doing a good job playing Daddy, until I started to notice all the stress I caused your mother. Charlotte Jean Carter... Wow, that woman was a gem." he stated with a smile. "She was caring, loving, and so mature for her age. She was too good for a knucklehead baby boy like me, but we were best friends nonetheless." he continued as Londyn listened attentively. "Even when things were getting rocky in our marriage, we made a promise to one another that no matter what, we'd always look out for each other. I've never been able to live with the fact that I let that accident happen to her."

"You didn't make that happen to her, Daddy. Shane's mom did."

"We all have our downfalls, Londyn. Had

Shane's mother not been dealing with whatever she was dealing with at the time then she never would've been behind the wheel in her condition... and, if I would have just picked up some milk from the grocery store earlier that morning like she'd asked, then your Mom wouldn't have been in the car in the first place. She wouldn't have even been there." Gerald sniffled as he shut his eyes tightly.

Londyn was taken aback, as this was the first time in a while that she'd talked about the car accident with her father. She reached over and laid her hand on his hand, and squeezed it tightly.

"My point is, we can 'what if' and point fingers all day, but none of that will bring her back. I learned that the hard way. I couldn't even look at myself in the mirror for months after the accident. When I'd look at my reflection, I could feel what I thought was her disappointment staring through my soul. I didn't know what to do, so I just ran. Believe me, leaving you and Tony for all those years was the most selfish, terrible thing I've ever done in my life, but it didn't stem from a lack of love. I was just lost, and didn't feel worthy or qualified to teach you and your brother how to grow up. I hadn't grown up myself." he said as he squeezed her hand.

"I'm sorry Daddy... all these years, I've never even taken the time to think about how losing Mommy affected you too." Londyn replied as she stared at her father's sincere eyes.

"You don't have to apologize. Bottom line is, I should've been there, and I'm sorry Londyn. I've done my best to be the best father I could be ever since I got you and Tony back, but I know there's nothing I can do to replace those lost years. You're the light of my life, and I want you to know that you mean the world to me. I don't want you to think I'm trying to replace your mother, with Tammy... or even you, with Sabrina. That's impossible. But I'd be a fool to look at that innocent, 5-year-old little girl in the face everyday and repeat my mistakes. I may not be her biological father, but when I married her mother I made a vow to stand in his place, and I'm going to do everything in my power to be the dad I should've been 21 years ago. That's the thing about life. It might not go as planned for us, but we always have another chance to make it better for somebody else."

"Yeah... I guess I never really thought of it that way."

"Sabrina needs you too. You're her big sister, and whether you realize it or not, she looks up to you." he said with a smile as he pointed out the window at a smiling, energetic, Sabrina who was jumping and waving at Londyn.

As Londyn giggled and opened the car door, Sabrina jumped onto her lap.

"Londyn, can you and me watch Doc McStuffins on the big TV in your room? Mom says only if you say yes." she asked, with her mouth covered in crumbs.

"Sure." Londyn replied with a smile, as a single tear ran down her cheek.

"Why are you crying? Are you sad?" Sabrina asked.

"No, I'm not sad. I'm just happy to see you." Londyn giggled as she looked at Sabrina's big brown eyes.

Up until that point, she'd never once thought about how big of blessing it was to be a big sister all over again. Let alone, how selfish she'd been towards such an innocent, loving little girl.

"How about you go dress up in your Doc McStuffins costume and I'll get the DVD ready in my room, okay?" Londyn asked with a smile.

"Yayyyyyyyyy!" Sabrina cheered.

"Come on big baby. Let's wipe these crumbs off your messy face." Tammy stated as she pulled Sabrina out of the car and walked back towards the house.

Just as Londyn was about to get out of the car, Gerald lightly grabbed her shoulder. "One more thing," he began, "you can still talk to her you know. It's not the same as hearing her talk back, but if there's one thing I'll never forget about your mother, it's how great of a listener she was. She's right, here." he said as he reached over and poked the area above her heart.

He kissed her forehead, and got out of the car, leaving Londyn alone to think. She rested her head back against the headrest, and closed her eyes as she took one of the deepest breaths she'd ever taken.

"Hey Mommy," she began as she clinched the "C.J.C." locket dangling from her neck, "it's me, Londyn. I miss you. I don't know if you can hear me, but I just pray that God lets you listen in, just this once. I've been going through a lot, and I really wish you were here. Not a day goes by that I don't think of you. I hope you're proud of me. I know it's been a minute since I talked to you. I'm sorry about that. It's just that, after you passed away, I'd close my eyes every night and envision you talking to me. It was comforting and painful all at the same time, replaying your voice in my mind, over, and over. But it made me feel closer to you... well, somewhere down the line, your voice got dimmer and dimmer, until one day I couldn't hear you at all. I know you're still here with me Mommy, but I just wish I could hear your voice one more time. I wish I could remember. So please, ask God to restore that memory for me. That's all I want... to hear you. I love you, and I'll see you again one day."

Chapter 25

"Good Morning Londyn. What are you up to this lovely morning?" Reagan asked over the phone.

"Hey Reagan. I've been up since like 6am, thinking."

"Really, about what?"

"A lot of stuff... God... and how I need to get back to going to church. I used to go all the time with Shane... I think I'm going to go today."

"Dang, I wish I could come, but I have to work at the studio today."

"It's okay... I know it's something I need to do, for me."

"Do you think you'll run into Shane there?"

"I don't even know... I'm not planning on it, I just really miss Bishop and First Lady Brooks. They really helped me grow while I was going there..."

"Oh yeah, I feel you."

"...But, if he just so happens to be there, I can't lie, it would be nice to see him."

"It would. I wonder how he's been doing lately. It's still so weird not having him around."

"Yeah it is... but hey, that's life right..."

"That's life..." Reagan replied.

"Well, I'll call you after you get off work later."

"Okay sounds good. Talk to you later Lo. Have a good day at church."

The weather was sunny and warm that morning, so Londyn chose a pastel pink pencil dress, and nude heels. With her hair slicked into a sleek top bun, and her natural glow, she looked like a pure angel. As she walked into the sanctuary of New Hope Missionary Baptist Church, ushers and fellow churchgoers immediately greeted her. While she was overjoyed to be back in church, she felt somewhat empty being there without Shane. She walked to a center aisle pew, and took a seat next to a family that she'd seen a few times before. She was only a few minutes late, but service had already begun.

"Okay, I think you all know this next song. It

goes a little something like this... Lord, we lift your name. We lift your name! He is mighty. Yes, He is. Yes, He is." Sister Stephanie, the praise leader sang.

"His name is greatly to be praised," the praise team joined in.

As Londyn stood and clapped along, she looked around briefly to see if Shane had made it to church.

"Stop it, Londyn. You're not here for him." she thought.

After a few more songs and morning announcements, Bishop Booker got up to begin his sermon. "Please open your bibles with me and stand for the reading of the word. Turn with me to the book of Matthew, the 18th chapter, and the 22nd verse. When you got it, say amen." he said in his booming, deep voice.

"Amen." echoed the voices of the congregation throughout the sanctuary.

Just as the Bishop began his sermon, in walked Shane, who quickly found a seat near the back of the sanctuary near Aunt Ryn.

"Let us read together," Bishop Booker began, "Then Peter came up and said to him, 'Lord, how often will my brother sin against me, and I forgive him? As many as seven times?' Jesus said to him, 'I do not say to you seven times, but seventy times seven.'" the congregation read together.

"The title of my sermon today is simple,

Forgiveness is necessary."

"Amen, Bishop." yelled one of the women in the sanctuary.

"You may take your seats."

Before he could sit down, Shane noticed Londyn a few rows ahead of him. He was so entranced by her beauty, that he still stood standing once everyone else had already sat.

Aunt Ryn chuckled as she tapped him on his leg and motioned for him to sit down. "Boy you look like you just saw a ghost."

"More like an angel." he said as he pointed towards Londyn.

Aunt Ryn smiled and nodded her head.

"You see, forgiveness is a concept that many of us haven't been able to grasp." Bishop Booker stated. "We think that forgiveness makes us a punk. We think that by forgiving someone, we're telling them that what they did was okay, or that we're giving in, and letting them win. But I'm here to tell you today, that forgiveness is not about anyone else, but yourself. Can I get an amen?"

"Amen." everyone shouted.

"Let me tell ya, when you hold onto unforgiveness, bitterness, and hatred... you ain't hurting nobody more than you're hurting yourself. We let the things people do to us linger in our minds for so long that they have no choice but to grow and take over our lives. How many of y'all know, that when you're bitter you start acting different. You start talking different. You change, for the worse."

"Preach Bishop." yelled Brother Robinson from the front row.

"I was reading a book, called Epiphanies Within: When Mediocre Living Is No Longer Enough, by a best selling author by the name of, Brittney Michelle, and one point in particular stood out to me. She said 'Let yourself out of the prison called unforgiveness,'" Bishop Booker shouted, "'the one where you constantly torture yourself with the memory of how much someone hurt you. Unforgiveness in your heart keeps you stagnant and stuck in the past. So why voluntarily enslave yourself to circumstances or people? You have to let it all go in order to move on and be able to accept the next phase of your life.'" he continued.

"Do I have anyone here today, who wants to be freed from their own mental strongholds, rooted in unforgiveness? Anyone here tired of carrying weights that other people threw on them years and years ago. If that's you then I want you to run here to the altar right now so that we can pray with you. Is there one?" he asked.

Slowly but surely, people began to spill over into the aisles.

"Don't let this moment pass you by. There is power in forgiveness." he continued as soft melodies played from the piano.

As she sat alone in the pew, Londyn twitched in her seat as she thought about how badly she needed to let everything go.

"Today, you can break free. Today, you can break free." Bishop Booker echoed softly. "A wise man once said, 'Unforgiveness is like drinking poison from your enemy and then expecting them to feel sick.'" Bishop Booker continued as weaved in and out of the crowded altar, touching several shoulders and heads with oil.

Londyn couldn't bare to sit still any longer, and decided to press her way to the aisle.

"Excuse me." Londyn whispered softly to the person sitting next to her.

"Let's stop making ourselves sick because of what other people have done to us."

He paused and stretched his hand to the ceiling before continuing. "Father, God, I come to you today and ask that you soften the hearts of every single person here at this altar. Allow them to let go of their past hurt, so that they can move on to what you have in store for their lives, God. Help them to break free from the chains of unforgiveness. And even if it is themselves who they need to forgive, help them to do so. We know that there is power in forgiveness. Your amazing grace pardoned our sins on the cross so that we can be forgiven... so we must do the same for our fellow brothers and sisters. Replace their broken hearts with whole hearts, hearts filled with your love. The Bible says that God heals the brokenhearted, and holds them close to Him. Allow Him to set you free. Don't stay in that dark place you've been stuck in." Bishop Booker continued, as he signaled the praise team to rise.

"I've been freed from the chains that once held me down. I'm delivered from all my guilt and shame! No weapon formed against me shall prosper, because I'm covered in Jesus' name..." Sister Stephanie sang.

The band, as well as the rest of the praise team immediately joined in, singing the classic gospel song.

"The enemy and his schemes have no power." Bishop Booker sang.

Londyn slowly extended her arms to the ceiling and closed her eyes. She quietly whispered the words of the song, and felt a load being lifted as she released every bit of pain, bitterness, and unforgiveness from her mind. She felt the pressure of a man's heavy hand on her right shoulder, but did not look up to see who it belonged to. Instead she continued to worship and pray.

"Sing it with me, No more chains. No more fear!" Bishop Booker sang loudly along with the praise team.

As tears streamed down her face, she opened her eyes and looked to her left to see that the hand on her shoulder was none other than Shane's. With one hand on her shoulder, and the other hand extended fully towards the ceiling, Shane poured his heart out in song, his eyes closed shut.

"No weapon formed against me shall prosper, because I'm covered in Jesus' name..." they sang.

Chapter 26

"I am so glad to finally meet you, Miss Londyn. I've heard nothing but wonderful things about you." Aunt Ryn said as she hugged Londyn tightly.

"Oh it is soooo good to finally meet you too, Mrs. Jackson."

"Chile, please. Call me Aunt Ryn." she chuckled.

The warm sunrays beat heavily against their skin as they stood in the church parking lot.

"You look beautiful, Londyn. How have things been with you?" Shane asked.

"Thank you, you're looking good yourself," she smiled, "and I can't complain. Things are working themselves out..." she replied.

"Aunt Ryn, I'm hungry." Uncle Buck's son 13 year old Brian Jr. whined.

"Me too Aunt Ryn, can you, pleaseeee get me and Bucky something to eat?" his 10 year old brother, Troy asked.

"Well, let me head on home so I can feed my growing nephews." Aunt Ryn stated as she swept them both under each arm, "Shane I'll meet you back at the house."

"Okay, cool I'll catch y'all a little later."

"Bye sweetheart. You be good now." Aunt Ryn cooed.

"I sure will." Londyn replied cheerfully.

"Bye Londyn." Bucky and Troy cheered.

Shane and Londyn waved goodbye as they watched them walk over to Aunt Ryn's car.

"It was really nice to finally meet her." Londyn stated as she turned back to look at Shane.

"Yeah... it's been really cool having her around again." Shane smiled.

"I'm sure..." Londyn replied with a head nod.

"Yeah....so, are you busy, like right now? I was wondering if we could grab a bite to eat... catch up a little, maybe? That is if you're free..." Shane asked.

"Ummm.. Yeah, yeah, sure... I have a little bit of time."

"Oh right, Sunday dinner at your Granny's"

"You know it... 4pm." Londyn replied.

"...and not a minute sooner." Shane chuckled. "I miss her. How's she doing?"

"She's doing well. Still as feisty and loving as ever." Londyn smiled.

She squinted and shielded the sun from her eyes with her hand.

"Good... So, where do you want to go eat?" he asked.

"How about your favorite spot?"

Shane smiled and nodded his head.

"That works... Do you wanna ride together or...?" he asked.

"Let's drive separately, that way I can just swing to Granny's afterward and you won't have to worry about bringing me back to my car."

"Okay, that's cool. Well, I'll just see you there."

"Alrighty." Londyn replied as they parted ways and headed to their cars.

"*What did I just get myself into...*" Londyn thought.

After about 5 minutes, her phone began to ring. She quickly answered it, while keeping her eyes on the road.

"Hello?"

"Heyyyy. How was church?" Reagan asked.

"It was very nice. I'm so glad I came, for real."

"Was Shane there?"

"Yeah.. he was actually... and so was his Aunt Ryn. She's just as sweet as she can be."

"Awwww, so that means you talked to him. I'm glad to hear that... was it weird?"

"A little bit, but I guess that's to be expected when we haven't seen each other in months. But, we're about to go meet up at the Riverwalk now and catch up I guess... This should be interesting."

"Whaaaaat. Wow, this is big!" Reagan squealed.

"I know right... I definitely didn't see this one coming. Who knows if anything will come out of it, but it can't hurt, right?"

"It'll be fine. Despite everything that's gone on between you two I know that the love is still there. This could be a fresh start."

"Maybe... I guess we'll see."

"Yeah, well, this commercial break is about to be over so let me get back to work. Call me tonight and fill me in."

"I will."

"Okay, bye girl."

During the 15-minute drive from the church to Downtown Detroit, very similar thoughts raced through both Shane and Londyn's minds. Both wondered what they were getting themselves into, and whether or not the conversation would be productive or a waste of time. Most of all, they wondered if they'd ever be able to work things out between them. Shane pulled into the parking lot next to Mojo's first, with Londyn arriving just a few seconds after him.

"This brings back some great memories." Londyn said as Shane helped her out of her car.

"Sure does..." Shane replied as he reminisced on their first trip to the Riverwalk after their first date at Mojo's.

As they neared the water, Shane led Londyn towards a park bench on a small hill that overlooked the river.

"Did you still want to order something from Mojo's?"

"I'm okay... I'm not all that hungry." she replied as she nervously looked forward at the river.

The Detroit Princess boat sailed across their view, and happy passengers waved as the captain honked the horn. As Londyn smiled and waved, she wondered why her stomach was in knots. Little did she know, Shane's nerves had his stomach turning in somersaults as well. After the dramatic ending they'd had, he just wasn't sure what she thought of him. They stared ahead at the beautiful view in silence for a few moments, until Shane hesitantly slipped his hand around hers. He was quite certain she'd politely pull away, but to his surprise, she didn't. Instead, she intertwined her fingers in his, and caressed his hand with her thumb. Now feeling a bit more comfortable, Shane decided to cut right to the chase.

"Londyn, I really miss you, a lot."

"I miss you too." she replied.

"I've been doing a lot of thinking, about everything... a lot of self reflecting, and really dealing with a lot of the issues I've kept built up inside of me for so long."

"Yeah, same here. I guess I never realized how much stuff I actually needed to deal with all this time. Like with my dad. We actually had a talk about how I felt about him getting remarried. It's been interesting, to the say the least. But, I'm feeling really good. I can feel myself growing."

"That's good to hear. And yeah, I've just working on myself, and my family relationships. Desi and I are really getting along great. We picked back up right where we left off back in the 90's." he chuckled.

"Good... I'm really happy for you."

"Thank you... And yo, I even wrote a letter to my mother."

"Wow, really?"

"Yeah. It's 5 pages long, about everything that she missed in my life, and how I felt about her disowning me. I haven't found the courage to mail it yet though... but just writing it and facing the facts has helped me tremendously."

"I'm proud of you Shane."

"Thank you, Londyn. I'm proud of you too."

"It's crazy..." she began. "I mean, who ever would've guessed we'd end up like this. Not together, growing on our own."

"Ever since we started dating, I always imagined us being together forever. I know that might not be possible now, but I just want you to know that I will never, ever stop loving you." he said with sincerity.

She leaned over and gave him a kiss on the cheek, and smiled as she laid her head on his shoulder.

"I'll always love you too." she replied.

"I don't expect you, or your family for that matter, to ever be able to accept me, you know, considering... everything." he said.

Londyn sat up straight and looked him directly in his eyes.

"Shane, what happened is not your fault." she began. "Listen to me, you can't carry that burden around for the rest of your life. My family and I, we've been dealing with her being gone the best way we know how for the past 15 years. The fact that your mother is the cause of it all does make this a little more complicated, but it doesn't make it impossible. My love for you is deeper than your mother's mistake."

Shane was speechless as he leaned in and gave Londyn the longest hug he'd ever given her.

"Everything is going to be okay." she said as she rubbed his back.

As he squeezed her tightly he was reminded in that moment that Londyn was indeed the most special woman he'd ever known.

"Thank you, Londyn. Thank you."

Chapter 27

For the next two weeks, Shane and Londyn caught up on all they'd missed in each other's lives. They went on cute dates, and talked into the wee hours of the night just as they'd done when they first met. At Londyn's request, Shane agreed to join Londyn's family for Sunday dinner at Grandma Hattie's home.

"Don't worry, it'll be just fine." Londyn reassured him as they walked up the driveway towards the front door.

"I hope so." he replied as he followed quickly behind her.

Considering the circumstances, he was extremely worried that the dinner would be much more awkward than he was prepared to handle. After all, he hadn't seen or spoken to the James' family since he abruptly left Grandma Hattie's birthday party months prior. Now that they knew who he really was, he was prepared to be given the cold shoulder.

"There goes my sweet babies! Come on inside here and give me some sugar." Grandma Hattie said from the doorway.

She gave Londyn a big hug and ran her fingers through her long silky hair.

"Babygirl, you look so pretty, I haven't seen your hair like this in years." she cooed.

"Yeah I decided to try something different this week." Londyn smiled.

"Well I like it, I think it looks nice. Any hairstyle you wear looks nice. Curly, straight. I love it all. " Grandma Hattie continued.

"Thanks Granny."

Grandma Hattie released Londyn from her grasp and looked at Shane, who stood patiently at the bottom of the porch steps.

"Well, get on up here Shane and give me a hug. Don't act like a stranger. Come on!" she exclaimed.

"How are you, Grandma Hattie?" he asked as he walked up the steps.

"I am alive, and I am surely well. It's so good to see you." she said with a smile as she wrapped her arms around him.

He sighed a huge sigh of relief as he walked into the house. To his pleasant surprise, Londyn's family welcomed him with open arms, just as they'd always done. He made his way through the house and exchanged hugs with everyone inside.

"Now y'all go wash your hands, so we can eat. We've been waiting on y'all." Grandma Hattie ordered.

"Go ahead," Londyn said as she pointed towards the bathroom door, "I'll go to the bathroom upstairs."

Shane walked into the bathroom and quickly closed the door behind him. He was overwhelmed in the best way possible, at the love Londyn's family showed. As he washed his hands, he glanced at the mirror, and paused. As he looked at his reflection, a thought that had been stirring for months came to the forefront of his thoughts... his mother.

"If these people can treat me like family, no matter how tragically we're connected, then I owe it to myself to finally mend things with my own. I'm going to mail the letter. " he thought.

No matter how hard, or how painful it'd be, he decided in that moment that he was going to start fresh, in every area. He dried his hands on the towel and walked over to the kitchen, joining the family in prayer for the food.

Together, they ate, laughed, and talked about any and everything under the sun. Although Londyn's family treated him as though nothing at all had changed, Shane still felt the need to acknowledge the overt elephant in the room.

"Can I say something?" he asked.

"Go head baby. Everybody hush for a moment, Shane has something to say." Grandma Hattie announced.

Shane looked around at the long rectangular table at the faces of Londyn, Grandma Hattie, Gerald, Antonio, Tammy, and little Sabrina, and took a long, deep breath. As he sat there face to face with the family most affected by the actions of his own, his fear of rejection sweated profusely through his palms. He scooted his chair back, and stood up from his seat as he placed his napkin on the table. Londyn looked up at him apprehensively, unsure of what exactly he was about to say.

"I just want to say thank you, to all of you. For embracing me the way you always have. It's not something I can say I'm used to, growing up the way I did. When I found out, well you know... about how my family was connected to yours, I was scared to ever come back around. I didn't know how anyone could ever accept the son of the person who's responsible for such heartache in their family," he continued.

Gerald put his fork down on his plate and listened attentively.

"...but this whole situation just shows how great you all are, you know. I'm so, so thankful, to Londyn, and all of you. You've taught me things in a little under a year, that I never understood in my entire 22 years of life." he stated as he sat back down in his chair.

Grandma Hattie got up from her seat, walked over to Shane and embraced him in a warm hug.

"Listen to me," she began as she grabbed him by the shoulders, and looked at him with a look that only a grandmother could give. "You have got to forgive her, you hear me. I know it's not easy, and I can't say I know exactly how you've felt all these years, but I do know that there is a peace that comes from letting go. All of us, Me, Gerald, Londyn, Antonio, we all had to forgive your mother for what she did, a long time ago. Yes, what she did was tragic, and yes, she took someone so precious from us, but we know that it was a mistake. Nobody is perfect, and on a bad day anyone of us at this table could have found ourselves in your mother's position. We had to let the hatred, anger, and animosity go Shane, so that we could go on with our lives and remember Charlotte for all of the right reasons. It took a long time, but we had to find it in our hearts to forgive your mother, and we did that. We forgave her long before we knew you. So the fact that you are her son doesn't change a thing, baby. It doesn't change a thing, because we've already dealt with that. Now, it's your turn Shane, it's your turn, to forgive. To make peace."

"Thank You." Shane whispered in Grandma Hattie's ear as he gave her another hug.

He sniffled a little, but as always, didn't drop a single tear.

"So have you talked to her at all, your mother?" Grandma Hattie asked as she returned to her seat at the table.

"No ma'am. She's written me about 5 letters, but I haven't mailed any of my responses. I'm definitely going to do it, very soon."

"Have you ever thought about actually going to see her?" Tammy asked.

"I've thought about it briefly over the past few weeks, after reading all of her letters over and over. I just don't know if I could bring myself to do it. I really do want to forgive her, and move forward... I just don't know where to start."

"I think you should go to the prison, and talk to her face to face. It could give you closure to one chapter, and hopefully open the door to another." Tammy said.

Silence fell across the room as Shane thought about Tammy's idea. Now that he'd heard it from someone else, it sounded more and more like the right next step to take.

"I'll go with you..." Londyn said kindly.

He looked at her in utter shock and amazement. As he opened his mouth to respond, Antonio interrupted him.

"Yeah I'll go too, bro."

"Are you two sure about that?" Gerald asked. "That could be a lot to handle."

"Yes, they're sure. They are adults who can think for themselves, Gerald." Grandma Hattie replied. "I would go with you too baby, but I'm old, I can't travel that far. So, I will be there in spirit."

Tammy nudged Gerald, but he took too long to chime in, so she spoke up for the both of them. "...and WE will go with you too, if you need us Shane, right honey?" she asked as she looked over at her husband.

Gerald swallowed the food in his mouth and took a sip of water. He looked over at Londyn, and then back and Tammy. "Right. Yeah, yeah kid, you have our support," he began. "Anyone this special to my daughter is most definitely okay in my book."

While the thought of seeing CJ face-to-face again after all this time saddened him, he'd do anything to support Londyn.

"Wow. I'm in awe." Shane stated. "...and please don't take this the wrong way, because I truly thank you all from the bottom of my heart... but if I'm going to do this, then I think I need to do it alone. I hope you all understand."

"Of course we do. We'll be supporting you from right here. Don't you worry." Grandma Hattie replied.

Chapter 28

His pulse was racing as his body softly swayed from left to right. His hands wouldn't stop shaking, and his feet tapped a mile a minute on the cold, hard floor. Exactly 5 days after his decision was made at Londyn's family's Sunday dinner, Shane sat nervously in the waiting room of the Chicago State Penitentiary. Each time he heard the screech of the door hinges turn, his heart jerked inside his chest.

He looked up, and in walked a woman in her early 20's, dressed in an orange jumpsuit, with her hands down at her side. She walked past Shane to a little boy, who smiled from ear to ear at a table next to his. The little boy embraced her in a hug, and she cried on his small shoulders. Shane was surprised at how much he remembered being in that little boy's shoes. The pervasive smell of disinfectant overshadowed by urine in the air brought back the prison visit memories he'd tried to erase all these years. As he looked at the little boy, he couldn't help but wonder what'd it would feel like to hug his mom.

"Or do I even want to hug her at all?" he thought.

He hadn't felt the warmth of his mother's body against his since right before the accident when she put him in the backseat of her car. All while she was in prison, the only visits she was allowed to have were those separated by a thick sheet of glass. But now, due to good behavior, she'd been permitted a face-to-face visit. Shane squirmed in the plastic chair as he anxiously stared at the door.

"What if I'm making a mistake. It's not too late to back out now." he wondered.

As he contemplated whether or not he was making the biggest mistake of his life, the hinges screeched and the door opened wide again. He looked up from his spot at the small round table for two, and felt a large lump form in his throat. In walked a short, petite woman, with shoulder length black hair. With her hands covering her mouth, and a face wet with tears, Shane watched her slowly walk his way. She smiled as she looked her now, adult son in the eyes for the first time in 12 long years. Unsure if he'd be receptive, she opted to take a seat rather than immediately overwhelm him with a hug.

"Hi Shane," she stuttered, "it's, it's so good to see you."

"It's good to see you too." he replied nervously.

"So, how have you been? How's life?" she asked.

Shane sat in silence for a few seconds as he gathered his thoughts. He scratched his head and then put his hands on the table in front of him.

"How's life... How's life?" he chuckled sarcastically. "You know. I've been racking my brain trying to figure out what I would say when I finally mustered up the courage to come here and talk to you. But no matter how hard I thought about it, I couldn't think of what I'd say until now. My life hasn't been the easiest. It's been rough growing up without a mother. Aunt Ryn, she did a great job raising me, but no matter how much love she showed, she couldn't undo the damage you caused. Do you know how many times I felt worthless because the woman who gave me life abandoned me? Do you really understand how it felt as a little, helpless boy, to watch you walk away and never look back? Do you know how much I needed you?" he asked as he stared in her eyes.

While CJ's mouth remained silent, her facial expression was worth a thousand words. She was ashamed.

"I needed you. I needed a mother, and you weren't there. You weren't there not because you couldn't be, but because you chose not to." he said as a single tear streamed down his face. "Growing up it was so hard, to love myself... to receive love from others, to show others love, because my issues were so deeply rooted. I didn't even know who I was for most of my childhood. I mean, come on now, my name is Shane Solomon Jr. I'm a JR., the namesake of a man who I've barely ever known, and the son of a woman who left me to die alone on the inside. How was I supposed to know how to be a good man without one single positive male role model in my life? How was I supposed to know how to love when the person that was supposed to love me the most pushed me away?" he continued as he wiped the tear away from his face. "It wasn't until going to counseling in high school with Aunt Ryn that I realized how I've always veered away from close relationships, because I didn't want them to end the way mine ended with you. I was so messed up on the inside that I almost pushed my girlfriend Londyn and her family away, that is until they showed me that not everyone is like you. Not everyone's parents treat them the way mine have. Some people will say they love you and actually mean it. They'll actually show it, unconditionally. You know what really changed me though... I found God. I always knew He was there, but I actually got to know Him. And He's blessed me and kept me, and held me safe in his arms no matter what situation I was in. So because of all of that, I can't be angry with you. I have to forgive you, because He's forgiven me for all the messed up stuff I've done. So, I guess I just wanted to come here and give you the peace of mind in knowing that no matter how many messed up choices you've made, your son is a survivor. I'm strong. I used to think that I had no purpose, and that I was here on this earth by accident, but God's grace has saved me, and it can save you too. I'm not perfect, I've had to fight my own demons, but if I can come out of this then so can you. So I forgive you," he continued as another tear dropped from his eye. "I wholeheartedly, genuinely, forgive you, for everything... because, if my angel of a girlfriend can forgive you for killing her mother, then who I am not to show that same love."

CJ's mouth nearly dropped to the floor as she processed the news Shane had just given her. She was completely stunned, and couldn't bring herself to say a single world.

Shane took a deep breath and continued. "Look, I don't think I have the strength to talk through this whole thing today, but I learned in counseling that the first step to getting through this was to be open and honest, and not hold anything back. So, there it is. That's how life has been."

CJ sat emotionless, like a statue in front of Shane, who was growing more emotional by the minute.

"I'm gonna head back to Detroit now, because my girlfriend's graduation ceremony is tomorrow morning, and I won't miss that for the world. I finally know what it feels like to have a big family now, and I want to show support to those that support me... but don't worry, I'm different than you were. I'm not going to turn my back on you forever. If you'd like to see me again, then I'll be back. And hopefully, we can one day figure out how to start this whole mother and son thing over from scratch. I won't beg you this time though... It's all on you."

He paused and waited for a response, but to his disappointment she said nothing at all.

He pushed his chair back, and stood next to the table where his mother sat with her head hung low. After all that he'd just poured out to her, it cut him deeply to know that she didn't have a single word to say.

"Goodbye CJ." he said as he turned and walked away.

He clinched his fist tightly to try and hold his composure, but another tear raced down his face. His heart felt free, yet broken all in one. Just as his hand touched the cold metal doorknob, he heard his mother scream.

"Wait!!!"

He quickly turned his head, only to see CJ running towards him with open arms. He felt his voice crack as a sobbing whimper escaped from his chest.

"I'm so sorry, son. I'm so sorry." she cried as she wrapped her arms tightly around his body. "I love you. I love you so much."

For the first time in a long time, Shane let out a much-needed cry in the arms of the woman he'd longed for, for years.

"I love you too, Mama."

Chapter 29

The next morning, Shane sat in the stands of East Lincoln University's football stadium, surrounded by Londyn's cheering friends and family. It was Sunday, May 29, 2016, and Londyn was graduating with a Bachelor of Arts degree in Broadcasting.

"How did it go with your mother yesterday?" Grandma Hattie asked as they waited for Londyn to cross the stage.

"It went well. It was intense to say the least, but it was good. I know it'll probably take some time, but I'm hopeful." he replied.

"That's great baby. These things take time, but with God, you two will get through it." Grandma Hattie said with a huge smile.

"You're right!"

"Look there they are!" Tony yelled.

"Where?" Gerald asked as he raised his camera to capture the moment.

"Right there!" Little Sabrina replied, "Yayyyy, Sissy!"

"Oh! I see her! Hey Londyn!" Gerald yelled, "I'm so proud of my Babygirl."

Their entire section waved and jumped with joy as Londyn and her friends approached the stage.

"David DeAngelo Tyrone Lewis." the announcer read as David walked across the stage and dabbed with his diploma in hand.

"Reagan Raquel Graham!"

"Yeaaaaah. Go Reagan!" Tony yelled.

"What is that dance she's doing?" Gerald asked.

"It's called hit the folks, son. Get hip." Grandma Hattie teased.

"Okay guys, you ready? Londyn's up next!" Tammy exclaimed.

"Londyn Marie James!"

"Yeaaaaahhhhhh!!! Let's go Londyn! Go Londyn. Whooo Hooooo." they yelled, cheered, and clapped as Londyn walked across the stage and curtsied.

"Look at my Londyn!" Gerald said. "She did it."

"Yes she did." Shane said as he high-fived Gerald. "She did it..."

About 20 minutes later, the ceremony ended and the family headed outside to greet Londyn with lots of love, flowers, and congratulations. Londyn flashed a smile and ran towards her family as soon as she laid eyes on them. She looked stunning in her all white dress, and forest green heels to match her cap and gown.

"Londyn, I'm so proud of you Babygirl." Gerald said as he gave Londyn a big hug and a kiss on the forehead.

"Thank you Daddy!" she smiled.

"Don't thank me yet, wait until you see your graduation/early birthday gift!" he chuckled.

"Daddy you didn't have to get me anything!" she giggled. "But what is it?"

"Daddy got you a new car." Sabrina blurted out.

"Sabrina!" Tammy snapped.

"Sorry. I tried to hold it in like you said." Sabrina said with both hands on her cheeks.

"Whaaaatttt. Are you serious?" Londyn screamed.

"I guess you'll have to wait and see when we get home!" Gerald laughed.

"Congrats Londyn!" Tammy said as she reached in and gave Londyn a hug.

"Congrats Sis. I'm so proud of you!" Tony said with a hug and a high-five.

"Thanks you guys. Thank you. And Granny! Thank you for coming! I know you hate being around big crowds like this."

"Now you know I wouldn't miss this day for nothing!" Grandma Hattie said as she reached in to give Londyn a kiss.

"This is just so surreal." Londyn squealed.

"Ahemm." Gerald grunted as he pointed over at Shane.

Londyn turned and noticed the huge bouquet of pink roses that Shane held in his hands.

"Congrats Beautiful!" Shane said after politely waiting his turn to congratulate Londyn.

"Oh my God, these are gorgeous." she said as she leaned in and kissed him lightly on the lips. "Thank you so much, baby."

"Watch it now, just because you have a degree doesn't make you grown!" Gerald laughed.

"Sorry Mr. James." Shane giggled as he wiped Londyn's lipstick from his lips.

"I love you all so much!" Londyn cheered with a huge smile.

"We love you too, Lo." Shane replied.

"Well, let's take pictures!" she squealed as she whipped out her cell phone.

As they all laughed and snapped selfies, Londyn felt an unexplainable joy. She realized in that moment, surrounded by the people she loved most, that the joys and pain she'd experienced were all just apart of the circle of life. Nothing would ever be perfect, but she could find beauty even in the struggle. At the end of the day love conquers all.

"Babygirl, where did you park your car? Can we just follow you over to the restaurant if that's cool." Gerald asked.

"I rode with Shane, his car is right over there." Londyn replied as she pointed a few feet away at Shane's car.

"Shane. How the heck you get that good parking spot, man?"

"Londyn had us here super early, that's how." Shane chuckled as he stuffed his hands in his suit pocket. "I can ride you all to your car if you want?"

"No, we're okay. We can use the exercise." Tammy giggled. "C'mon, Sabrina. Let's go work up an appetite for Sissy's graduation dinner!"

"Speak for yourselves!" Tony laughed as he spotted one of his lady friends walking past. "Ayeee, LaKeisha. You think you can drop me off at my car?" he yelled as he ran off and wrapped his arm around the pretty girl's shoulders.

"That boy is a fool." Gerald began. "Well, I think I know how to get there. I'll just GPS it and call if I get lost."

"Okay, cool." Londyn replied.

"I'm proud of you." he replied as he kissed her on the forehead.

"Thank you, Daddy."

"Alright, drive safely Shane, precious cargo right there." Gerald yelled to Shane as they walked away.

"I got you Mr. James." Shane chuckled.

"She did it! My Babygirl did it!" Gerald yelled as he fist pumped in the air and ended with a classic Mu Psi spin.

"He's team too much." Londyn giggled.

"He just loves you, that's all." Shane chuckled as he opened the passenger door for Londyn.

"You're right... he does." she replied.

After sitting down in the driver's seat, Shane immediately reached over Londyn's lap and opened the glove compartment.

"What's that?" she asked as he pulled out a blank CD.

"It's part one of your graduation gift." he began as he opened the cd case. "So, somehow, Uncle Buck and one of his Supervisor's at the plant got to talking... and your Mom came up... turns out, his wife was your Mom's guidance counselor back in the day, and she wanted him to pass this along to you." he continued as he inserted the CD into the sound system.

Londyn looked puzzled as she waited for the CD

to start playing. Seconds later, to her complete and utter surprise, the most beautiful voice she'd ever heard echoed from the speakers.

"Greetings Mackenzie High School. I am your valedictorian, Charlotte Jean Carter."

Londyn's jaw dropped in awe, and the purest joy she'd ever felt filled her mind, body, and soul as her mother's angelic voice passed through her ears.

"He did it..." Londyn whispered as she clutched her mother's locket around her neck.

"Who?" Shake asked.

"God..." she smiled.

After all these years, she could finally hear her mother's voice again, and this time she'd never forget.

"Now, I won't be before you all long today, because I know everyone is ready to celebrate. However, I want to offer a few encouraging words of advice to the Class of 1991. First and foremost, I want to thank all of you who've been there for me this past year as I've grieved the loss of my dear mother, Evelyn Joyce Carter. Although it hurts, I know that she's proud, and that she's looking down on me from above. Today, my friends, we enter the world of adulthood. We're now more responsible for ourselves and our futures than ever before. All of the preparation over the years, by our teachers, our families, and ourselves have lead to this very moment. If you haven't yet realized it, the future is no longer on its way. The future is here! The time is now. Now is when we create the legacy that people will read about long after we're gone.

Now is where we lay the foundation for our children, and our children's children. This is where life begins. There will be some rough patches, because, well, that's just apart of life... but the good news is, it doesn't matter how hard you fall, as long as you find the courage to get back up again. So go after your dreams, no matter how scary they sound. Class of 1991, be proud of yourselves. Reflect on how far you've come, and be excited about the days to come. I'm just a girl from the west side of Detroit, Michigan, who was determined not to be another statistic. I didn't come from much, but with love from God, and my family- I've made it. If you don't remember anything else from this speech, it is my hope that you'll remember this: No matter where you come from, no matter who your parents are, you too can be somebody. You too can make it. Class of 1991, go out and be the person that God created you to be. Live without regrets, laugh until it hurts, and cherish the people in your world. That's life. That's love. Thank You."

The End.

Bonus Chapter

On July 4th, 2023, 7 years after Londyn graduated from college, she sat at the kitchen table of Aunt Ryn's home in front of a plate of potato salad, baked beans, hot dogs, and potato chips. Her wedding ring shined brightly as her hand lay on her very pregnant belly. Shane leaned in and kissed her belly as Man-Man snapped a picture on his iPhone.

"My little nephew is getting big!" Man-Man smiled.

"I know right, 3 more weeks!" Londyn giggled.

"Little Emmanuel Solomon." Man-Man chuckled.

"Yeah right." Londyn laughed. "Daddy would have a fit if you didn't take on his name." she cooed as she leaned down and whispered to her big stomach.

"That's right. Shane Solomon III is a strong, kingly name. He's destined for greatness." Shane chuckled.

"Yeah, little Tre is going to be something special." Londyn smiled.

"He sure is, and his little God-sister Raven can't wait to meet him either." Reagan said as she rubbed her big belly.

"I still can't get over the fact that y'all are having babies at the same time." Londyn's now 12-year old stepsister Sabrina squealed. "I can't wait to babysit."

"Oh yeah we are definitely putting you to work." Reagan chuckled.

Aunt Ryn's 4th of July cookout was going strong as the sound of hip-hop music and the aroma of barbecue filled the summer air. Although a quick rain shower caused them to move the party indoors, they were still having the time of their lives.

"So are you excited about your promotion?" Desi's husband Josh asked as he fixed their 6-year-old son Kenny a plate.

"Yeah man! I can't wait, and that salary increase is super clutch." Shane chuckled.

"I know that's right. I'm happy for you man."

"Thanks bro." Shane replied as he looked around and smiled.

Shane was ecstatic to have all of he and Londyn's family together under one roof again. A few years after college, he and Londyn moved about an hour away to be closer to his new job at a new Blackmond Hill site. As of the 1st of the month, he'd accepted a new Lead Project Manager position, making him the youngest in his department to take on such great responsibility. As he, Londyn, Reagan, David, Aunt Ryn, Gerald, Tammy, Tony, Sabrina, Uncle Buck, Danielle, Bucky, Troy, Desi, Josh, Kenny, and Man-Man all sat around eating, cracking jokes, and playing cards, he couldn't help but to smile. He thought back to years prior, and was humbled at the fact that two families once connected by tragedy would soon be blessed with a greater connection, one based on love, and a new baby boy. Suddenly, the doorbell rang, interrupting Shane's thought.

"I'll get it." he stated as hopped up from his spot in the kitchen.

He walked around the corner, through the living room to the front door.

"Now who could this be?" he mumbled as he turned the knob.

As the door thrust open, he stood in shock like a deer in headlights.

"Babe, who is it?" Londyn asked as she waddled over to her husband's side.

"Surprise, son... I'm out!" CJ smiled. "Aren't you happy to see me?"

........To be continued

Also By Brittney Michelle

Epiphanies Within: *When Mediocre Living Is No Longer Enough.*

Epiphanies Within is a self-help natured book written for women who have a desire to activate their best "self" while becoming a better, stronger, wiser and happier woman of God. (Non-Fiction/Self-Help)

BM Webster Publishing, LLC.

publishing@itsBrittneyMichelle.com

About The Author

Brittney Michelle is a purpose-driven author, publisher, entrepreneur, and advocate for teenage girls. After graduating from Grand Valley State University with a B.S. in Biomedical Sciences, she decided to pursue her lifelong dream of becoming a published author. She is committed to inspiring people across the world to activate his or her best selves, while unapologetically pursuing their gifts and passions. Brittney is the founder and CEO of MISSion.31 Incorporated, a non-profit mentoring organization on a mission to teach, mentor, and inspire young ladies in grades 6-12. She is also the owner and executive publisher of BM Webster Publishing, LLC. She has been a proud member of Alpha Kappa Alpha Sorority, Incorporated since 2010.